WHY

PAUL EBERZ

A
JUST
SUGAR
PRODUCTION

WHY

World News

BREAKING

"...the continued postponement of public disclosure of such information (classified JFK documents) is warranted to protect against an identifiable harm to themilitary defense, intelligence operations, law enforcement, or the conduct of foreign relations that is of such gravity that it outweighs the public interest in dis closure."
Statement by the White House - President Joe Biden - ABC NEWS Dec 15, 2022

PAUL EBERZ

Editor: Carrie Murgittroyd, Editor extraordinaire.

Cover Design: Paradox Book Cover Design & Formatting.

ISBN
Hardcover 978-1-7352566-1-0
Paperback 978-1-7352566-0-3

A
JUST
SUGAR
PRODUCTION

DEDICATION

To my grandchildren, the next generation of hope

ACKNOWLEDGMENTS

Bob Ficarra - mio amico

PART ONE

IT BEGINS. 1944 - 1947

CHAPTER 1

UNIVERSITY OF TEXAS AT AUSTIN. JUNE 26, 1944

HE WAS TALL, taller than the average Texan, taller than almost any man. Standing six-feet-four, he towered over his constituents even when they wore ten-gallon hats. He was lanky, weighing only 170 pounds, and walked, slightly bent over, as if he were constantly leaning down to speak to smaller people.

A high forehead rose to meet short thin hair parted slightly off center, which gave an odd balance to his disproportionally long nose and oversized ears. A person might assume he was older than his years due to the dark circles beneath intense, narrow brown eyes. His daunting appearance allowed him to appear in control at all times.

Not many of the students paid attention to him as he walked toward Kozmetsky Center. Some traveled at a canter, holding books tight, hurrying along apparently late for class. Others were strolling from the shade of one live oak to another, occupied by conversations of the young and hopeful. But anyone close gave space to the man who walked without waver down the center of the sidewalk.

The bells atop the twenty-five-story tower in the center of campus announced the top of the hour. On schedule, doors of the McCombs School of Business building opened and a small crowd of students and faculty entered. It was his destination and where this United States Congressman for the Tenth District was to give a speech.

The surroundings of this auspicious campus were familiar to him even though he wasn't an alum. Lyndon Baines Johnson came from very humble beginnings and could afford to attend the much less prestigious Southwest Texas State Teachers College. During his campaigns however, he adopted UT in Austin, making speeches, garnering press, and most importantly, connections. He never hesitated to use his association with UT's administration, faculty, and academic status whenever possible, endeavoring to be viewed as well-educated. Despite the effort to appear scholarly, he was instead respected and feared for his cunning and political savvy. Some came to know him as ruthless, but all knew of his relentless ambition.

Ducking down an alley, he used a side door putting him in a hallway leading to the backstage of the auditorium. It wasn't his first appearance at UT. He had spoken during each of his three previous runs for office. Cooler air was welcome even to the man who seldom paid attention the heat of the Texas sun. The dark corridor, lined with a wainscot of tile, echoed his bootsteps.

"Lyndon." A voice called his name from a small anteroom just off the hall, near the stage.

Edward Clark, the Johnson for Congress re-election campaign manager, financial advisor, and lawyer, gave LBJ a small wave and a nod.

"Clark." Johnson entered, pulled his Stetson off, and looked for a hook. Finding none he tossed it to an empty chair. "Who's in the seats?"

"Nice to see you, too." Clark had gotten used to the candidate's pre-game jitters. Four congressional election campaigns taught him when to be truly offended by LBJ's ill-timed rebuffs. A foot shorter, going bald and sporting wirerimmed glasses, Clark became almost non-existent when appearing with the congressman. Without Clark, however diminutive, Johnson would still be teaching high school, in the border town near the Mexico border.

Lyndon paid no attention to the remark and stepped back to the door, peering down the hall at the opening at the edge of the curtain.

Edward Clark cleared his throat, trying to redirect Johnson's attention.

LBJ stepped back inside, plopped into a chair, and asked again, "Who's in the seats?"

Clark took a breath. "Right... mostly students, some faculty, but mostly undergrads in poly sci, public admin, public policy, or just the curious. Obviously, they're all bright new pennies, full of optimism and impressionable. I would recommend you stick to your New Deal speech, that should prove effective for this crowd. But... just keep in mind... why we're here. Most of them aren't old enough to vote, even if they were registered in the tenth district, which they're not. You're not looking for votes... you're looking for recruits."

Johnson grunted. "Uh huh."

Clark spoke with more intensity. "You helped block the repeal of the oil depletion allowance so we have money from Hunt and Murchison, not to mention what you've gotten from Brown and Root, but that's just the money. We need boots-on-the-ground to put that money to work in the field."

Johnson seemed disinterested, concentrating on brushing the dust from his pants.

Annoyed, Clark asked, "Are you listening to me?"

Lyndon raised his head as he placed both hands on his knees and leaned forward, his eyes narrowed and focused. "I don't need this lesson. I know why I'm here. Recruits. Do you have names?" Lyndon sighed and eased back.

"There are two; Horace Busby and Malcolm Wallace. Both are politically active on campus. Wallace is President of the Student Body and Busby, editor of the paper."

Lyndon remained quiet, eyes now staring at the floor.

"I see Busby as a behind-the-scenes guy. He's very smart, ambitious and has a reputation for being devious. He's kind of an odd-looking guy, so even if he had potential for something more visible, which he doesn't, he can't be in front of anything. Strictly behind the scenes."

"Wallace?"

Clark grinned slyly.

A figure suddenly appeared in the doorway. "Congressman."

Lyndon turned to the student stage manager.

A toothy grin said, "Five minutes."

Johnson, without acknowledgment to the student, turned back to Clark and the boy disappeared.

"Malcolm Wallace... our friends on the faculty said he's a liberal. I'm told he's a big fan of The New Deal. He won President of the Student Body mostly because he's big, tough and handsome so he appeals to the jocks and the girls. After graduating high school in '39, he enlisted in the Marines. Went through boot camp with flying colors but was injured in an accident, had surgery on his back, and received an honorable in 1940. He recovered, enrolled here but, get this...when the Japs hit Pearl, he tried to re-enlist."

Clark looked for approval or at least a nod from Johnson.

"He's a patriot."

The congressman maintained a stoic demeanor.

Clark moved on. "He's an Economics and Finance major, near the top of his class."

"So, a couple of years in the service, and now a senior, that makes him what... twenty-three, twenty-four?"

"Twenty-three."

"Not married?" Lyndon's faced got tight, he squinted and pointed a finger. "He's not a fag, is he?"

"Ah..." Clark was surprised.

"We can't have any of them working on my campaign." LBJ got loud. "There is all that homo shit in the papers about what's going on here. They are accusing the President of this University of not getting rid of a whole ring of them... professors and students... letting a bunch of fags stay on campus. I mean, Rainey better do something or he'll be gone like a fart in the wind."

Clark offered a weak response. "Lyndon, he's an academic, not a politician."

Johnson slapped his legs, preparing to rise. "Yeah well, if he doesn't act, he's going to be an academic without a job."

Conversation from the crowd in the auditorium drifted into the room.

LBJ stood, picked up his hat and fingered the edge. "Do you know what your two candidates have to say about this?"

"Busby wrote an article in the paper and is against any move to remove Rainey. I'm not sure about Wallace."

Johnson grimaced then flipped his hat onto his head, still fingering the brim. "This Wallace guy... Marine you say."

"Yep."

Johnson stepped to the doorway and stood pondering, his back to Clark.

"Lyndon?"

"Make sure he gets behind Busby in this. Let's get them involved but keep both in the background like you said. I want people we can use who don't have ties to me in case something goes wrong. Everybody knows I'm way past yonder on fags. Way, way past. If they have a record of supporting these homos it will give them distance from the campaign." Johnson turned around and lowered his voice. "We're going to need special help when I run for the Senate."

"Can we win this one first?"

LBJ scoffed. "Can't lose, Clark. I'll beat Buck Taylor in the primary by a country mile and the Republicans aren't even running an opposition in the general. I'll be running unopposed. This is in the bag and you know it."

"Of course, and I know you want the Senate but we will need soldiers, a lot of them."

"Okay, okay. You get them onboard, but like I said, and I mean it, keep them at arm's length."

Clark nodded, straightened his tie, and rose to follow his leader.

LBJ walked out of the room, heading for the stage.

Clark followed him down the hall, but remained behind the curtain.

The stage was well lit. About a hundred or so bodies quieted down as a man with black hair, Clark Kent glasses, and broad shoulders took the microphone. "Ladies and Gentlemen, it is my privilege to introduce the four-term Congressman from our great state of Texas, Lyndon Baines Johnson."

Malcolm Wallace, smiling broadly, stepped forward extending his hand.

Edward Lorenz, a scientist/mathematician/meteorologist at MIT, developed a hypothesis called the Butterfly Effect. His highly respected work stated that minor, almost imperceptible occurrences can affect the path of a future event however great, causing the eventual chaos. Lorenz theorized even the flap of a butterfly's wings could have influence on the path of a tornado. He developed this award-winning mathematical formula proving even an insignificant moment of influence could alter the track of a massive force.

On June 26, 1944, a handshake at a podium became the flap of the butterfly wing which altered the course of events nineteen years later, November 22, 1963.

CHAPTER 2

UNIVERSITY OF TEXAS

MARY ANDRE DUBOIS BARTON lay on her stomach, her knees bent, bare toes dancing. Long red hair framed a face that wore a devilish grin. Mac wasn't giving her his undivided attention but she knew it was just a matter of time. No matter how hard he tried, the textbook he was trying to read was no match for her, mirror practiced, Rita Hayworth stare. She let out a perfectly executed sigh.

"Would you please stop." He, laying on his stomach as well, looked up and slapped his hand on the open book. Mishkins, The Economics of Money and Banking, was now the wall between them. "I have midterms in three days and I need to study."

She riveted her eyes to his and tilted her head slightly, letting her curls hang loosely to one side. She had carefully chosen a soft purple skirt and yellow silk blouse, colors that complemented the blue blanket. She was picture perfect.

His stern look disappeared.

She wiggled her toes. A sense of satisfaction warmed her face.

But then his tone changed, voice lowered and he became serious, "Andre, I have to study. Please."

The warmth turned cold and a response came instantly. "Are you still pining over... what's her name... Norma?"

"No, absolutely not." Mac responded immediately—a little too fast.

"I think you are. You date her for years and she throws you over and... is now going to marry... a... what is he anyway, like or doctor or something?"

"Podiatrist."

"See... I knew it. You know all about him and her. I'm right."

"You couldn't be more wrong." Mac summoned his fortitude. "Do we have to do this now?"

Her face remained frozen.

"I love you. I've never met anyone like you... ever. You are everything to me. And if I had met you while I was seeing her, she would have been the one dumped."

The words hung for a second or two.

"Good answer." A small smile of victory curled her lips. "So then...," she seductively ran the tip of her tongue over her bottom lip, "can we go back to your apartment, now?"

He shook his head slowly, pleading. "Andre, please, I got out of the apartment so I could study." He looked around, then whispered, "I can't get anything done there. All you want to do is... you know."

"Fuck." Her voice was normal but the word was not.

Mac's face got red and for a moment she didn't know if it was embarrassment or anger. Either way it turned her on.

"Andre. If you don't stop, I'm going to get up and go to the library."

She stared at him in defiance.

The stare down was broken when Mac lowered his head and started reading.

Exasperated, she rolled on her back, hands folded across her

11

chest. She smoothed her skirt that had a hem a little higher than acceptable, and often got sneers from the other girls on campus.

A bird flew by and landed in a live oak nearby. Several students were milling about on the green. A study group was close but not too close. It was a beautiful, clear November day in Austin, finally nice enough to be out in the sun in the afternoon. A gentle breeze occasionally played with the ends of her hair.

A soft sigh of boredom went unnoticed.

Newly painted fingernails tapped together as a new plan formulated. A minute or so went by but then the tapping stopped.

Her fingers moved up to the buttons on her V-neck blouse. She unfastened a top button, waited a few seconds then unbuttoned the next one. She bent her head down and could see the curve of her breasts and the bottom clasp of her bra. She gently shimmied over, remaining on her back, positioning herself so the top of her head was across from Mac's. Then she arched her back like she had taken a deep breath.

She braced her pose with her elbows and bedroom whispered, "Mac."

He raised his head from his book and his eyes went immediately to her wide-open blouse. "Oh my God. Andre, what are you doing? Everyone can see."

"Let them." She flipped over onto her stomach, put her head in her hands, and her elbows on the blanket. A position that offered a view into the new year only to Mac.

"Still need to study?" She tilted her head to the Haywood pose again, but this time he didn't look away.

A very weak voice squeaked out, "Yes."

She adjusted her elbows, squeezing the light and shadow that framed her chest. She had control and the warm feeling returned. "Really? You don't want to—"

"Mac." Horace Busby came up on them unnoticed.

"Fuck." Andre whispered and dropped her hands to fasten the buttons and end the show.

Mac rolled to his side bending one leg, concealing his enthusiasm. "What's up?"

Horace suddenly aware of what was going on, turned his head and pulled on his tie nervously. "Ah…right… Mr. Clark… You know… Edward Clark? Well, he works for a congressman in the tenth and he wants to meet to discuss a possible opportunity for us to work in a re-election campaign."

"Clark?" Wallace was also stumbling, trying to regain his composure.

"We met him at the Homecoming dinner, remember?"

Mac shook his head, then quick glanced, checking on Andre's progress.

Horace turned to look, then away again quickly, and continued. "Doesn't matter, he remembers us. This could be a great opportunity."

Mac slapped his book closed, sat up, and crossed his arms. "This is ridiculous, I'm just not going to get a chance to study."

Andre stuck out her tongue.

"It's Lyndon Johnson. He's running again for Congress, which in itself isn't anything too big. He'll win going away, but Clark said he wants us on board now to work behind the scenes for Johnson's run for the Senate.

Andre, fit for public, sat up. "That sounds exciting. Undercover work, spying? Wow. Cool beans."

Busby paid her no attention. "Clark wants to meet with us tomorrow night. Will you come?"

Mac sat up straight, removed his Clark Kent glasses, wiped them on his shirt, pausing before responding.

Busby tapped his foot, impatient.

Andre had a fixed gaze. Malcolm Wallace became more interesting every day.

"Where?" Mac put on his glasses and slicked his hair back.

"Where what?" Horace suddenly looked nervous.

"What do you mean where what? Where does he want to meet?"

Horace leaned down and lowered his voice. "The Social Club."

Andre squealed with delight.

Mac did not. His mouth dropped open. "Hattie Valdez? You mean—"

"Austin's own famous… no infamous… house of prostitution." Andre small-clapped her hands. "What fun."

"No." Mac pointed. "No, I won't go."

There wasn't a chance for Horace to build a case. Andre took over. "Of course, you're going. You graduate in four months. What are we going to do after this? This is a chance for you to make the right connections and…" She reached out, took his arm with one hand and stroked his bicep with the other. "I want to hear about every detail."

Both men looked at her with male disbelief on their faces.

"What?" Andre looked genuinely surprised.

CHAPTER 3

SOLOMON CORTEZ WASHINGTON stood in the foyer, awaiting the arrival of the next member of Hattie Valdez's Social Club. He was tall, thin, with distinguished close-cropped grey hair and always wore a white long-tailed jacket over black tuxedo trousers. The pants were supported by suspenders given to him by the madam of the house some forty years prior. Serving as the head of staff and sergeant at arms, he knew the pecking order of all the members and their expected level of service. He knew which members drank at the bar, socialized, then had dinner before partaking in the delights offered on the second floor. He also knew who wanted privacy and how to surreptitiously guide them up the back stairs without much interaction. He knew how to break up bar fights that sometimes occurred when members who had too much to drink fought over the same courtesan.

When the brass door knocker announced an arrival, Solomon opened the door then guided most members and pre-approved guests to the main lounge. A few, because of tenure or social position, were escorted to a magnificent private parlor. Solomon treated them all with courtesy and respect, though some were not worthy of either.

Hattie appeared from her office down the hall and walked across the foyer. "Solomon, Mr. Clark has informed me that two young men will be arriving, shortly."

"Ma'am." He nodded slightly.

"They are his guests, a Mr. Busby and a Mr. Wallace. Please escort them to meet Mr. Clark in the parlor. They are to be offered all the benefits of membership."

"As yo say, ma'am."

She nodded then crooked her arm. "I'm ready now. Please walk me to the lounge." It wasn't a command, more of a tradition. Solomon always took an arm and cleared the way for her nightly, dramatic entrance.

They started down the hall, but she paused momentarily to fluff her hair and examine her dress in a full length, gold-framed mirror.

She wore a silk, form-fitting, dress with a deeply cut neckline accenting her best feature. She was not as attractive, or as alluring, as her much younger employees, but she wasn't unattractive either. Men still fawned over her, though she rarely if ever bedded one. Pushing the second half of her sixties, Hattie had long curly hair needing color often and her face normally modeled a little too much makeup, but she walked like the belle of the ball, with the confidence of an independent woman. She owned a prosperous business, had a fat bank account, and the protection of her well satisfied clientele. She also had a pink Cadillac.

Side-by-side, Hattie and Solomon continued down the long hall to the main lounge. The biggest room in the spacious house stretched forty feet in length, had a vaulted ceiling, and harshly painted deep red walls. There were tall windows on each side-wall covered with plantation shutters. Heavy drapes hung from the ceiling on thick rods. Privacy from prying eyes was a necessity.

A painting, perfect for a Texas men's club, hung on the expansive back wall. General William J. Worth was portrayed storming up Federation Hill, leading six companies of Texas Rangers during The Mexican War. Oversized leather couches, an assortment of tables and chairs, and a few oriental rugs over a wide plank floor and a well-stocked bar completed the room. Above the bar, fitted between two glass-shelved cases filled with amber colored bottles of liquor, hung a life-size portrait of a young Hattie Valdez.

Several girls politely clapped as she entered, and the men in the room raised a glass.

Solomon, his duty done, took a step back.

She gripped his arm. "Remember now, don't bring Mr. Clark's guests here. He's waiting for them in the parlor."

"Ma'am." Released, he returned to his post, put his back against the wall, and waited for the next knock on the door.

Edward Clark had arrived early, well before the recruits were due. He usually arrived in advance of a meeting of any kind. Being late for something was disrespectful and an opportunity missed. Being first sometimes meant picking up on perhaps some valuable morsel of useful information. He sat in a high-backed leather chair in the corner of the parlor, quietly watching four other men socialize. He sipped a vintage Sherry from a slim crystal glass. A fitting drink for his image though he didn't really enjoy the taste. He rationalized drinking something he didn't like would keep him from drinking too much of something he did like.

His approach to alcohol mirrored his self-imposed dress

code. He usually wore a dark suit, a fully buttoned vest, white collared shirt, and a black bow tie. He was very particular of his public image and always dressed accordingly. That evening, though the temperature didn't require it, he wore a long light-weight overcoat topped by a black Fedora with a wide black silk band. He had given the hat and overcoat to Solomon, but held onto his favorite walking stick. The tapered, solid oak staff topped with a silver knob now rested like a scepter against the arm of the chair.

He rested the drink on a table, laced his fingers together across his chest, and studied the other four members in the room. The parlor was really just a VIP lounge, a smaller room with better furnishings, reserved for a few of Hattie's best clients. It was more for prestige than privacy. However, a para-mount requirement of all attendees was discretion, which for all patronizing a brothel occurred out of necessity. Hattie's Social Club was the worst, best-kept secret in the city of Austin. Everyone knew about it, but no one spoke of it, or acknowl-edged membership, nor did anyone try to close it down. Oper-ating for more than fifty years, it stayed a favorite haunt of some of the most powerful men in Texas. The last thing that would happen in any conversation was, "You'll never guess who I saw at Hattie Valdez's last night," because to say it was to admit attendance which no one in this devoutly Christian town would own up to.

From his leather perch, Clark recognized and raised his glass, ever so slightly, to the nervously fidgeting President of the First National Bank of Austin who was drinking bourbon and branch water. The short fat man returned the acknowledgment, his face blank and void of expression. Clark could see he was still trying to drown out the death of his wife.

Clark knew the banker, whose membership was recent, toler-ated the Club over the years, though it went against all his beliefs, because it was in his best interest to do so. Some of

Hattie's best clients were not only the most influential people in the state, but also the banks best customers. He could ill-afford not cooperating with Hattie.

Clark at first was offput by the bank manager's presence in the VIP room, as his station in society was well beneath consideration. His title was manager but he was basically just a clerk. Hatti explained to Clark that the manager had always treated her like every other client who favored his bank, something she didn't get from other establishments. Despite his beliefs, the bank manager always maintained a respectful business relationship and dealt personally in handling her, mostly cash, business. She also explained she returned his kindness by quietly offering the Club's accommodation about a year after his wife died. It took him six months to knock on the door, but soon after his first visit, he became a regular monthly visitor.

Clark also nodded and received recognition from the Democratic Party leader of the 2nd district who was laughing and patronizing two men Clark assumed were guests being positioned for support in the leader's upcoming election. The ward leader possessed the brass of a marching band, and was not to Clark's taste, but the man had provided valuable work for LBJ's previous congressional campaigns and would be needed when Johnson ran for the Senate. Clark watched as the ward leader filled glasses and slapped backs. However distasteful it was to watch, the rude and crude man would eventually maneuver his two guests into contributing large gifts to the party.

Clark reached over to the small table and picked up a cut glass carafe and, while refilling his glass with Sherry, noticed a slim man, dressed in a dark suit with wide lapels, standing in a dimly lit corner of the room. Through the shadow, Clark could see that the man had a pencil-thin mustache and slicked-back, dark hair. The man had a saucer in one hand and was sipping from a China cup with the other. Clark made a mental note to discover the odd stranger's identity.

Like the bank manager, he abhorred this club, feeling what went in the rooms on the second-floor appalling. However, the existence of this private room was extremely useful for private business. A meeting here was different than clandestine meetings in restaurants or parks. He observed how differently men behaved here. It was where the weaknesses of both his opponents and his friends were exposed. He, however, was ever vigilant, guarding his own secrets, while waiting, like a spider at the cobweb edge, watching every move his victim made.

He was a very patient man, but Clark checked his watch, and noted that the boys were late. He shook his head, but then decided it would be for the best. The ward leader was pushing his guests out of the door toward the lounge, the bank manager easing out as well, leaving only the shadowy man, still in the corner, still sipping from his cup.

Clark checked his watch again. He knew who was at fault which reinforced his effort to replace the culprit.

Hattie Valdez breezed into the room, looked around, and announced, "Drink up, dinner will be served in just a few minutes." She bowed slightly at the waist but didn't lower her eyes.

Clark admired her. She would have made a formidable opponent if she had chosen a normal existence instead of the madam of a whore house or, if she were a not a Mexican or, if she were a man. He respected her resourcefulness and diligence, the way she solved problems quietly, and even in difficult circumstances was able to make alliances that benefited her future. He knew her to be as tough as any man he had met, and a heartless bitch when it came to the business and her whores.

One of Hattie's Club traditions was a Wednesday dinner party, a night in the middle of the week when married men could find an excuse to attend and single men rarely missed.

The man in the corner deposited his cup and saucer on a

table as he moved quickly from the shadow through the open door.

Minutes passed and Clark drummed his fingers on the arm of the chair.

Activity in the foyer caught his attention; through the open door he watched about a dozen girls come down the stairs. They descended single file, giggling, then gathered in a group in the foyer. Hattie clapped once and waved a finger. The group performed a well-rehearsed maneuver to where they ended up in a straight line. Two were short, two were tall, several blonde, several brunettes.

A heavy girl stood next to a skinny thing and both were bookended by a brown girl on one side and a black girl on the other. All but two were dressed in long gowns of various colors and materials. The two non-conformists had chosen a different look. A ponytailed girl decided on a Western hoedown costume. The other sported a black silk tuxedo jacket with no blouse, but still donned a bowtie.

Hattie pointed, and three of the girls, who apparently had been requested especially for the occasion, left the line and took their place beside the Democratic Party Leader and his two friends. Hattie then took an exotic-looking girl from the line and led her to the bank manager who blushed red when the girl took his arm. The rest of the lineup broke ranks as the group of men from the main lounge darted after the bevy of quail like pointer dogs on the hunt.

He took another sip of sherry and leaned his head back against the chair, allowing his mind to drift. Partaking in the pleasures found on the club's upper floor was not for him. His membership was political not social and certainly not personal. Everyone knew him, including the other members, as silent and aloof.

Clark removed a cigarette case from an inside pocket,

opened it, and withdrew an unfiltered Pall Mall. The inside of the lid of the silver case was inscribed.

A winner never quits
Lyndon

He snapped the lid of his birthday present closed. Even in a gesture of kindness, LBJ was positioning himself as the lead dog, a position Edward Clark relinquished soon after recognizing the candidate had unrelenting ambition which superseded good manners, good taste, and good morals. Nothing would stand against Lyndon's unstoppable will.

Edward was happy in the background. He knew he could never be the politician Lyndon was. He learned this lesson as a young man when he suffered an overwhelming defeat running for office as a low-level county commissioner. He realized in that defeat, in spite of the fact he was overly qualified for the job, he was totally unelectable. He realized there were two ways to obtain a position of power, be born to it, or take it by any means possible. Edward knew he was neither, and decided to become indispensable to the man he was convinced had the drive to take what he wanted and the power to change everything.

He and Lyndon spent almost ten years building the power base needed to take the next step up from congressman. The run for a seat in the United States Senate was next and soldiers were needed to prepare the battleground.

The foyer had emptied and the sound from the knocker on the front door echoed back into the parlor.

Two young men stepped past Solomon, their heads darting from side to side, eyes wide, and their faces lit up with expectation.

Solomon ushered them into the parlor then closed the double doors behind them.

"Mr. Clark." Busby, wincing at the volume of his voice, added, "Sorry."

Wordlessly, Clark stood and gestured them forward.

Horace approached first, sporting a broad smile. The taller, more handsome boy followed a step behind.

Clark shook Busby's hand then looked to Mac. "And this is Mr. Wallace, I presume?"

Horace answered. "Yes sir, Malcolm Wallace." Busby reached behind, placed his arm around the taller boy's shoulders, and pulled Mac forward.

Clark offered his hand to Wallace. "A firm grip, that's good."

"Ah... thank you, sir." Wallace's voice cracked.

Clark didn't say anything else, quietly waiting at the edge of the web.

The differences between the two young men were dramatic. Horace dressed well, but his counterpart wore a cheap suit that was too small for his form and shoes that had a military shine, but were old and desperately needed new soles.

Busby and Wallace remained standing as Clark returned to his chair.

Clark finished the last sip of sherry from his glass. "Please." He gestured to them to sit.

The two pulled chairs around to face Clark.

"A few years from now a very powerful man is going to run against Coke Stevenson for the Democratic nomination for US Senate." He paused to see if they knew what that meant. Not seeing recognition, he decided to explain. "The nomination of the democratic party is really the election even though it is just the primary. A Republican hasn't come close to winning in a general election in Texas since 1870. The man Stevenson will face will be Congressman Lyndon Baines Johnson."

The name registered on both faces.

"LBJ is running for reelection now but that is already in the bag... he's in front by more than twenty points. It's a two-year term, and there will be one more which he will also win. That will bring us to 1948. During these years we will prepare the ground for a campaign for the United States Senate."

Clark put his hands on the armrests and pushed himself up to his feet, now standing over the two who fidgeted not knowing whether to remain seated or stand.

"You're the lawyer, right?" Clark looked at Busby who nodded. "We might need you in the office occasionally."

"That would be a great—"

Turning to Wallace, Clark cut Busby off. "And you're the marine, correct?"

"Sir." Wallace nodded now standing and almost at attention.

"I have been told that you can get things done and be quiet about it. Is that true?"

Wallace said nothing at first, and then nodded his head almost imperceptibly.

"Answer the man," said Busby who hadn't noticed.

"He did answer." Clark nodded to Wallace with a wry smile.

Clark dusted his sleeve with the back of his hand. "You two should stay, have dinner and… enjoy yourselves. Hattie knows you're my guests. We'll be in touch." He turned picked up his walking stick, and sauntered out the door without turning around.

Busby looked at Wallace and whispered in Clark's wake. "We're in."

Wallace looked concerned. "In what?"

Hattie saw Clark heading for the door and came out of the dining room. He gave a nod toward the parlor and she headed to retrieve Clark's guests.

Solomon reached for the door handle.

Clark's attention was drawn to movement in the hallway.

The thin man Clark saw earlier in the parlor was now well-lit and headed up the stairs with a girl with long yellow hair.

"Who was that?" Clark's puzzlement caused him to pause and stare.

The dark suited arm was draped around the shoulders of the girl. They were taking the steps upstairs quickly. The blonde bent an ear toward the man then giggled at something unintelligible.

Clark's face went white. It was the walk that gave it away. Inquiry into the identity wasn't necessary.

The dark suited head turned sideways, speaking to the girl again, giving Clark a very distinguishable profile. The pencil thin moustache was painted on.

The slicked-back hair, the long nose, the narrow face, the tall lanky frame, belonged to Josefa Johnson, the candidate's sister.

CHAPTER 4

JULY 22, 1944

THE SMELL MADE his heart beat a little faster, blood flow a little quicker, and caused his memory to flash to the past. Dozens of campaign workers spending endless hours jammed into the forty-by-twenty storefront generated a pungent odor. Perspiration mixed with women's perfume; men's cologne combined with a cloud of cigarette smoke hanging in now undisturbed air. It invigorated his mood and caused his exhausted frame to straighten and the humorless expression on his face to change. A grin appeared. It wasn't a big, toothy, politician walking up to a microphone smile. It was a no-witnesses grin of his power. The corners of his mouth turned up ever so slightly from the satisfaction of the smell of the mindless, powerless, minions devoted to his success.

The Lyndon Baines Johnson reelection headquarters had been filled with volunteers just hours before. From early in the morning, they jammed together, their voices raising a din that made conversation difficult, and, as the day wore on, accounted for an ever-increasing volume of noise. It had been, as usual, a hot day in Austin. There was no breeze, a clear sky, the sun had baked the sidewalk to frying pan heat. Inside, the workers were sealed in a Dutch oven. It was empty now and as the door closed slowly behind him, and he paused, hands on his hips, hat tilted slightly to the side, surveying the empty space. It was over. Polls closed and the staff had left to eat and drink and, no doubt, celebrate when the results were announced. Piles of now obsolete hand-bills and stacks of envelopes waiting to be stuffed, lay next to silver-dollar sized campaign buttons bearing a badly touched-up picture of him that looked straight from a mortician's obituary. Everything was strewn about on long tables. All now worthless.

He sucked in another nose full of air.

"68%."

Johnson startled, peering through the shadows to the back of the room.

Ed Clark emerged from a makeshift office door and headed toward him.

"You sure?" Johnson took a step. "The polls have only been closed for a couple of hours."

"Positive." Clark gave a knowing grin, then restated his educated guess. "I had five staff at every polling site asking who people voted for. When the count is finished, you'll have won by almost 70%."

Johnson pulled the hat off his head and kicked a metal chair into sitting position. "Was it ever in doubt?"

Clark gave him the same grin again. "Never." Ed Clark pointed to a chair then pulled one out from a table for himself. "It's important we get a press release out right away empha-sizing the margin of victory. You beat Buck Taylor so bad in this primary that the Republicans won't even think about putting anybody up against you in '46. You'll run unopposed."

Clark waited a few seconds for a reaction but just got a nod. "Right..." he continued, "this virtually assures you staying in

Congress for four more years, which brings us right up to the Senate race in '48."

Again, no reaction.

"We have to start that campaign now." Clark put both hands on his knees and leaned forward. "You know that, right?"

Johnson nodded again.

Clark's expression seemed uneasy at Johnson's silence.

LBJ was stoic, seemed indifferent and detached.

Clark sat back. "What's wrong?"

"Who's coming?" Johnson remained stiff; his arms folded.

"How did you...?" Clark's face gave up that he indeed had a hidden agenda. He sputtered then spit out his plot. "Right. Okay. First, we... I mean, you... need to put someone in place to run the Senate campaign now. You don't want me in front of an unannounced senate run while I still do what you need done in Congress."

LBJ closed his eyes and leaned back a bit. His response came out almost under his breath. "Who?"

"Cliff Carter. He's from Bryan, Texas. I met him when he volunteered for your campaign for Congress in '37. Ironically, he wound up serving under me when I was a captain in the 36th Infantry. He won the Bronze Star, Legion of Merit, and the French Croix de Guerre."

LBJ grumbled impatiently. "Cro de what? And... who in Texas gives a flying fuck what some Frenchy..." Johnson suddenly stiffened his back and leaned in close to Clark, almost nose to nose. "Why are you hot on this guy?"

Clark didn't move back. He kept his face close and responded slowly. "He is loyal. He understands how the system works and doesn't need to know... the why... to follow orders."

Johnson pushed back, shaking his head. "A campaign for Senate... no. No, I'm not putting myself in the hands of any rank amateur." He stood up, now not looking tired. He looked angry.

Clark put both hands up in a stop sign gesture but remained

seated. "Lyndon, it's four years out. Let Carter get involved now. I'll watch closely, keep you insulated and informed, but we need to get started."

Johnson stood silent.

"I know that Coke Stevenson intends to run. He's the sitting Governor. He's been positioning for it just like you but you're a congressman and he's the Governor. You have a good reputation but you're not that well-known outside of the tenth district."

Johnson kicked the chair. "How sure are you that its Coke?"

"Certain. My wife is on a charity committee with his wife and she's already talking about what living in Washington will be like."

"Fuck. He'll be tough to beat."

"Yes, he will. So, you agree then, we need to start now?"

Johnson nodded. "I know you know him… this Carter… but did you really check this guy out?"

"Our friend in Washington ran the background through the FBI in Austin and he's clean."

Lyndon turned his back to Clark, pondering again, hand scratching beard stubble on his face. "Okay, I'll meet with your Mr. Carter."

"Good, he should be here any minute." Clark looked relieved at first then quizzical. "Ah…I have to ask. How did you know I had someone coming here tonight?"

Johnson turned and looked hard at his trusted assistant. "Well, I might tell you, someday." He put a big paw on Clark's shoulder and smiled. "Then again, I might not."

The front door swung open.

Clark gave a half wave and raised his voice. "Come on back."

Cliff Carter was average height and an average face, but he walked like a Texan, head up confident and seemingly unafraid.

Johnson gave him a stern face, a once-over look, then finally broke into a smile. "Cliff Carter. Your former captain filled me in on your war record. How long have you been back?"

"I got back last December. Not long really."

LBJ puffed up. "You know, I won the Silver Star when I was in."

Carter shot a concerned look at Lyndon.

Not noticing, LBJ pushed on. "I never made a big deal about it in the press, but MacArthur gave it to me, personally."

Clark looked a little confused. "I didn't know you served, sir. Army like us—"

Carter cut him off and redirected back to the original question. "Tell Lyndon what you've been doing since you got back."

Carter stuttered a bit. "I… I'm managing a bottling plant."

Johnson nodded. "Sounds profitable. Beer distribution, correct?"

"No, sir. Not beer, 7-UP. It's a pop drink out of St. Louis."

"Oh. Is that a money maker too?" LBJ turned to Clark. "Maybe we should look into that Ed."

"Well," Carter said cautiously. "It's not like were making Coca-Cola nervous but we're doing okay. It's catching on."

There was an awkward silence, broken by LBJ. "Clark tells me you can follow orders. Is that correct?"

Carter almost snapped to attention. "Yes, sir."

"All orders?"

"Yes, sir."

LBJ resolved, turned to Carter and gestured. "Fill him in."

Clark turned his full attention to Carter, leaned forward, and lowered his voice.

LBJ walked away, chose a table to sit on, pushed the remnants of the campaign to the floor and sat, dangling his boots. Carter would handle this and if he didn't there would be a price to pay. Johnson turned off the external sound and tuned into his internal voice.

I'm going to need a ton of money.

CHAPTER 5

MARCH 1945

MAC WALLACE WALKED up the wooden stairs which creaked with the weight of each footstep. He started counting them but dismissed the tabulation, afraid the result would equal thirteen, the same number that led to a hangman's gallows. He needed good luck, not bad omens. When he reached the second-floor landing, he bent forward peeking through the yellow curtains framing the window of the apartment's door. His eyes darted and, not finding her in the kitchen, he put his forehead on the glass, straining to see into the living room. The limited view revealed only her legs, crossed and elevated, resting on the back of the couch. A radio was providing the music, and her toes were keeping the beat.

He stood up and stepped back, ducked his head, and took a deep breath. He spun away from the door and put his hands on the railing. Looking down he saw an empty trash can, its lid off and leaning on an old, rusted lawn mower. He gripped the wood rail hard, trying to summon the courage he needed to face her. He was a big man, a good athlete, played football, been tough enough to be a marine, and popular enough to become the student body president of the University of Texas. Yet some-how, she made him feel like a little boy. Mary was different than any girl... any woman... he had ever met. He could see her in his mind's eye. Inside, laying on the couch, a cigarette burning in the ashtray, holding a bottle of beer, and reading some trashy paperback. She was nothing like who he thought he would be with— that would always be Nora. But then again, he never thought he would be in the position he was in now either. Maybe, he should not tell her and just go. Maybe, it wasn't too late to try to talk to— he shook his head back and forth trying to rid himself of doubt.

Stop. Just stop.

Suddenly, the music coming from the radio inside got much louder and he spun around to see Mary in the open door, feet apart and arms crossed.

"Hi." Mac said weakly.

"Hi yourself. What are you doing out here?" She glanced over the side. "It isn't high enough to jump."

He chuckled and stepped toward the door.

There was an instant of hesitation, but she moved back inside as he passed by.

Mac walked to the refrigerator, pulled out a beer, popped the cap with the can opener screwed to a cabinet door, and took a long swig.

"Thanks for offering." She still had her arms crossed.

Mac spit a bit. "Oh, right, sorry. You want one?"

Mary Andre DuBois Barton nodded. "Uh huh."

He grabbed a beer, removed the cap, and held out the bottle.

She let it hang there for a bit, then snatched it from his hand. "Well?"

He looked at her for a second, decided to be mysterious, walked into the living room, and plopped onto the couch.

She followed behind, slowly, sat close, but was careful not to touch him.

He took another pull from the bottle.

Mary followed suit. A moment passed, then she shrugged her shoulders impatiently.

He grinned.

Her hard façade cracked. "What? Tell me."

"Horace and I met with Ed Clark. He wants Horace to work in the office in Austin."

"And?"

"He said he needs me to get some experience, so I can help them do some things for the campaign over the next couple of years."

"What does he mean when he said, 'things?' I don't understand."

Mac's expression signified his lack of an answer. "Yeah, things was a little vague but—"

"But what? I swear to God, if you don't tell me, right now, I'm going to—"

"He wants me… to move to New York."

This moment of silence was different than the previous one. She was wordless, then after a beat, "New York?" came out like a whisper. It got louder, "New York." Then a scream of delight. "New fucking York."

Mac nodded, still grinning.

She dropped the beer on the carpet and threw herself at him, coming to rest sitting on his lap.

Caught off guard, he managed to hold on to his beer while dealing with her commando attack.

"Oh my God. You're not talking the state of, right, but New York, the city?"

"Yep, New York City, three blocks from Greenwich Village."

She pushed back, stiff arming his shoulders, mouth open, and speechless again.

He let the glorious silence continue.

A full minute went by before her shoulders and arms

relaxed, her elbows bent, unpinning him from the back of the couch. Her cheeks were flushed, almost matching her lipstick. She gulped in a breath and weakly eked out, "when?"

"Now. I mean they want me there as soon as I can manage." He could tell she was still stunned and decided to dump everything all at once. "I stopped by the Dean's office before I came home, withdrew from class, and resigned as student body president."

For the first time in their short and tumultuous relationship, he was in control, and he smiled.

This is fun.

She was shifting around on his lap and he was getting aroused. Her silk blouse was undone to a third button and her unrestricted breasts were in and out of visibility. The moment was brief.

Suddenly, her expression stiffened and she stood up, hands on hips and bent at the waist. "Why?"

His mood didn't change as fast. "Huh?"

"Why? Why the rush? What could possibly be so important that you have to quit school three credits short and two months from graduation?"

He held up two stop sign hands and pumped the brakes. "Woah, cowgirl. Everything is going to be fine. I've been enrolled at The New School for Social Research. It's a highly recognized graduate study for social reform programs. It's what I've been pushing for the whole time I've been at UT."

"Social reform?"

"Ed Clark told me I will begin to learn the ins and outs of social theory, policy and economic justice all based on the political philosophy, psychology and historical analysis of capitalism, migration, critical journalism and current gender and sexual movements."

She shook her head and frowned. "You memorized that whole speech?"

"I did... just for you." He laughed and reached up, grabbing her by the arms, dragging her back to his lap. "These guys are giving me the opportunity of a lifetime. They set this up so I could do research for a man who wants to be the next Senator of Texas. Clark told me Johnson will be running against the governor, Coke Stevenson. And he is going to be tough to beat. Clark also said the two men will split the usual Texas vote but the one who gets the most fringe votes... like the liberals, will win. Johnson is a Roosevelt-New Deal guy but that's just him following a popular vote in Congress. Clark thinks Johnson will need to add some original planks to his platform that will attract new voters without losing the base."

She just stared at him blankly. "So, they want you to suck up to a bunch of New York liberals, like the Jews and the coloreds, so this Johnson guy gets a few more votes in an election that is happening three years from now?"

"Actually, the election is two years and nine months from now, but yes. I will report to Clark and he will give me directions. Meanwhile, I get a front row seat in a major political campaign."

She seemed unconvinced, and pointed a finger at him. "They're using you."

He gripped her arms. "Of course they are using me. So what? It's how the system works." He gripped her harder and shook her a little. "Don't you get it? This is my... I mean, our, ticket."

Her face softened and her body slackened a little.

"Well? What do you say?"

One eyebrow raised over her now twinkling eye. "Did you say you were going to study sexual movements?"

He laughed out loud then pulled her to him.

She kissed him hard. Her mouth open and tongue probing. She shifted her weight in his lap, grinding against him.

He pulled back, breathless.

35

She was not, and used an open palm to pull his head back to her mouth. She took control, her passion heating the moment to a boil.

When her mouth moved to his neck, he murmured, "Will you come with me?"

She bit his earlobe.

"Will you?" he repeated.

She moved her lips to his ear. "You're not ready for me, yet." She sucked on where she bit. "I will suck you, and I will fuck you."

His breath was short, his heart beating almost out of his chest. "Will you come?"

She pushed his face into the back of the couch then got eye to eye. "I always come."

CHAPTER 6

OCTOBER 1945

THE CITY WAS NAMED for the infamous Sam Houston, soldier, politician, leader of the revolution against Mexico, and the first President of the Republic of Texas. The second president, a man who founded public education, the University of Texas, and brought economic stability to a frontier state, had his name memorialized on a street and a dingy downtown building.

Edward Clark stood on the sidewalk staring at the Lamar Hotel. Although the building dominated Houston's skyline, it took no part in adding nuance or beauty. Its facade had few adornments, looked more like a factory than a luxury hotel, and Clark thought the dark shadow covering the front to be its natural color. The juxtaposition between where this meeting was being held and the meeting of the equally powerful men of Houston was as definitive as the path of the sun.

He was wearing a dark suit, white shirt, a tie, and his Washington D.C. Fedora. His suit was wrinkled, his body sweaty, and he was hungry and very tired. The forty-eight-hour train ride was torture, his claustrophobia preventing sleep, and his apprehension concerning the outcome of this meeting caused a migraine that seemed relentless.

He looked both ways, as was his habit, then crossed the road and took quick steps up to the front door. There was no uniformed doorman but, to his surprise, inside was substantially cooler than the city's midday sun. In the lobby, a few tall chairs were clumped together and positioned under the mandatory stuffed head of a giant longhorn steer. Two men sat apart reading newspapers and a couple was either checking in or out at the counter. He knew where he was going and headed directly to the elevator, and Suite 8F.

A mechanical whine got louder and his feet began to shuffle nervously as he waited for the door to open. He boarded and stood gripping a brass rail wondering if the heavy oak paneling lining the walls, or the overweight operator, were straining its cables.

"The eight floor popular today, sir." The man dressed in a nicely creased uniform nodded and smiled politely at his passenger.

"Uh huh." Clark grumbled.

"Yessier. You my ninth trip this mornin.'"

"Uh huh."

"Here we are." The elevator jerked to a stop and the steel wire gate slid open, and the wooden door on the eighth floor followed.

Clark stepped off quickly, barely acknowledging the operator who was tipping his cap. He had been on this floor many times and had come to hate the hotel, the city and the power posturing of the men he had come to see. Waiting for him was a small group composed of the biggest builders and developers in Texas, owners of banks, insurance companies, a newspaper, CEOs of major companies and a few of the lawyers that kept all of them off the radar.

Construction magnets George and Herman Brown were the

two most influential of the group. Their holdings exceeded the total of all the others combined. They were rich, powerful, stopped at nothing to further their agenda, and didn't hesitate to use the others in the room as pieces on their chessboard. Their vote always carried the day because everyone in the 8F Group benefited from their moves, especially Lyndon Baines Johnson.

In the beginning, the brothers impressed by the wiry ex-schoolteacher's non-stop energy and relentless ambition, helped Lyndon get elected to the tenth district Congressional seat. Their support was rewarded almost immediately when the freshman congressman pushed through special legislation that allowed the brothers to continue construction on the multimillion-dollar Mansfield Dam project. Since then Johnson's entire political career had been conducted from one small district in Austin, but now, after twelve years as one of many in congress, the time to become one of the few in the Senate had arrived. Today's meeting was to inform the group that his position on the chess-board was about to change.

A man who looked like a bulldozer without the blade stood guard outside the room.

"Edward Clark."

The man nodded, opened the door, and stood aside.

Clark felt very small passing by him into a small foyer.

"You're late." A terse voice came from a room behind open double doors.

Clark decided not to answer. It was strategic and designed to give weight to his presence and reason for meeting. He walked in slowly. A white oak table centered a conference room that was long enough for eight chairs on each side and wide enough for two chairs at the head. George and Herman Brown sat side-by-side, one sipping coffee, one tapping fingers.

George bellowed. "I said, you're late."

The force of his voice caused Clark's resolve to buckle. "The train didn't... arrive on time."

Herman grunted.

Clark started for the empty chair at the end of the table while trying to resummon his fortitude. In addition to the Browns, the chairs were occupied by bankers, Jesse Jones and Gus Wortham; James Abercrombie, who was steel and iron in Texas; Insurance giants, William Vinson, Jim Elkins, and Albert Thomas; and the publisher and owner of the Houston Post, William Hobby. The eighth man was Hugh Cullen, a D.C. lobbyist and one of Lyndon Johnson's most vengeful enemies.

Vinson, a portly man with a thin mustache and a slicked back comb-over tried to ease the tension. "Ed, you look like you could use a glass of sweet tea. It's hotter than a burning stump out there." He beckoned to a tall black man wearing a white jacket and matching gloves standing in the corner. The man went to a server cabinet and poured a glass from a pewter pitcher.

To Clark's surprise, George Brown, in a much more civilized voice said, "Boy, I'll have a glass too."

Vinson, pleased with his interaction, gloated a bit. "Clarky, the insurance business has been doing good for me, but the new regulations coming out of DC are like hugging a rosebush. I mean, I like the flowers, but it's painful if'n you aint careful."

Herman thumped the table. "Shut up, Vinson. We're not here for that stuff today. Clark, you wanted this meeting, or more accurately, Congressman Johnson wanted it, but neither of you would tell us what it was about."

A white glove deposited a glass in front of Clark.

Herman continued. "You're here, and you got a nice glass of tea. So... please tell us why we're here?" He folded his fingers together in front of him and stared at Clark.

Ed didn't speak. Instead he picked up the glass and took a pull. When finished he set it down carefully using two hands to position it on the center of a coaster. He pushed it forward then spoke. "Congressman Lyndon Johnson is announcing his candidacy for the Senate next week."

George and Herman simultaneously said, "So what?"

"So… we want 8F to support him in his run for office. He will be against Governor Coke Stevenson, which of course you already know, and several of you support." He raised a hand adding quickly, "Before you object, Lyndon knows some of you can't openly support him."

Bill Hobby sitting across from Clark, responded angrily. "You're right about that. My paper won't have a reader left if we endorse Johnson."

Hugh Cullen's face was red and he spit when he yelled out, "He's a Roosevelt New Dealer, not to mention he's as crooked as a barrel of fish hooks. No… no. I won't do it. He'll get nothing from me."

Clark responded calmly. "First, we aren't looking to your newspaper, Bill. And second…" He faced Cullen and raised his voice one decibel, "that New Dealer, as you call him, made some people in this room pretty healthy on the Mansfield Dam project."

"Enough." George Brown stopped Cullen who seemed to get even more red faced and addressed Clark. "You said you don't want support. I don't understand."

"No, we want your support, but we're not looking for an endorsement."

No one spoke.

Clark started to stand but then thought better of it and just shifted around in his seat. Standing would be overplaying his hand. He looked around the room slowly. They were puzzled and waiting for an explanation.

Clark took another drink then began addressing himself to the Browns. "Lyndon wants you to remember in spite of whatever political persona he deems necessary to win his seat, that he continues to stand, as he has demonstrated many times in the past, for you… on everything that matters."

George nodded. "Obviously you want money, but I still don't understand what you're saying."

"There will be two Democratic candidates in the primary, LBJ and Coke Stevenson. Like always, the general election doesn't matter. A Republican hasn't won in a hundred years and that's not about to change. The Senate seat will be decided in the primary."

"Come on Clark, you're hollering down a well. Everybody knows that." Bill Vinson seemed pleased with his folksy saying but no one else did.

"Lyndon wants you to understand nothing will change when he wins."

"When." George Brown chuckled.

"Yes, when he wins." Clark looked directly at the Browns. "Coke is Governor and widely known in-state so his name recognition is good. LBJ is from the tenth district, gets occasional press, but is not a household name. That makes the campaign tough and it is where we will focus our campaign. You, however, need to understand electing Stevenson may help on local state issues but he is virtually unknown in Washington. LBJ, on the other hand, is a powerful force in Congress. His influence has already proven very beneficial to this group, and will continue in the future, for example, the upcoming construction contracts for the Naval Air station in Corpus Christi are pending."

Herman, now paying close attention said, "Noted."

"This will be a tight race decided by a very slim margin. Coke will rely on his reputation and the good old boy network and LBJ will need to work twice as hard."

George Brown piped in. "Your point, Clark?"

"We want half. Half of all the money you choose to put into this election… exactly half. You all knew Coke would run. Every

Governor looking at an empty Senate seat runs. Naturally, he would expect your support, but know this: if Coke wins, you'll still have influence, no doubt. But when LBJ wins, you'll have a young, energetic advocate in the United States Senate that has been in the past, and will be in the future, extremely advantageous."

Bill Hobby pointed an inquisitive finger. "So, if my paper endorses Coke?"

"Don't care. Those votes are already counted. Nobody who reads the Post would vote for LBJ. We are confident we'll split the conservative vote. He'll just need the outliners to win."

"The niggers and the Jews." Cullen spit again. "I knew it."

Clark stared at Cullen. "Hugh, I've been coming here for years and I just can't believe how stupid you really are. You couldn't be more wrong. The Negroes don't vote in large numbers because of the poll tax. It costs them money they don't have and to the Jews, sure maybe we get some to vote but just exactly how many Temples are here in Houston?"

Cullen had no response but spit anyway.

"LBJ is going after the rural vote. The city vote will split but the country vote is up for grabs. It's a lot of territory and that's why the money is so necessary. We are counting on Coke taking your money and spending it all on votes he already has."

George and Herman both pushed back in their chairs.

Clark thought he heard one of them whisper, "Smart," but he wasn't sure which one.

Minutes went by. Looks were exchanged.

George Brown looked like he was about to speak.

Herman put his hand on his brother's arm. "We were expecting Johnson to be here today. So, why are you here instead of him coming himself? I have to say, we don't cotton to being stood up."

Clark spoke without emotion, clear and strong. "Lyndon is in Austin as we speak. He's meeting with Clint Murchison, H.L.

Hunt, and the other oilmen with the same deal. I'm here at his instruction because Lyndon didn't want either group to feel like they were a second choice and to alleviate any misgivings about equal representation."

George looked at Herman who nodded again. He then looked around the table. Everybody except Cullen, who had his head down and was mumbling under his breath, nodded. "Okay, Ed. Tell Lyndon we'll split the money evenly. But, as usual, we want distance so when he does help us in the future nothing can be traced back to us directly."

"Of course." Clark nodded.

"Do you have somebody in New York?"

"Yes. A good boy from UT in Austin. Picked him myself. Been there about nine months."

"Good. We'll open a position for him to work at Nation Bank of New York. We'll funnel the money through contacts to him and he can watch over the accounts. You know Baily from my office?"

Clark nodded.

"He'll be in touch with the details. What's this fella's name?"

"Wallace. Malcolm Wallace."

CHAPTER 7
DECEMBER 1945

New York City, in the snow, at Christmas, is a magician's illusion on the grandest scale. Multicolored lights are affixed to row upon row of signs and billboards that rise into the night. Glaring spotlights reflect off black windows and glisten like tinsel. And here in Chinatown, paper lanterns, like giant Christmas balls, hang from lamppost to lamppost. The falling snow surrounds the non-stop commotion on the street absorbing the usually relentless noise. With collars up and hats pulled tight, people move in a muffled but synchronous ballet. For a very brief period of time, the city changes its aura and becomes a living, breathing, snow globe.

Growing up in Texas, Mac had seen snow flurries several times and once he awoke to a thin coating on the front yard. When he joined the marines, he hoped to be stationed near someplace that actually had all the parts of a real winter not just wind and cold. But after training at Parris Island, South Carolina, where snow is equally as scarce as Texas, he was assigned to Hawaii, never coming close to experiencing real snow.

He had dressed in a hurry, left in a hurry, and was moving faster than the bundled-up pedestrians. The meeting was set for seven o'clock at Uncle Lou's Chinese restaurant, near Columbus Park, only a few blocks from his Mulberry Street apartment. He checked his watch and, realizing he would be early, slowed his gait. Yesterday's phone call from Ed Clark was unexpected and very unusual. Mac usually reported to a man he had never met, Mr. Baily. He reported the week's activities of the accounts set up by Clark and what to expect in the coming days. Always routine. Always dull. However, yesterday he picked up the receiver and found Ed Clark on the line asking if Mac had a suggestion on where they could meet. They had only spoken a few times since he left Austin, the last time when Clark told him to drop out of the New School for Social Reform. He was needed to fill a position that had been opened for him at the Nation Bank of New York.

A wave of anxiety ran up his spine.

Did I fuck up?

He crossed the street and could see the white sign with bright red letters with the restaurant's name hanging out over the sidewalk. He liked the place and ate there often. The food was good and compared to most New York restaurants was cheap. Baily paid the rent and utilities on the apartment but Mac had to live on what the bank paid a clerk which meant a some-what austere lifestyle.

A contributing factor to his lack of funds was the need to save money to entertain Mary. She was far from austere and he did his best to show her all the attractions and popular night spots when she visited. They had decided she should finish her degree. Her father, a Pastor at a Baptist church, and her mother were paying for Mary's college experience. Neither of Mac's assignments paid much and Mac assumed it was like boot camp and he was paying his dues. He was convinced he would move up the ladder quickly if he could prove himself worthy. Mary, overwhelmed with the nightlife, was less than impressed with his living conditions. Mac hoped tonight his future might be discussed in more detail.

The aroma from the restaurant hit him before he got to the door. Inside was dark and warm. The room was long and thin and filled with brown lacquer tables and round back chairs covered in bright red fabric. It was about half full of diners and most of them were Asian which is always a sign of good food in a Chinese restaurant.

"Table sir?" A petite woman with jet black hair held a menu which was almost as big as she was.

"Yes, please and…" he surveyed the room and pointed to an unoccupied area of tables in the far corner. "May I sit there, please?"

"Of course." She bowed slightly, her delicate hand pointing in that direction then led the way.

After he sat down, he was able to speak almost eye to eye with the sweet lady. "I'm expecting a man to meet me for a business dinner which is why I wanted the privacy."

She nodded and handed him the menu. "I'll watch for him."

Mac felt moisture on his head, shook off the residual snow, then used a napkin to dry his hair.

"Just get out of the shower?"

Mac looked up and into the eyes of the lady holding another menu and Ed Clark standing beside her. He started to stand up which went awkwardly.

"Relax Mac. Its just me." Ed Clark took the menu from the waitress, bowed slightly, and said, "Xie Xie."

She smiled and left.

"It means thank you." Ed put his overcoat on top of Mac's, which was on an empty chair, carefully placing his hat in the middle.

Mac grunted a little, nervous and clearing his throat.

"Mac really, relax. Everything is good."

A waiter showed up and interrupted the proceedings.

"I eat here a lot. The dim sum is good, and so is the hot and sour soup."

They ordered and hot tea arrived.

"I suspect my visit has caught you off guard."

Mac responded quickly. "It did."

Clark adopted a superior being look. "Nothing to fear young man, we are very impressed with your performance so far."

Mac's face became grimaced and looked puzzled at the same time. "I haven't done anything. I wasn't at the school long enough to learn much. All I came away with was a list of all the names and addresses of everybody who worked there. At the bank, I just deposit checks into the account you set up, and write checks to whom you want. There's some bookkeeping but any secretary could do the job."

Ed Clark remained stoic. His face showed no emotion. "Mr. Wallace, do you remember many months ago when I asked you if you could follow orders?"

Mac resisted going to marine attention. "Yes sir."

"Well, you were asked to accept an assignment, which turned out to be a dead end. You were then reassigned to the bank where as you say, you're doing clerical work. As you described it's a nothing job." Clark took a sip of tea. "But you see Mac... you were in fact doing nothing... but it seemed like nothing only to you."

Mac's voice got softer. "I don't understand, sir."

Clark poured more tea. "I usually don't explain, but I think you will have a future with us and some illumination is necessary."

The food arrived and, hungry, Mac started eating.

"The first assignment, the school, was more a favor for a friend in law enforcement. He needed some knowledge of the interworking of the organization and although you were unaware, what you supplied was very helpful."

48

Mac knew it was a mistake before he finished the sentence. "Who was the friend?"

Ed Clark got a little red in the face, locked his jaw, and whispered. "Don't ever ask that question again. Your job is to follow orders. Understand?"

Mac was conflicted, but said, "Yes sir."

Clark ate a bit, drank more tea then continued. "We moved you to the bank because we needed someone we could trust, to handle incoming checks and money orders and disperse wire transfers as instructed. On Monday morning you will send the balance of the account to this account number, then resign." Clark removed a folded piece of white stationary and handed it to Mac.

Surprised, Mac put it in the inside pocket of his jacket. "Of course, sir."

"When that is accomplished, go home and pack."

Mac was stunned. "Where am I going?"

Ed looked down and swirled the tea in the cup.

"Sir?"

Clark looked up and grinned. "You're going back to the University of Texas. You've already been enrolled in the class you need to finish your Bachelor's degree. Following that you will be accepted into graduate school to pursue a Master's in Economics. Naturally, there will be graduate housing and meals and in addition, we've arranged for a professor's assistant job for extra income."

"I'm speechless."

"Of course, you are." Clark tapped his spoon on the table.

"That's a lot." Mac, still stunned, added, "Why?"

"Again, with the why." Clark shook his head, paused a moment, and looked at Mac. "However... I understand, and I guess answers to your curiosity are warranted in this case. Simply put, you've done well and we know your success will be our success." He said the last part extending the last s.

"But..." He sat up and raised a finger. "We do have an ulterior motive."

Mac chuckled. "I know, you want me to kill somebody."

Clark did not see the humor, grimaced, but moved on. "Before you start school, you'll be working on Homer Grainer's election campaign for Governor."

"Dean Grainer is running for office?"

"Yes. I know he's had some history at UT but you supported him during his troubles, but before he was ousted. You'll be accepted onto his campaign with open arms."

"Do you think he can win?"

"Not a chance in hell. He's a card carrying Socialist and was removed as the President of UT because he wouldn't fire the fairies teaching there." His voice had gotten louder. He paused and took a breath. "To tell the truth, we can't figure out why he's running. It might be so he can raise some money. There are some fools that would donate. But I digress. Mac, you'll be working all over the state and we need information that will help LBJ's Senate campaign. What you will discover while helping Grainer will be invaluable to us."

Neither man spoke.

Clark tapped a spoon on the table then pointed. "Your food is getting cold."

"Right." The spell broken; Mac dived back in.

"You accept the new assignment?"

"Of course."

Clark paused a beat. "There is one thing that has caused a little concern."

Mac looked up. He had a whole dim sum in his mouth. "Uhhuh."

"What is your relationship with Mary Barton?"

"Mary?" Mac looked stunned.

"There is some talk that's not good and I'm asking if she will be a problem… and by the way I've been told she is insisting on being called Andre instead of Mary. Is that right?"

"Ah.. yes she is."

"Andre, it's a man's name."

"It is and I, actually, don't know why." Mac straightened his back and put on a sheepish grin. "She's a wild one that's for sure. Kinda, an unbroken colt. But now that I'm coming back to Texas, I'm sure she'll settle down."

Clark looked unsure. "Hmmm. I had heard you were in a serious relationship with a Nora Ann Carroll. What happen there?"

Mac's face went white. "I was, but we broke up, and she got married. Why is this important?"

Without comment, Clark looked down, pulled his vest tight, then checked his watch.

Oh yeah, I can't ask why.

"Right. Well, it's getting late, and I have a train to catch."

"You're leaving tonight?"

"Indeed. 9:50 train to D.C. Much to do." Standing quickly, he took his hat and draped his coat over his arm. "I got the check."

Mac stood, stuck out his hand. "Thank you, sir. I won't let you down."

Clark smiled and started for the door, stopped, turned around and came back to the table. "Will you be taking the train back to Texas?"

Mac nodded.

"Good. Leave on Friday afternoon and get off in D.C. Call Baily in the morning. He'll get you a room for the night and give you an address. There are some people I want you to meet. Wear a suit."

"Yes sir. Of course, sir, and thanks again."

Clark headed for the door.

Mac yelled to his back. "Merry Christmas, sir."

Clark raised his arm and gave a backward wave.

Mac plopped back into the chair.

Back to UT... invited to a party in Washington D.C., damn, I'm on my way.

He grinned then looked around for someone to get take home boxes. Suddenly, he remembered then end of the conversation.

What did she do now?

CHAPTER 8

JANUARY, 1946

MAC WALLACE STOOD, one hand in his pocket and the other holding a perfectly mixed Martini. He was alone, looking through the wavy, rippled glass, of a hundred-year-old window wondering, 'what am I doing here?' His thoughtful moment was interrupted by a reflection in the window.

"You made it. Good." Ed Clark came up behind him and put a hand on his shoulder.

Mac turned to shake hands.

"I see you have a drink."

"Sir." Mac raised his glass slightly.

"Good, good. I want to talk to you, but I need to say hello to the host first. Walk around. This house stands just as it was built over 125 years ago, except for the indoor plumbing and air conditioning." He chuckled then leaned forward to share a gossip, "I think you'll find it interesting— even the horrible decorating couldn't screw it up."

Mac smiled nervously, and watched Clark exit to mingle. He finished his drink and looked for a place to leave the empty glass. Deciding the bar was the likely depository he made his way through the gathering. The guests were standing in small groups, each of which was apparently in good humor. Several uniformed servers had trays of what he learned was called heavy hors d'oevures. A few other white coats were keeping glasses full of wine or champagne. The quarters were close and he had some difficulty maneuvering the gauntlet.

"Headed to the bar?"

Mac's shoulder was bumped by a woman almost as tall as he with straight black hair, only slightly longer than his. "How could you tell?"

She grinned and pointed to his glass. "Needs a refill."

He grinned back, "Indeed."

"You're too polite. Follow me."

The woman was markedly different than the other women present. She had no jewelry nor makeup and wore a dress that had little shape, but looked expensive. He followed behind as she took a straight heading, extending both arms and pushing though narrow gaps. "Pardon me. Excuse me. Pardon me."

They reached the bar in a flash. "That's how it's done at a ritzy Washington D.C. hoedown." She snapped fingers at the bartender saying, "Manhattan up and a..."

"Martini."

She looked at him, not satisfied.

"Vodka."

She looked to the bartender, who nodded.

"Josefa." She hesitated a beat, then held out her hand.

He shook it. "Malcolm... Mac."

She put an elbow on the bar and leaned back, her hip bones pronounced against the satiny fabric. Her eyes began an inspection which started at his hair, then took a long slow trip down to his shoes.

When she finished, she straightened and said, "You here for the food or the politics?"

"Neither. I was just told to be here and wear a suit."

"By?"

Mac looked around and nodded toward Ed Clark who was talking to a couple on the other side of the room. "Him. Tall man, grey hair, blue suit… by the window."

When she saw who Mac pointed to, her expression changed. "Edward Clark?"

"Yes. You know him?"

"You work for him?"

The bartender handed the drinks across the bar.

Mac took his glass, saying, "I think so."

She didn't pursue his vague answer. She just stood there looking down while stirring her drink with the maraschino cherry. "Do you know who he's talking to right now?"

Mac looked again. "No idea."

"That's the Secretary of the Navy." She started pointing with a little finger at other men. "That's a Senator from Wyoming, that's the Chairman of the Appropriations Committee, and the man with his hand resting on the ass of the wife of the Majority Whip is the CEO of ConocoPhillips, one of the biggest defense contractors in the country."

"Jesus."

"No… God is not present in this room." Her voice was a little loud.

He looked around to see if anyone was paying attention.

"Don't be nervous. People here know who I am and what to expect."

He stood patiently, not speaking.

"Good boy." She smiled. "You must be a quick study."

"I try."

"You didn't ask about me. So, obviously, you know how to conduct yourself in public. The question then is, are you a good fuck in private?"

He tried to maintain a straight face. His mind immediately went to Mary.

"I see you have found some company." Ed Clark pushed up next to him, bumping his shoulder and causing his drink to slosh over the side of the glass.

"Indeed, he did... Edward." She drew out the name.

"Having a good time, Josefa?" Clark gently started to pull on Mac's arm.

"Yes, I am. I've met your friend and who not only looks like Clark Kent but I think he has a secret identity as well." She took a step forward, her demeanor changed, her limbs tense, jaw tightened. She spoke flat and even, like a professor at a lectern. "The ones I pointed out... they're just pieces of shit." She looked at Clark and stuck a finger in his vest. "But this one... this one, is evil."

Clark grunted, red-faced.

She downed her drink with one gulp then patted Mac's cheek. "Nice meeting you, honey boy. Look me up if you ever get to Austin. I'm in the book."

Clark, pulling harder on Mac's arm, led him away in the opposite direction.

They walked single file around the edge of the room to a corner near the front door. Clark signaled to a white coat.

"Malcolm, you've been doing a fine job for us."

Mac started to object.

Clark raised his hand. "You have followed the instructions we gave you to a tee, and without question. By the way, every transaction you made at the bank was perfect. Not one mistake. Which is important. One mistake at this point could sink the ship."

Mac looked confused.

"Look, it's not necessary that you understand what's going on. You just need to always remember you do not need to know the why. Understand?"

Mac nodded.

A white coat appeared.

Clark held out his hand to Mac. "Your coat check."

Mac took a round numbered button out of his pocket and gave it to the man who retreated down the hall.

"You will be working remotely. Your only contact will be me. So, it will be difficult to see how what you're doing fits into the big picture." Clark put his arm around Mac's shoulders. "Well, son, look around. This is the big picture. What you will be doing is important. Very important. I wanted you to stop here tonight because I wanted you to see for yourself that you will be helping Congressman Johnson at the top level of government."

"Is he here? Can I meet him?"

Clark shut him down immediately. "No. He's not here, yet, and even if he was you won't be seen with him."

Mac's confusion was verbal and physical. "What? Why not? That's—"

"Everywhere he goes somebody is taking a picture and you can't be in any. How can you be effective if people know you're a Johnson man? Get it?"

Mac took a beat then took a chance. "Who's Josefa?"

Clark stopped walking.

Mac could see he was calculating his answer. It was the first time he saw his boss waver.

"She is... she is..." he stammered then spit it out. "She's the Congressman's sister, Josefa Johnson. She is also trouble, a wild child and an embarrassment to the Congressman and his family. If by any remote chance you should happen to run into her again, you'll be wise to keep your distance. Understood?"

"Sir." Mac said smartly.

"Good boy."

That's what she said.

They reached the door.

Clark paused, looked like he was about to reveal something, then apparently dismissing the idea, spoke quickly. "Baily arranged a room for the night?"

"Yes, sir."

"Ticket for the train?"

"No. He said you wanted to talk to me tonight about that."

"I do. You'll be working out of Houston for now. Rainy set up his campaign office there."

"Houston?" Mac was surprised, disappointed, and confused all at once.

"Listen, Malcolm. You need to be focused, and like I said, you cannot draw any attention to yourself. Think of yourself as a spy and the press is the enemy."

Mac nodded like a good soldier.

Clark opened the door and started Mac out. "Good, good. You should head back to your hotel. Okay? You'll be able to catch a cab at the corner— they're everywhere in Georgetown. I'll be in touch. Good night then."

The door closed behind him. It was cold, his breath clouding the air. The snow on this street in Georgetown wasn't the same as the snowfall he witnessed in New York. It wasn't a picturesque moment of time. It was pushed up in piles. It was grey with black streams of dirt trailing down to the ground. He stuck his hands in his pockets and walked the brick sidewalk to the corner. There wasn't a cab anywhere.

CHAPTER 9
JULY 1946

He heard the phone's first ring as he arrived at the door. While holding his briefcase, he shifted a stack of files from his right to his left arm then searched his coat pockets for the key.

three… four… five

The key slid in the lock. It clicked and he kicked open the door. When he hit the wall switch, the files slid out of his grip, scattering when they hit the floor. The phone was on the nightstand, across the room.

six

He grabbed the receiver on seven. "Hello. Hello." All he heard was dial tone. "Fuck."

It was Mary.

He checked his watch, 11:08, then flopped on the bed, exhausted. A streak of blinking neon light annoyed him, but not enough to make him get up. The curtain on the room's single window was open, probably because the maid vacuumed his room today. He just lay on the neatly tucked-in bedspread at the Cortez Motel. It wasn't much, but there was a radio that worked, the room was clean, and the water was hot. There was fifty dollars left in the line-item budget for his room. Five dollars a night. Exactly enough for another ten days, right up to the primary.

Mac got up and walked to the dresser for the bottle of whisky and a glass. He poured three fingers, splashed in some water from the tap in the bathroom, and returned to the bed. He propped up the pillow, grabbed the phone by the base off the night table, and set it on his chest. He had one hand on the receiver and the other on the glass.

It was Mary who called. It had to have been her. It couldn't have been anyone from the office or even Rainey. They all left the campaign office when Mac did, and the soon to be x-candidate for Governor of Texas would be getting on the train to Dallas right about now. Raines had no chance to win the Democratic Primary, which like every other election in Texas for the past hundred years was the real election. No republican had ever made a serious run at a high office and this race was no exception. Homer Raines would lose and lose big.

Staying away from the staff in the office was fairly easy— no friends there. He sat alone in the back of the campaign office functioning as the accountant, bookkeeper, and monitor of the meager election fund. The people in charge, volunteers, and Raines's staff focused on the campaign events, fund raising, and speeches. They had little time for the quiet accountant who received invoices, made budgets, and wrote checks. His meek office persona was the perfect cover to do his real job, spy for Ed Clark. He copied everything and sent it along to Clark's office man; a man whom he'd never met, Bob Butler. He didn't know if the information had any relevance to Johnson's upcoming run for Senate, or how it was used. He didn't care. He just wanted this to be over, get out of this stinking city, get back to Austin, and Mary.

Being assigned to Houston was disappointing, but he tried to make the best of it, keeping in mind going back to the University of Texas was his reward. Mary accepted it, at first, and in the beginning would arrive on a two- or three-day visit, enthusiastic, and insatiable. The short stays were okay with Mac. Towards the end of each visit, Mac would be worn out from working all day then romping with Mary most of the night. When he got to the room after work, they would drink, have sex, drink while eating dinner, have sex, drink some more, then have sex till one of them fell asleep. On the occasion he could manage a whole day off, the order of eating and drinking was exactly the same. The exception was that the falling asleep part changed to who passed out first. Mac was convinced that he was the luckiest guy in the world. He thought she felt the same but as the months dragged on, Mary stopped coming. She liked the nights together and loved the sex. But she didn't like being alone all day with nothing to do.

It might have also been because Mac was not responding to the occasional hints Mary dropped about marriage. They were veiled and playful at first, but became more obvious and deliberate. She said she loved him, and wanted him all the time. Mac was a little wary because the only time she said these things was when she was naked and smoking a cigarette after sex. She was also impatient about what he was doing. She wanted to know more about what his future held.

So did he.

The phone rang and he lurched, spilled the drink, and almost dropped the glass.

"Hello." He pulled the corner of the bedspread up to blot his pants.

"Hi… Honeyboy."

"What? Honey who? Who is this?"

"Forget me already? Washington, D.C., a couple of months ago."

"No. I mean yes. Wait, I'm sorry, who is this?"

"Josefa. I met you at a party in Georgetown."

"I don't remember." His voice started solid but wavered at the end.

"Ah…yes. See, you do." She laughed. "I'm unforgettable."

Seconds of silence followed.

Josefa broke first. "Got it yet?"

"Yes. I remember you, now."

"Good boy."

His voice was firm and defiant. "Okay, we met… and how did you find me?"

"Do you remember my name?"

The defiance went away but he remained firm. "Yes, you're Lyndon Johnson's sister."

"I am, and I found you because you work for my brother's prince of darkness, Edward Clark."

Mac just grunted.

She became a little softer, not much but it was perceptible. "Listen Honeyboy, I will explain everything tomorrow night. Dinner, Roof Garden Restaurant, Rice Hotel, downtown. Nine o'clock."

Firm was left in the dust. "I don't understand."

"What don't you understand? The big boss's sister is telling you… dinner, tomorrow night, be there."

"I—"

"And Honeyboy," she paused a long beat, "believe me when I say, you won't regret it."

"I—"

"Don't be late."

Mac heard the other end disconnect. He replaced the receiver, set the phone back on the nightstand, and lit a cigarette.

"Damn."

He finished his drink and the smoke, then decided it was too late to call Mary.

She was alone at a table for two in the back corner of the restaurant. He saw her in silhouette, her chin raised, one elbow resting on the table, back arched, and a stream of grey cigarette smoke drifting from her lips. Her eyes were fixed on a less than architecturally perfect cityscape through the tall windows of the seventeenth floor.

Without turning her head to his reflection in the glass, she said, "You're on time."

"You sound surprised."

"Would you like a drink?"

"Of course."

Still without turning to face him, she raised her hand into the air, and a waiter appeared. She waved her glass. "Two of these, Por favor."

Mac remained standing.

She turned and looked at him. "Please." Josefa beckoned to the empty chair across from hers. "Vodka Martini, correct?"

He nodded, impressed with her memory for details.

She wore a thin strapped evening dress that was cut straight across her chest. The fabric glimmered in the light when unpainted fingers moved to place a long cigarette holder to her lips. She was unadorned— no jewelry, no makeup, no pretense.

"So… why?"

She laughed a little. "You waste no time. I like that, right to the point."

"We met once, months ago, and obviously you went to a lot of trouble to track me down. I guess you could say I'm curious."

"First, it wasn't that much trouble and," she blew a smoke ring, "second, it wasn't the first time we saw each other."

"No, I'm pretty sure that was the first time. I would have remembered you."

There was a twinkle in her eye. "I wasn't me, when I saw you the first time."

That startled him. "I don't understand?"

"I saw you at Hattie Valdez's Social Club."

Mac reacted like a child getting caught in a lie, embarrassed and in denial. "What... no. I never—."

"Stop. Don't even try. You met Clark there. You were with that little fool, Busby."

"Ah... I—"

The waiter saved him, arriving with their drinks.

"Don't be embarrassed. I knew it was your first time there." She leaned forward a bit and smiled devilishly. "It wasn't mine."

"Wait... backup, you said, 'you weren't 'you'. What does that mean?"

"What it means is, girls who like girls sometimes look like boys."

He was stunned and had no response.

She smiled then pointed to the menu. "You should look at that, like every restaurant in Texas, you can't go wrong with the steak."

He was sure he still had a blank look on his face, but picked up the menu, and tried to read.

She gently shook her glass side to side. "Have another drink and order dinner. And... don't fret Honeyboy, the night is young."

He knew she was right; another drink was needed.

She waved her hand again, summoning the waiter. They ordered steaks and another round.

"The fact that I saw you at Hattie's was purely coincidental. You just happened to be there." She grinned as she twirled her olive. "I like going there, not exactly a regular but it's where I can express myself without any consequence because—"

"Nobody talks about what happens there because they would have to admit being there."

"Correct." She smiled then spoke more directly. "I love sex." She looked up to the ceiling with a matter-of-fact expression. "I like sex with men, but sometimes… I want to have sex with a woman the same way you do. Understand?" She didn't wait for acknowledgement. "You didn't notice me at Hattie's that night, because I chose to be more… masculine. I dressed in a black suit, a white shirt, and a black silk tie. I had my hair slicked back and even used highlighter to pencil in a thin mustache. I spent the night with a girl with long blond hair… and a beautiful body."

Mac suddenly had the vague recollection of that night, after Clark had left, seeing a thin man, sitting alone, staring at him. "Wait… you are a…" He didn't finish the sentence.

"Uh huh." She smiled, enjoying his embarrassment. "As you can imagine, if a sister of a United States Congressman who is sleeping with random men and women became known, it could be a tremendous detriment to an election campaign."

Mac nodded.

"I've been discrete, most of the time." She waggled her head a little. "I try to live normal, and in point of fact, I met you at that party… by chance again… because I just happened to be in Washington finalizing my divorce. The husband was a good man. We just didn't see eye to eye… sorta."

"Wait. This is way beyond small talk." Mac put both hands on the table. "Why are you telling me all this? There must be a reason."

Another smile, this time a knowing, in-control smile. "You really have a thing for the why, don't you?"

"Not the first time I've been told that."

"You're correct. There is a reason which needs some explanation." She finished her drink and waved for another. "As you probably already know, my brother, Lyndon, has more ambition than anyone you will ever meet."

Mac responded. "I don't know."

"Don't know?"

"About his ambition, in fact, I've never met him." He raised a hand. "Wait, that's not exactly true. I met him once. I introduced him when he gave a speech at UT."

She seemed surprised. "You work for my brother, and never met him?"

"I don't work for your brother; I work for Ed Clark."

"Edward Clark is a lawyer, whose only client is Lyndon. Lyndon tells him what he wants and Clark tells you."

"I don't know anything about that." He started his next thought but knew it sounded strange even as he said it. "Actually, I've only met with Mr. Clark a couple of times."

She put her glass on the table and stared at him.

"I communicate through Bob Baily."

She burst into laughter. "Oh my God. You are so in the dark."

He started to get mad, but the waiter came with their orders and stalled his response. The interruption gave him time to reflect. She was right. He was just following orders.

"Isn't the steak good?" She had cut a small piece off a huge slab of meat and was chewing politely. "People have been hung for serving a bad steak in Texas."

He changed direction. "Why?"

"Sorry?"

"Why did you call me?"

She took a long breath. "My brother knows beating Stevenson for the Senate will be tough. The prediction is Lyndon will come in a close second, in a field of ten candidates, in the primary. That will force a run-off between the two top candidates. Lyndon and Stevenson. My brother will get the same votes he got in the first primary but to win the run-off, he'll need the votes of the ones who lost, and from every fringe voter he can find." She took a sip and continued. "Normally, my bohemian lifestyle is a huge liability. He'd get a lot of bad press if my... dalliances, came to light. The conservative church goers would run for cover. However, assuming I stay under the radar, I can bring some votes to his column. I meet with the arty types, from the big cities like Houston, Austin, and Dallas even San Antonio. So, for this election... and only this election, I serve a purpose."

"Doesn't he already get a liberal voter? I mean, he supports New Deal policies, and civil rights."

"Please... he hasn't voted for a civil rights bill... ever, and the New Deal... that's mostly about construction contracts. He will say anything and do anything that will get votes. He plays both ends against the middle all the time."

"But he seems so genuine."

"Genuine." She almost came out of her chair. "Listen Honey-boy, my brother is the only man you'll ever meet who can strut sitting down. It's all about getting elected, staying in office, and making money."

Mac didn't speak much after that. He digested what she said and his dinner, washing both down with more Martinis.

Eventually the waiter came and cleared the table.

She put a cigarette in the holder.

He lit hers, then one for himself. "So, back to the beginning. Why did you call me?"

She put both elbows on the table and leaned forward.

He felt her foot on his leg.

"I heard about you. You were almost a Socialist in college, supported Rainer, which makes you perfect for this 'mission.'" She used air quotes which he hated. "I think you're ill-informed about what these guys want from you."

He looked down. "I want to succeed. They are powerful men that have made some things happen for me, so far."

She stared at him, leaning forward and tapping her fingers on the table. "Just be very careful. If they get something on you... like what they have on me... they'll use you till you're all used up."

Mac saw she was earnest which caused him to wonder if that was her only motive. "That's it. You just wanted to warn me about Ed Clark and your brother?"

The devilish grin came back. "My mama used to say I was wilder than an acre of snakes."

Her foot moved up and down one leg then moved to his other.

"I'm involved with somebody. I can't—"

"Yeah, know about her." The grin got wider. "Rumor around the campaign is she's a real wild one… like me."

"Rumor?" His face instantly reddened. "Who was talking about her?" He smacked the table; the silverware rose and fell.

"Calm down. Don't be gettin' your tail up."

He spread out his fingers, pressing hard against the tablecloth.

She reached over and put her hands on top of his. "Good, good. The women we are surrounded by all act the same, church going, soft spoken, hair done… staying at home and raising the childrn'. They meet, and talk, and gossip." She paused a beat and puffed her cigarette. "They don't talk much about me, but if they do, they're real careful. Because, I can be a pretty scary bitch. Now Honeyboy, I've heard your girl is a lot like me… a lot. Which is fine. Actually, I'd love to meet her sometime." She blew smoke out in a thin stream. "Your problem is like mine, if you get caught living… large… you'll become a liability."

"And?"

Her voice became sincere. "What do you think happens to liabilities in the world of powerful men?"

Mac stared at her for a long time.

She finished her drink.

He finished his.

She tapped one finger on the table. "I have a pitcher of Martinis in my room."

He was calm, resolute.

She picked the napkin from her lap and dropped it on the table. "Enough of this." She scrunched her shoulders together and leaned forward, the crest of her breasts rising above the cut of the dress. Her face was flushed and her eyes sparkling. "Honeyboy, I'm going to fuck you like you've never been fucked before." She grinned but stayed seated, waiting for the response.

"Unlikely. I've been schooled."

She laughed and pushed her chair back. "I love a challenge."

PART TWO

POWER. 1948 - 1951

CHAPTER 10

JANUARY 1948

LYNDON JOHNSON STOOD at the window, parting the curtains with one hand and holding a carefully folded frontpage section of the *New York Times* in the other. Cliff Carter was ten minutes late, which upset him, but trying to read the article in the paper made him angry. His fury had nothing to do with the newspaper, it was the frustration of not being able to find his glasses. In the Texas campaign office, there was always someone there to respond to his needs, a secretary, assistants, volunteers, even the campaign manager, Carter. In D.C. he also had staff, but it was Ed Clark who was his professional 'wife', always there watching, protecting him. But there was no staff allowed here— not at home. Here, and in their house in Austin, there was only Bird and the girls.

So far, Carter had proven to be good at his job. He followed directions well, occasionally took cautious initiative, and, most importantly, didn't question orders. Ed Clark had chosen well. Carter was a man who had served under him in the war, believed what he was told and acted accordingly. Lyndon was nervous when Ed Clark told him of the money men's demand for an immediate sit down, especially when Clark put Carter in charge of coordination. Cliff was hired to be a manager, and aside from now being twelve minutes late, had successfully managed to pull all the difficult schedules together.

LBJ tapped an empty shirt pocket.

He grabbed his jacket off the desk chair, and searched the pockets. He scanned his desk top, shifted a pile of papers, nothing. Frustrated, he yelled, "God damnit, where are my glasses?"

"Lyndon!" Lady Bird stepped into his home office at this inopportune moment. Her expression silenced him.

His voice lowered and he meekly said, "Sorry, Bird."

She shook her head back and forth in disappointment, her Aquanet hair frozen in space.

LBJ tossed the paper to a chair and returned to look out the window. He got close to the glass and stared intently, then quickly peeked to see if his wife was still there. She was.

She stood with arms crossed and a stern look. "Dinner is at six. Will you be here?"

He mumbled, "Maybe, not sure how long this will take."

"But it's Sunday, Lyndon, you promised the girls." She walked behind his desk and picked up the glasses off the floor.

"Can't be helped." He saw the black Lincoln coming down the street and left his post, grabbed his hat, and headed for the door.

She held out his missing glasses. "Try to make it short, Lyndon. You promised."

He took the glasses from her hand, nodding as he passed. There was no thank you, and no kiss goodbye.

The street was narrow, houses close together, and it only took twelve steps to get from the small Forest Hills three-bedroom house to the car door. This wasn't home, wasn't comfortable, and definitely wasn't in Texas. Living here was a compromise, giving up proximity to the Capital for schools for the girls. It was the least he could do and the least that he did.

"You're fucking late." He slammed the car door. "Move. Come on, let's go."

"Sir." Cliff Carter hit the gas, and the big car took a moment to respond.

LBJ didn't want an explanation. It didn't matter. Giving even the slightest upper-hand to H. L. Hunt was a mistake and he could afford none.

Fortunately, it was Sunday, and the traffic on Connecticut Avenue. was light. The normal twenty-minute ride took twelve. He wasn't worried about being stopped for speeding, not with a license plate that read Federal Government United States Representative.

Carter checked his watch and looking relieved said, "I'll pull to the front and valet. Ed will be waiting in the lobby."

"You were late, you pay for the parking." He swung around, leaning over so his nose was close to Carter's. "Don't be late... ever again."

Carter squeaked, "Sir."

The St. Regis Hotel lobby was fitting of the finest hotel anywhere, and especially for Washington D.C. It had a ceiling rivaling a Smithsonian Museum, accented with finely engraved columns and arches. The floors were covered with Italian marble and plush red carpet embossed with gold thread. All these accouterments served as a frame for huge hundred-year-old paintings and museum quality period furniture.

Ed Clark stood waiting, and Johnson with Carter in tow, walked past him without a word. The finery of the surroundings was summarily overlooked by the trio who headed to the elevator.

Clark pushed the call button. "They're here, private room, top floor."

Johnson looked straight ahead. "What's the lineup?"

"Hunt, Murchison, Larry Bell, in from Buffalo, and..." Clark hesitated, "George."

Johnson was surprised. "Brown, here?"

Clark nodded.

"You said George, no Herman?" LBJ looked puzzled.

Clark nodded. "I think he may be ill. Not sure."

Johnson grunted.

The bell announced their arrival on seventeen and they headed down a similarly decorated hallway.

Lyndon's demeaner changed. His baby-kissing charm turned on as the door opened.

Larry Bell answered their knock. "Lyndon, good to see you. Gentlemen, come in."

Shaking hands vigorously, LBJ glad handed the other three men in the room. Clark and Carter nodded but remained near a wall and out of the way.

Bell, apparently acting as moderator, gestured to five chairs positioned in the middle of the room. "Shall we get started?"

George Brown sat first, and watched as Hunt and Murchison took their places.

Lyndon, like an intruding male in a pride of lions, circled slowly before sitting down.

H. L. Hunt cleared his throat, then coughed. He was a short, almost physically nondescript man, and one of, if not the first, billionaire in the country. There was only a paper-thin difference between him and J D Rockefeller. "Lyndon, we're concerned with your recent public stands on issues, but more importantly, we're not happy with the results you're getting for us in Congress."

Murchison adjusted his giant black-framed glasses and followed suit. "You've always held our interests first, but since you set your hat for the Senate seat," he looked at the other three, "which we are financing, you've been making a lot of public remarks that we don't like."

Lyndon remained quiet.

Clark and Carter looked at each with a surprised look on their faces.

"You're pushing an increase in income tax, eliminating the voting poll tax here in Texas, and advocating signing the treaty for the Organization of American States." He slapped the arm of his chair. "God damn it, you're costing us money while backing those commie countries down south... and," a blue vein started to push out on his forehead, "you wanna let all the niggers vote. What's gotten into you boy?"

Lyndon looked slowly around the room, one face at a time. The only one who cowered was Larry Bell. He was a loyal supporter but his aeronautics company was struggling and he was not even close to being in the same financial league as the others.

LBJ beckoned to Clark, making an empty glass hand signal.

Clark moved quickly, filled a glass with ice water, then handed it to Johnson.

Nobody had spoken and Lyndon let the silence continue.

The men in the chairs did not seem fazed.

Lyndon placed the glass on the table beside his chair, leaned forward, and addressed one of the richest men in the world. "H L... that was about the dumbest thing I've ever heard you say... and I've heard you say some really stupid shit."

Hunt blustered, "Nobody—"

LBJ cut him off. "Nobody what? Nobody ever tells you you're wrong? Well, I'm telling you, you're wrong. Way wrong." He shifted and pointed around the room. "Ya'll think this too?"

George Brown held up a hand. "Let's slow down, here."

LBJ pushed back in the chair.

Brown continued. "Lyndon, we came here, to you, because you couldn't come to us while Congress was in session. Obviously, that means this is serious." He pointed at Clark. "What's our total in the campaign so far?"

Clark paused a second. "All of your money together... about

three hundred and fifty thousand."

Murchison whistled. "That's what I pay about a hundred workers a year, and twice maybe three times what we've spent in any other election."

Brown held the floor. "That will no doubt double... if we stay in."

"If?" LBJ's face got beat red.

Bell stood up. "Gentleman, I know I'm low man on the pole here, but I'm still in the room and I think Lyndon needs a chance to explain his position."

Lyndon focused on Hunt. "You're the biggest oilman in the country. You have almost total control of supply and demand in the U.S. ... for now." He paused for effect. "There are thirty-four countries in the OAS including what could be your biggest oil competitor, Venezuela. Betancourt, their President, right now... today... is trying to nationalize the oil industry like Cardenas did in Mexico, in 38. Do you really want a country with ten times the oil reserve we have to be in control, or would you like to continue to influence oil production and price?"

Hunt made a sound which was more a grunt than a no.

"Next, its true I'm supporting a tax bill that raises taxes on anybody making over three hundred thousand a year. So what? It won't make any difference to you. Not a speck. Ya'll have more loopholes than flies on cow shit. And as for the nigras... again, why the hell do you care?"

"It's the first step. You give them the vote and the next thing they'll be eating in our restaurants, pissing in our bathrooms, and sending their little monkeys to our schools." Hunt's face was red and he sputtered and spit when he spoke.

Murchison chimed in. "It's the commies. You're pandering to the commies. Taxes, civil rights, signing a treaty with the commie countries. I'm not—"

Johnson yelled, drowning out his objection. "I haven't sponsored or voted for one single bill that advocated for civil rights in my entire career. Not one… so far. My banter about the poll tax is political bullshit. It won't pass, that's a guarantee." He had their attention. "But it will, one day. The tax increase will pass also but the deal will include no changes to the oil depletion allowance. So, ask yourself what is more important, people you don't know paying more taxes or you losing millions and millions every year if Congress votes to reduce the depletion allowance."

Johnson sat back in the chair, put his hands on the arms, then continued. "Gentlemen, I can't keep doing this exercise with you. You have to trust my interests are the same as yours. I know what I'm doing, and I will say whatever I have to say to get elected. I will do whatever I need to do to stay in office… and, because this is a democracy, sometimes compromises are necessary… if you want to stay in control. You must believe when I'm in office, you have control. If I'm out… so are you."

Brown chuckled arrogantly. "You think you're the only pair of pants we own in this town?"

"Own… me?" Lyndon chuckled then pointed his finger. "I know you have influence with at least a half dozen including Speaker Rayburn, but I know I am better than any of them by a country mile." His stare became fixed. "And so do you."

Murchison chimed in. "We have more than just influence in Congress, my friend. We have serious business connections as well. There's J.D. Rockefeller and D.H. Byrd and of course, Joe Kennedy got his kid, Jack, in there."

"Gentlemen, you only have influence, that's all. I am the one, on the floor, wrangling all that influence you think you have to a single up or down vote. And as for the Kennedy kid, he's going nowhere. He's all grin— no substance."

Brown's face contorted with anger. "Lyndon, who do you think you are? We didn't come here to get a lecture from the likes of you. You are hired help, that's it, and nothing more. You started out dirt poor. Your salary from Congress is, what, twelve thousand a year, and on that you have a house in Washington, and in Austin, and rumor has it, you're looking to buy a ranch." He leaned forward. "We all know how the radio stations were acquired, don't we? You've come a long way from Southwest Texas State Teachers College. Lyndon, you'd better get a grip. Everything that you are… is because of us. We bought you, and lately we're thinking we're paying too much."

LBJ broke out into laughter. "Too much, too much. That's hilarious… you pompous prick."

Clark and Carter both sucked in air at the same time.

LBJ spoke rapidly. "You got some balls on you. You were about to go tits up until I rescued your Marshall Ford Dam contract. Since then, you've gotten government contracts for miles and miles of roads, a dozen bridges, you opened a ship building company and got contracts to build hundreds of boats even though you've never built one… ever. So, please tell me exactly how I'm costing you money."

Brown retreated back into his chair.

It seemed like it took a couple of minutes for Johnson's words to stop reverberating off the walls.

LBJ dropped his voice and tone. "You're right George, I come from where I didn't have a pot to piss in or a window to throw it out of. And I guess because of that I can be arrogant and rude. That kind of poor is what drove me, gave me the ambition to rise above my station, where now I'm on the verge of repre- senting Texas in the United States Senate." He looked at Brown. "I'm telling you… this Senate seat will open up a world of possi- bilities that go way beyond what I can do in the House. It's a big step for me, no doubt, but it is the key to the vault for you."

Again, there was silence until Hunt looked over at Carter. "Would you get me some of that water?"

In the moments before the request was met, a silent decision was made. The money men, the tycoons, the men of power, looked at each other and nodded.

Larry Bell gestured at Clark. "I'm curious, you said three hundred and fifty thousand dollars so far. My question is, is there a law saying how much a candidate can spend on an election?"

"Yes, governing law passed, in 1907, amended in 39. and amended again just recently Taft-Hartly. Officially... a candidate can spend ten thousand dollars on a primary, twenty-five in a general election."

"What? You mean—"

"All in, thirty-five." Clark summarized.

Hunt followed up. "And what's Stevenson spent so far?"

"About the same, we think, and he's spending where we thought he would, on votes he already has. The problem is he has more of that section than we do. To win we need all the fringe voters; the liberals, the negros, and most importantly, the farmers and ranchers. The latter, because they're so scattered and remote, are hard to get to in a timely fashion. The effort will intensify as we get closer and the schedule will be non-stop till election day."

LBJ, like a boxer before the bell rings, put his head down. "This'll be a dog-fight all the way."

"Lyndon, you know I'm behind you a hundred percent." Bell scratched his head and glanced at the others. "I put into the fund, not at their level, but I'm in, you know that."

LBJ nodded.

"Bell Aviation is a rising star and I believe it will, given your help in Congress, get to be the biggest manufacturer of helicopters in the world. We have the engineering and the capacity."

"Is this a TV commercial?" Hunt impatiently rolled his fingers with a get-on-with-it gesture.

"Right, so if I understand correctly, you're only able to legally raise twenty-five thousand dollars for this campaign."

"Ten, we're only allowed ten in the Primary. Twenty-five in the general." Clark's correction drew several stern looks.

Bell went on. "You said we need to reach the rural vote, which is scattered and remote. Your man, Carter, suggested a helicopter was needed."

"That would help tremendously." Lyndon nodded.

Bell grinned. "My question is, if I give you our protypes Sikorski S-51helicopter, which is still not in production, can we write it off as a very, very long test flight?"

LBJ smiled for the first time. "That'll work."

The Lincoln was obeying the speed limit. There was no need to hurry. Cliff had an elbow bent resting on the rolled down window. No one had spoken since Lyndon, Clark, and he had left the meeting. When Clark left them on the sidewalk to take a cab, he just nodded and walked away.

"What time is it?" Lyndon was in the backseat and had a fixed stare out the window watching one government building after another go by.

"Ah… 5:48, sir."

Lyndon grunted.

"Dinner with the family, then sir?"

LBJ looked up and saw Carter smile into the rearview mirror.

Lyndon grunted again.

Clark apparently didn't get the message and pressed on. "I thought the meeting went well. Before we left, Bell told me to expect the money to start to be deposited in the same manner as before."

Johnson didn't grunt but also didn't respond.

"Can I say sir, I think you spoke very powerfully. I was in awe."

Johnson looked back out the window. "I told them exactly what they wanted to hear."

CHAPTER 11

"JESUS H CHRIST BOY, you look like you got one wheel down and you're dragging your axle." Horace Busby stood in the open door of the Lyndon Johnson for U. S. Senate campaign office with both hands on his hips and a satirical grin on his face.

"I feel worse than I look." Mac pushed past his tormentor.

"That's impossible." Busby pulled the door closed behind them. "That must have been some honeymoon."

Mac was waiting for a motherly tisk, tisk, but it didn't come. He walked directly to a coffeepot and poured what looked like day-old mud into a paper cup.

"You've been back in Austin, what, two weeks, and you got married, already?"

Mac grunted then took a sip. It was awful. "Got anything else to drink?"

Horace stood, judgmental, with arms crossed. "There's some bourbon in the top drawer of the corner desk."

Mac's eyes brightened a bit, and he headed across the room.

"You really need a shot of whisky at," Horace looked at his watch, "9:30 in the morning?"

"No, I don't— this coffee does." Mac's voice cracked a little when he spoke.

Busby waved a hand. "I could make fresh."

Mac waved back. "No. No need." He opened the desk and removed a pint bottle half filled with brown liquid. He held out the cup, his hand shaking a little, and added some flavoring.

Busby walked to a chair, sat down, and crossed his legs.

Mac took a long drink and perched on the edge of the desk. "How is married life?"

"Don't know, really— only got married yesterday."

"Yesterday? No, honeymoon?"

"We had the honeymoon first, as soon as I got back from New York, then we got married." He leaned forward as far as he could without losing balance, "Horace, I gotta tell you, we've been... ever since I got off the train." Mac paused, revising his thought. "Let me put it this way, Mary missed me... a lot."

"Okay, well, it shows boy, you look like shit."

"Thanks for pointing that out again, buddy. Appreciate ya." Mac took another drink then splashed more whisky into the cup.

Busby cleared his throat. "Right, let's get to business."

"By all means." His words were still slightly garbled.

"Cliff Carter needs you to do some recon work for the campaign."

"Recon," came out slurred.

"It's an easy assignment, but does involve a couple of days of travel, which might be inconvenient, given you just got married."

"No, it's not. In fact," Mac grinned slightly, "I need a break."

Busby shrugged and moved on. "You are to head south towards Corpus Christi. We want you to go to the county clerk's office in a couple of the ranch towns down there— Driscoll, Kingsville, and Alice."

"Alice who?"

"Not who, where." Busby shook his head and started to stand up. "You're not taking me seriously. This isn't going to work."

"Wait." Mac slipped off the desk. "I'm fine. I mean, I'll be fine. County Clerk, public records, names, in Driscoll, Kingsville and Alice, got it." He took another sip from his eye opener, turned to Horace. "Whose names?"

"Alice is a small town surrounded by ranches and farms. There are about 9,000 residents all spread out over the city limits which makes it hard to keep track of every registered voter. We don't want to draw any attention and let the Stevenson camp get wind of our strategy, so we can't do this through the Democratic Party. Coke has a lot of allies there. Your task, actually, is pretty simple. Show up, identify yourself as an assistant professor at the University of Texas, and you're doing research which requires access to public records. We went ahead and got the credentials from UT, which was easy, because you are, actually, an assistant professor. You'll start that job after you return."

"And this assistant professor is researching what?" Mac tried to ask a sober question.

Busby reacted as if he hadn't thought it through. "You'll think of something. What we need is a list of names. How you get them is immaterial."

"What names?"

"Yes, we need to know the name of every registered demo-crat in these three towns who died over the last two years."

Mac burped. "Excuse me." He chuckled a bit then said, "Why?"

Busby responded short and direct. "Just get the list."

Mac semi-saluted. "Aye, aye, sir."

Busby seemed frustrated and a little angry. "You know, Mac, I recommended you for this job and Ed and Cliff have been nothing but good to you. You had that posh job in New York and now you get to finish your undergrad and go for your master's. Meanwhile, you're getting paid and on a fast track."

Mac's eyes narrowed. "Fast track to where?"

"What?"

Mac pointed his finger at his friend. "I appreciate what you did, but believe me there was nothing posh about New York. I'm here and I'm excited about finishing my degree. But to what end? I'm going to collect names of dead people. Horace, this isn't what I signed up for."

Busby sat back down. "Listen Mac, you have to trust these men. There is a reason for everything you... and I... are asked to do. The drawback is, I admit, we don't always know why—"

"Never know why."

"Right, we don't, but this is the big game and you have chips in the game. When... and I do mean when... LBJ gets the Senate seat, we will both wind up in D.C. at the center of the federal government."

Mac didn't respond.

Horace let his defense rest.

"Okay, Horace. I'll be patient. It's just hard to explain to Mary... I mean Andre... what I do."

"I get it but that's the way it is for now and, by the way, can you explain that name thing? Your wife, Mary, wants to be called Andre now?"

"Something to do with equality, and pre-judgmental behavior of men towards women."

"I understand, I guess." Horace brightened. "She seems perfect for you. You were almost a Socialist in college and she sounds pretty far out on the left wing to me."

"Yeah, I had a lot of idealistic dreams back then. But the more I see in the real world, the more cynical I've become."

Horace put his hands together on his lap and laced his fingers. "I hear you Mac, but I believe in LBJ. I know it's not what either of us expected. It's mostly all politics and wheeling-dealing, but honestly, I think LBJ is going to make some big changes. I want to be part of that, and I hope you do too."

Mac stood up and threw the empty cup in the trash can. "Maybe you're right, but I gotta tell you pal, at this point, I'm running blind."

Horace nodded. "We both are."

They started walking to the door.

Horace put his arm on Mac's shoulder. "You're married now, and that's great. Congratulations by the way."

"Thanks."

"There's something else." Horace stopped walking and looked a little embarrassed. "I know about Josefa and you, and what happened in Houston."

Mac's blood shot cold.

"Don't panic. I don't think anybody else knows, and I really don't think Josefa will say anything."

"Really?" Mac pushed the door and stood in the opening and looked hard at Horace. "Who told you?"

"She did."

"Great— a steel trap of secrecy." Mac walked away quickly, letting the door slam behind him.

CHAPTER 12

JULY 24, 1948. DEMOCRATIC PRIMARY ELECTION.

THE MOMENT A PHONE was returned to its cradle, it rang again. Seven carefully selected volunteers stood, phone in hand, yelling into their receivers trying to be heard over the din filling the room. Democratic party captains from all over the state were calling in voting results to Lyndon Johnson's campaign headquarters. So far, the returns were as predicted by LBJ's optimistic staff, but exceeding the expectations of recent newspaper polls.

The *Dallas Morning News* and the *Houston Press* projected former Governor Coke Stevenson not only finishing first, but possibly reaching a fifty percent margin. Reaching that threshold, in a field of eleven candidates, would be an outright win. It would be a majority vote and eliminate a run-off election, which was often the case for a Democratic Party primary with a large field of candidates. The only newspaper that gave Lyndon Johnson a chance to lead the pack of eleven candidates was his hometown newspaper, the *Johnson City Record Courier*.

"What time is it?" LBJ was hoarse and struggling to be heard. He tapped his empty wrist.

John Connelly leaned closer. "A half past ten." Connelly

patted Johnson's shoulder. "You should head home, boss. The final tally won't be announced till tomorrow, but everything is looking great."

Ed Clark pushed past a few volunteers, holding a shaft of papers in his hand and bearing a grin on his face. "San Antonio has just reported and, combined with the returns from Dallas, Austin, and Houston, a run-off is almost an absolute. Coke is less than forty percent, and you are running at thirty-four."

LBJ squeaked painfully. "Peddy?"

Carter pulled one sheet from the pack and held up it up, smiling. "George E. B. Peddy has pulled almost twenty percent."

Connelly's mouth dropped open in surprise. "God bless. The votes for him kept the percentage under fifty."

Clark patted LBJ on the back. "You should get out of here. Go home. You're going to need all the sleep you can get. I just got off the phone with party headquarters and they said, if the vote holds, which of course it will, the run-off will be August 28th."

John Connelly seemed immediately flustered. "Less than a month? That's too fast. I'll make some calls."

LBJ's voice spoke in full volume. "No. No. Don't do that, John. We want it fast. I want to keep the momentum going."

"Okay, if you say so." Connelly sounded as if he had been scolded.

Johnson smiled as best he could. "John, do me a favor. Call Bird and tell her the news, please."

Connelly perked up. "Sure. My pleasure." He smiled weakly at Clark and headed toward the phone bank.

LBJ's face lost the smile and turned to Clark. "Don't let Connelly anywhere near the run-off. He has a lot of connections, and carries a lot of votes, but he still thinks he's the campaign manager. I lost the Senate race in '41 because of him. Public appearances with him are necessary but, dear God, keep him away from what... we have to do... to win. Understand?"

Carter nodded. "That's why we have Cliff. He can do the job."

"Are we prepared?"

"I... I mean, Cliff and I anticipated this situation months ago. We put a couple of men in the field to do the necessary groundwork."

LBJ nodded agreeably. "This was about the percentage of votes. Second place was all we needed. The run-off will count every single vote, from every corner of Texas. Get to George Parr, down in Jim Wells County, right away. He controls the vote in the south; Mexican American, ranchers, farmers." LBJ shook his finger. "It all might come down to what happens there."

Ed Carter put his hand on LBJ's shoulder again. "Stop worrying. I've already made the call. Go home, get some rest."

LBJ, head down, nodded.

"Tomorrow is Sunday. Go to church with Bird, and we will start fresh on Monday."

"Okay, but get me an appearance schedule." LBJ put both hands on his knees, stood up, then turned to Clark. "Send a photographer to the church, tomorrow."

"Understood. Go home."

They started toward the front door, volunteers and the staff clapping and cheering as he passed. LBJ acknowledged them, but only with half a wave, and an insincere smile. As they arrived at the door, Johnson saw his sister standing in the corner talking to a tall man wearing black glasses. Pointing to Josefa he said, "Who's she talking to?"

Clark looked over. "Mac Wallace. He's a... field guy."

"He works for us?"

Clark spoke close and low. "It's a problem but I'm handling it."

Josefa was drinking from a paper cup and saw him looking at her. She looked away without acknowledgment.

LBJ mumbled to Clark, "It was a big mistake letting her get involved in this."

Clark held the door open. "We need every vote, and like I said, I'm handling it."

"He looked like what the cat dragged in, didn't he?" Josefa raised her chin and blew a long stream of smoke into the air, instead of Mac's face.

Wallace leaned back against the wall. "I don't know how he's still standing. Horace said it's been nonstop."

She nodded. "I know…the helicopter… very clever. Most of those people in the sticks never saw one before and here comes Santa Johnson in a whirlybird."

"Did you hear about his hat?"

"The what?"

"His hat. Horace told me every time he flew into some barn-yard event, they would fly low over the crowd, then he'd open the door and throw his hat out. The crowd always loved it but after they landed, he'd send somebody to find it and ask for it back."

She grinned. "And what if they didn't give it back?"

"They'd buy it back for a dollar."

She laughed. "How much does my brother owe Horace?"

"Twenty-two dollars."

"Sounds like him, but still, a clever idea."

Mac took the last sip from his cup. "I need another. You?"

She looked at him curiously. "What's up? You've been hitting it pretty hard all night."

"Free drinks."

"Seriously, what's going on?"

"I have to go to New York."

Josefa tilted her head curiously. "Visit?"

"No. They want me there. Clark told me about a week ago. We're leaving on Monday."

She looked at the floor. "Shame. I was enjoying our… get-togethers."

Mac looked her in the eyes. "Me too."

"Why?" She smiled devilishly.

Mac stumbled and sputtered. "Because."

"What are you, ten? Answer the question. Why?"

Mac looked at his empty cup.

"Looking for courage?"

"No. I mean—"

"So, just tongue tied?" She changed her tone, and rubbed her leg up and down his.

"Because… you like me. I mean you like having sex… with me."

"Tell me something I don't know." She acted coy, slowly moving her tongue across her lower lip.

"Stop, wait, I mean, when Andre and I do it, it's like I'm not there. She's just all over me all the time."

"Sounds yummy."

"You don't understand. When we do it, you and me… it's like you want to do it with me, not to me. Understand?"

She withdrew, stood straight, and backed up a step. "Woah, pull the bridle, bucko."

Mac turned red. "That came out wrong."

"No, it didn't." She took a drink from her cup. "I like having sex, it's a lot of fun, and I like it with a lot of different people. And you, my dear, are… a lot of fun." She stepped closer and poked his chest. "I don't know that much about wifey, but it sounds like you have a tiger on your hands. Which, by the way, most men would love. So man up, and fix it."

Mac looked at the floor. "She's pregnant."

She sputtered, "That's… ah… wonderful?"

"I guess so."

Dismissively she said, "Well, you'll have time to figure all this out in New York, and by the way, you do know why they're suddenly sending you there, correct?"

He looked pensive but repeated what Clark had told him. "Yeah, they're sending me to Columbia for my doctorate and the semester is about to start. Clark said they want me at the Department of Agriculture by the end of next year. Why? It sounded like a good thing to me."

She laughed out loud, several people turned to look. "God, I'm worried about you. They want you out of town, out of sight, and away from any investigation that might come their way."

Mac looked hurt and stunned at the same time.

"Listen Honeyboy, you're a real smart guy, and I'm sure they have plans for you. But I'd bet the farm your sudden exit is about what you told me you were doing for them on your 'trips'. I've seen this play before and I'm telling you from experience. To my brother and his gang of thieves, you're important until you're not anymore."

He hated finger quotes.

"Did you really think that you were only doing research for them?"

Mac's response was almost military. "Doesn't matter. I don't ask why."

She looked at him for a long time. She put one foot behind her, a finger to her lip and looked him up and down. "Mac, sometimes for a smart guy you're pretty stupid, but," she grinned, stepped forward, and got close to his ear, "you are one great fuck." She stepped back and slipped her arm under his elbow. "Now, take me back to my hotel, and I'll give you a send-off you won't ever forget."

As if by magic, Mac's concerns turned into lust.

CHAPTER 13
SATURDAY AUGUST 28, 1948. DEMOCRATIC PRIMARY RUN-OFF ELECTION.

IT SEEMED to be exactly the same atmosphere as the Primary. Like thirty days prior, the same crew of volunteers was taking telephone calls from city and county precinct captains across Texas. The expectation was different, and so was the attitude of the staff. There could only be one winner and Coke Stevenson was leading in this two-man race.

In the back of the room, a few metal chairs were arranged for a view of a schoolhouse blackboard where totals from reporting precincts were etched in white chalk. LBJ was losing.

"There is no need to panic. It is way too early to get worried." Ed Clark spoke optimistically and looked like he was trying hard to seem calm.

"San Antonio will be reporting soon. That should tell the story." LBJ looked the same as a month ago, tired and drawn, but now, much thinner. He campaigned hard, working sixteen and seventeen hours a day, even holding off on a hospital visit when he experienced an almost crippling attack of gallstones. He made five speeches a day minimum and, in addition to the endless trips by car, put nearly four hundred hours on the helicopter. He was almost dead on his feet.

Clark looked at Cliff Carter. "I can see the numbers on the board, but where are we really?"

Carter glanced down at LBJ, looking reluctant to speak.

Clark waved his hand dismissively. "We both need to know. Where, exactly?"

"Were close but… down about 20,000 from where I thought we would be."

It was quiet for a beat.

John Connelly walked in the front door. Unlike other arrivals, the volunteers noticed him immediately, because he had an air of superiority about him that was also his main talent in life.

LBJ looked down and whispered to Clark, "Here he comes, my friend always in need."

Clark looked straight ahead and whispered back. "You needed him to placate the party's right wing."

Connelly had one hand looped through a red suspender and the other held an a unlit pipe. "Who reported in, so far?"

Cliff became a little less glum. "Only Dallas and Houston. Still a ton of uncounted votes."

LBJ nodded at the new arrival then leaned forward, his elbows on his knees and fingers intertwined. "San Antonio. We need to hear from San Antonio."

Clark gave a directional head bob to Carter. "Head up to the phones. Let us know as soon as they call in."

Carter walked away, talking and giving instructions to almost everyone he passed.

Clark sat on a metal folding chair next to LBJ. "Lyndon, I gotta tell 'ya. You look terrible."

Johnson waved him off. "Just get me some coffee. I'm fine."

Clark shook his head and started to get up.

Suddenly, Carter came back, sprinting in between the volunteers. "San Antonio called in. We picked up 10,000 votes on Stevenson's lead."

LBJ's head popped up.

Clark reached out to take the counting form out of Carter's hand. He looked at it, grinned, then handed it to Johnson. "About eighty percent counted and its better than we hoped."

LBJ pushed out of the chair and beckoned both men back to the small office. He spun around, pushed the door closed, then faced them while holding the paper in a clenched fist. "We can win this."

"Damn straight." Clark slapped the desktop.

Johnson continued, "Coke's got a thin majority in Dallas, Houston, and Fort Worth which John played a big part in keeping the conservatives happy."

Connelly puffed up. "They think you're a liberal and a Roosevelt New Dealer."

"They know nothing from nothing." Johnson spat in disgust. We are winning in Amarillo, Austin, and now close in San Antonio. We're splitting El Paso and the West, which will make the entire election hinge on Corpus Christi and the small towns in south Texas."

"Just like you predicted, boss." Clark affirmed.

LBJ sat in a chair and pointed to Carter. "This is Saturday, and none of those church going vote counters will work on Sunday. The election won't be decided tonight... or tomorrow, maybe not till Wednesday." He paused then motioned to Carter. "What's the time?"

"Eleven thirty."

"That's enough for tonight. Send everybody home. Thank them and tell them we'll see them at the victory party, but get rid of them. On Monday and the rest of the week, I only want key people."

Clark and Carter nodded. Connelly lit his pipe.

LBJ took a second then lowered his head. "I lost the last time

I ran for the Senate by a thousand votes." He looked up, his eyes narrow, his words slow. "A thousand fuckin' votes. I can't lose again. Nobody had ever lost twice, then won on a third try. It's not possible." His voice got louder and words came faster. "I'll be in the House the rest of my career. Our money friends will look for a fresh horse and all of us will be out to pasture. We'll be dead in the water."

The two men didn't speak, just nodded.

"A thousand votes... one thousand one hundred and seventeen to be exact." He looked at Carter. "Are you ready in case this goes that way?"

Carter snapped back like he was responding to a General. "I am, absolutely."

"If we do need to go that route... make sure nobody from the campaign is near it. If there's no one here they'll be nobody to answer questions."

LBJ looked at Ed Clark. "What happened to the field guy that was hanging around my sister?"

Carter held up both hands. "Handled. I sent him to New York. I called in a favor and got him enrolled in a doctorate program at Columbia. I told him he had to rush to get there before the semester started. He and his wife left a week ago."

"And Josefa?"

"She seemed like she didn't care one way or the other about her friend with the glasses. Also, we don't have to be concerned about her. Josefa told me she was leaving for one of those charity things she does in D.C. Said she was staying with friends for at least a month."

Johnson nodded but circled back to Wallace. "You sent her friend..."

"Wallace... Mac Wallace."

"Right, you sent him to Columbia. An Ivy league school? Seems excessive for a field guy."

Carter waggled a finger. "It's only for a year or so.

Remember the master plan, Lyndon. When you win...and you will win... we need a couple of inside people. We already have the guy in Justice and Commerce but we need someone inside the Department of Agriculture. We need a smart numbers guy who can take orders."

LBJ seemed unconvinced. "And?"

Carter's eyes darted to Clark.

LBJ nodded. "It's okay."

"Like I said, this guy Mac Wallace does what he's told and doesn't ask why. He just gets things done. For example, and to go to your concern about a too close for comfort election... he's the one we sent to Alice and Kingsville... Jim Wells County."

"Okay." LBJ nodded. "Did what you wanted?"

Carter nodded.

"Okay, good." LBJ stood up slowly. "I'll need to talk to George Parr on Monday."

"I'll set it up." Clark wrote a note.

Johnson stretched to full height. "I'm going home now. I'm fucking tired."

A young woman knocked on the glass panel in the door.

Carter waved her in.

"Rio Grande just called in. You are now only 854 votes behind, sir."

LBJ's expression didn't change.

"Great news, thank you." Carter dismissed her with a gesture.

Johnson gripped Carter's arm. "Ask somebody to get the car, Cliff. I need to get out of here."

"Sir." Carter exited quickly, closing the door behind him.

LBJ looked at Clark. "Make sure you keep Connelly away from this. I lost the last time because he wasn't prepared to do what was needed. Are you?"

"I am."

Johnson turned to the door. "It's gonna get real dirty from

here in, so keep him busy doing something else. Let him glad-hand the democratic committee. We may need them on our side. Besides," LBJ's eyes narrowed again. "I don't trust him when it comes to down and dirty."

Carter nodded. "It's definitely gonna be dirty."

CHAPTER 14

FRIDAY, SEPTEMBER 3, 1948. SIX DAYS AFTER THE RUN-OFF ELECTION

THE SMOKE in the campaign office had taken form, becoming a cloud so thick it obscured an entire section of the ceiling. When the front door opened, fingers of the grey mass became graceful tentacles rushing down to the opening, retreating back to its nest when the door closed. The dozen people milling around, most having nothing to do but smoke, seemed oblivious to the cloud, the smell, or lack of oxygen.

Day six began hopeful, but wore on without any announcement of the final outcome. The Democratic Committee of Texas, the judge and jury of the vote count, had been silent. The crew's anxiety built hourly resulting in outbursts of frustration and short tempers.

LBJ arrived late in the afternoon, and he and Edward Clark had holed-up in the small office in the back of the storefront election headquarters.

"You okay?" Clark asked, concerned.

"Yeah, yeah. I had to meet with our friends. They're nervous."

"Did you play nice?"

"I tried, but they are thinking Coke will be vengeful if he wins. They are certain he knows they were backing me."

"They gave him almost as much as they gave you. I don't get it."

"Stevenson thinks they shouldn't have given me anything at all."

Johnson sat in a chair far away from the paper coffee cups and cigarette butts stacked at the end of the only table. A smaller but equally offensive cloud of smoke hung over the Senatorial candidate and his lawyer/fixer.

LBJ looked through the office window and nodded toward Cliff Carter, who was perched on a desk staring at a phone. "What's he doing?"

Clark chuckled. "Willing it to ring."

LBJ looked tired but had actually slept the night before. It was the first time he had six uninterrupted hours of sleep in a month. Clark, dressed in a starched white shirt, pressed suit, and shined shoes, was his polar opposite.

Johnson stubbed out his cigarette. "I knew this was going to happen. I just knew it. We went from ten thousand down on Saturday night, to eight hundred and fifty-four on Sunday. We got to three hundred and ninety-four down on Wednesday, then Thursday morning it was only two hundred and fifty-seven. Then, late last night," he lit another smoke, "somebody in that office told a reporter the count was done, and Coke won by one hundred and thirteen votes."

"Lyndon, that wasn't official, you haven't conceded, and..." Clark looked at LBJ confidently, "it was the best thing that could have happened."

"What the fuck are you talking about?"

"They told us last night exactly how many votes we need to win."

Johnson took a second, but then nodded slowly. "We need one hundred and... fourteen."

"Well, maybe a couple of more," Clark grinned, "but yes, that's right. And remember, this isn't a state or federal election. It's just the party. The final count is the final count. We need a hundred plus votes and that's what's gonna' happen."

"I take it you made the call to Parr. He controls the—"

Cliff Carter pushed the door open, interrupting the conversation. He stepped in and spoke slowly and clearly. "Jim Wells County found a box of uncounted votes from the 13th District, which is the city of Alice. Two poll officials showed up at committee headquarters with a sealed voting box marked number 13. It contained two hundred and two ballots."

Neither Clark nor LBJ said a word.

Carter then spilled the rest of the news fast. "There were two votes for Stevenson… and two hundred for you. You won… you won by eighty-seven votes, Senator Johnson. The committee announced the official results to the press."

The staff had gathered outside the open office door. They began cheering, applauding, some jumping up and down.

Johnson rose, did a two-handed shake with Clark, then patted Carter on the back. A smile actually formed on his face. It had been a long time coming.

Carter looked past the volunteers and saw several members of the press coming through the front door. He hurried out of the office, hands up, gesturing the oncomers to stop. "The Congressman will have a statement in a moment." He backed up into the office and closed the door behind him.

Carter, looking like he was still recovering as well, gripped LBJ's arm. "I suggest you congratulate Coke on a fine race, thank the voters and promise them after you win the general election, you will represent them in Washington… etcetera, etcetera."

Clark echoed the sentiment. "You'll have to make a couple of speeches before the general election in November, but this is it. Congratulations, Senator."

"Thank you, both of you." LBJ turned to Carter, suddenly gripped with campaign exhaustion instead of victory adrenaline. "Don't let this go on too long. A couple of questions, then get me out as quick as you can."

"No problem, I'll send someone to get your driver."

Several flashbulbs went off the moment he walked into the room. There were only a few reporters there, apparently the main body of newspaper correspondents were covering the favorite, which wasn't him.

"Congressman, do you have a comment on the allegations from the Stevenson campaign that the ballots that showed up this morning were fraudulent?"

Ed Clark jumped in front of Johnson. "We have no knowledge of any wrongdoing, or how the committee counts votes. What we know for certain is the Democratic Party of Texas announced that Lyndon Baines Johnson will be the party's candidate in November."

Another reporter spoke. "Do you expect Coke Stevenson to concede without a fight?"

"We—"

LBJ stopped Carter with a raised hand. "Coke would argue with the statue of a cigar store wooden Indian. He likes to fight... but I'll tell you all a secret."

They went silent, leaned forward, with notepads and pencils at the ready.

"So do I."

Some laughed, some scribbled.

Clark grabbed LBJ's elbow and guided him toward the door. Cliff Carter followed close behind.

The car was waiting, the driver holding open the back door. He was a tall black man, with prizefighter hands and linebacker shoulders. "Home, sir?"

Johnson didn't respond.

Clark answered for him as he rounded the back of the Lincoln. "Yes, we're taking him home."

In the minute it took the driver to get behind the wheel, Cliff Carter pushed through the reporters and jumped into the passenger seat. His eyes were wide and his jaw clenched. "We have a problem."

"What?" Clark leaned forward.

LBJ leaned back.

Carter faced them over the front seat. "I got a call just now from Willie Healy over at the committee. The Stevenson people are irate. They got a look at the register from District 13. The two hundred and two signatures, for the ballots from Box 13, were listed last."

Clark interrupted. "Did that match the ballots cast?"

"Yes."

"Then what's the problem?"

"Every voter had to sign a register before they voted, and the last two hundred and two were written in black ink."

"So?" Clark's impatience was palpable.

"Every other signature was in blue ink."

Clark waved his hand dismissively. "Don't worry about it. The pen stopped working and they got a new one, so what?"

Carter clearly had more to say but hesitated.

LBJ spoke up. "Give me the bad news."

"All the names in Box 13 were in alphabetical order." He took a beat. "Nobody is going to believe that two hundred people lined up, a to z, before voting."

Johnson stuck a finger in Ed Clark's chest. "Get Abe Fortas down here, quick."

The driver pulled away from the curb.

Johnson looked out the window and shook his head. "We're going to need a good lawyer."

CHAPTER 15
SEPTEMBER 3, 1949. ONE YEAR LATER.

MAC WALKED up the concrete steps to the apartment building, careful not to trip on the broken third tread. The light in the common hall was out again, and he waited a moment for his eyes to adjust before entering. There hadn't been an incident in this building, but there were two muggings farther up 125th street, and he was being careful. Moving quickly down the hall, he pulled the apartment key from his jacket pocket, while checking the corners of the hallway for moving shadows.

"Andre?" The living room was dark, the bedroom door closed, and the only light came from the kitchen.

"In here, and be quiet. I just got the baby down."

The galley kitchen was functional and efficient. The appliances worked, there was just enough cabinet space, and there was room for a table and two chairs. It was also a virtual prison cell for Mrs. Malcolm Wallace.

Andre was seated in the chair near the sole window in the back of the one-bedroom apartment. The table was bare, save a glass ashtray which held the remnants of several hours of isolation.

Mac cleared his throat, causing her to avert her gaze from the window and its view of the alley. She looked at him with cold eyes. "Did you eat?"

He glanced to the empty stove. "Ah… did you?"

The cold eyes went to anger and so did her words. "You mean, did I make you dinner?"

"No… no." He held up his hands defensively. "I'm sorry I'm late, but I had a meeting with the dean and—"

"Liar. You stink of alcohol."

He hesitated a second, caught. "Okay, yes, you're right. I did have a meeting but I stopped at Ray's Bar. I needed to make a call to Washington, and you know I'm not supposed to do that from home."

"Really?" She added sarcasm to an unforgiving tone.

"There's a phone booth inside the bar. It's quiet, private, and I can call collect. You've been there with me. You've seen it. The old fashioned one with the glass door. And… it only took a couple of minutes."

"But you needed a few beers before you came home?"

It was more of a statement than a question and he had no defense.

She kept on the attack. "Sure, you had to call Washington. Mr. big deal. Mr. political spy. I don't buy it. I think it's just another reason not to come home." Her face was red and her voice got loud.

He gestured, hands out, palms down. "The baby is sleeping." He knew it was a mistake the moment it came out.

"Son of a … I sit here all day with nothing to do but take care of a four-month-old baby, and you're out doing God knows what, with God knows who."

"I had to make the call."

"And I'm stuck here all day, every day."

"I know this isn't easy for you," Mac tried a hard line, "but what I'm doing is tough too. My courses are Linear Algebra, and

Differential Equations. I need to study to have any chance of getting my PhD."

She grabbed the ashtray and flung it in his direction, hitting the wall instead of him.

"Nice." He glared at her, then took a beat.

Mac opened a cabinet door and removed a bottle of scotch and a glass. He tipped the bottle to its edge, and slowly poured it three-quarters full. He held it up examining the color, then turned to her. "Want one?"

She folded her arms across her chest. "Sure."

He took another glass from the cabinet and poured out the remainder of the bottle. Mac examined the two glasses for fullness, then equaled the difference. He held out both glasses for her to choose.

She reached up and took one.

Mac sat down and they both sipped the scotch. It wasn't a good brand, and the first swallow was harsh.

Andre put the glass down on the table. "We don't fuck anymore." Her tone was softer, almost normal.

He matched her volume and tone. "You have to take care of a baby, and I'm studying."

She frowned and shook her head slowly. "Studying? Tell me how that is possible when you're drunk, which is all the time."

"Why do we have to do this every night? I... I mean we, we're given an opportunity— "

"Not we... you," her voice rising again. "Your opportunity to go to Columbia means your wife, me, is stuck in this rathole, two blocks from Harlem, with no place to go, no friends, and nothing to do but take care of a baby."

He tried a different angle. "I was told to get a PhD so I could get a management position in the Department of Agriculture. They are taking care of me, because I helped get him elected."

She laughed. "You mean you helped... steal the election."

"The Supreme Court of the United States doesn't agree. Stevenson sued and they said LBJ won."

"What are you talking about? It wasn't the whole court; it was one judge, Hugo Black. Johnson probably owns him just like he owns you."

"Nobody owns me." He took a sip, grimaced and continued. "You're wrong about the judge too. It was Stevenson's mistake. Justice Black declined to hear the case because he said it was a state election and not federal. The Democratic Committee decided to declare Johnson official, because if they didn't, the Senate election in November would happen without a Democrat's name on the ballot. If they'd continued to argue in court, they would have handed the seat to the Republicans."

"He cheated."

"No." He took another swallow. "I think he just cheated better than the other guy."

"He won by eighty-seven votes that miraculously showed up six days after the election. Even the papers are calling him Landslide Lyndon. You're working for a thief."

Mac shook his head. "Not a thief— a politician."

"Same thing." She looked at her glass. It was almost empty.

Mac picked up the bottle and waggled it back and forth. "This was full when I left this morning."

"Yeah, so what?" She ducked her head down, her hair falling to cover her face. "I called you a drunk. I didn't say I wasn't a drunk too." She finished the last drop in her glass.

They were almost calm.

He sighed. "This will all be over soon. I promise."

She lowered her eyes, and gripped the empty glass with both hands.

A full minute went by. Neither spoke nor moved.

Finally, she looked up and stared at him. "I filed for a divorce."

He was stunned, speechless.

From the bedroom the baby started crying.

She put her hands on the table and stood. Standing still, looming over him, she said slowly, "I'm taking Mary back to Austin."

He drank the rest of his cheap scotch as she walked away.

"How far along are you?"

"Well, it's a two-year program. I've been here a year, so halfway." He immediately regretted his involuntary sarcastic tone.

Ed Clark let dead air follow Mac's response.

Mac changed hands with the receiver and pushed on the telephone booth door making sure it was closed tight. "Ah... sorry about that, sir. I'm upset, and that was uncalled for."

Again, Clark didn't respond.

"Last night, Andre told me she filed for divorce."

He heard a cough on the line indicating Clark was still on the phone.

"She's leaving me because she's alone in an apartment, in Harlem. It's all I could afford. I thought it would work out because it's only a block away from a park. But it's a bad neighborhood, and I guess she's not used to life in a city, especially New York City."

More silence.

"Sir?"

"I'm told you're both drinking a lot."

He instantly got mad. "Who told you that?"

A monotone voice responded. "Are you? Is she?"

Now Mac went quiet.

"Malcolm?"

"Yes."

"Answer the question. Are you drinking or are you not?"

"Yes, we are both drinking too much."

"That needs to stop. Also, you're further behind in your doctorate than what you've represented. We were hoping to put you into a high-level position at Agriculture when you finished but given your... situation, I'm going to move you now. We need information about what's going on inside the DOA, and now you'll just have to work harder to get it."

Mac stood straighter, his burden lifting.

"You will go to Arlington, Virginia, and start at the DOA in two weeks. Bob from my office will call you with the details."

"Sir. Yes, sir."

A pause was followed with a simple strong statement. "Malcolm, don't fuck up again."

"You can't divorce me."

"He said that?"

"Yes, he said divorce is a deal breaker. It's almost 1950 and everything is real modern and all, but placing someone who is divorced in Agriculture will cause too much attention. He said this needs to be under the radar with no issues." Mac stood as confidently as his lie would allow.

"And this is for real?" Andre had one hand on a hip and the baby on the other.

"Yes."

She looked at him, with judgment in her eyes. "Why are they still doing this? You told me you needed to get a PhD. What changed?"

"He said I would just have to work harder, or maybe they feel bad about putting me... I mean us, in this situation."

"Now I know you're lying. Politicians don't have feelings."

"I said I don't know why they're doing it. All I know is there is a job that pays well and it's in Arlington, Virginia, which is a lot better than Harlem."

She shifted the baby's weight. "When?"

"Two weeks. I have to withdraw from Columbia; we have to pack, and the movers will hold everything in storage until we find a place to live." He took a beat. "That is, if you agree."

She turned her back to him, opened the refrigerator door, took out a baby bottle, then turned around. "Okay, I'll withdraw the divorce."

"Great, I'll call them and say we accept."

She picked up a small pot, filled it halfway with water, put the bottle in and lit the stove. "If you lied to me, I'll refile."

"I didn't lie." He smiled and reached out, offering to hold the baby.

She turned her back to him, faced the pot, and waited for the water to boil.

CHAPTER 16

AUGUST, 1950

"You should've pulled up front and let the valet park the car."

Mac took Andre's hand, steadying her on the uneven surface. "It's one of the most expensive hotels in D.C. It would've cost a fortune to park with the valet."

Andre held tight. "If you had to walk in high heels, you'd pay for parking."

They came out of the shadows of the tree-lined sidewalk, and into the light of the porte-cochere.

"Look at this place. Isn't it fantastic?" Mac gasped in awe.

"I can see it's beautiful, bucko, I'm not exactly a hick from the sticks."

"Sorry. I just want you to have a good time tonight. I know it's been a rough year, but things are starting to loosen up, and I think everything is gonna be better real soon."

She looked up at him and grinned. "You're not going to start singing a show tune now."

"Very funny."

The valet looked at them strangely. Apparently, not many people attending a function at the prestigious Mayflower Hotel used public parking. After hesitating a moment, the man who sported a tight red jacket with brass buttons dashed forward and opened the etched glass front door. "Good evening."

Mac nodded, and Andre said, "Thank you."

The lobby was in keeping with other prominent Washington D.C. hotels. Its expanse was overwhelming and the appointments ornate. Only a completely jaded socialite would not take at least a moment to appreciate the hundred-year-old structure.

A tuxedoed usher pointed the couple to a bank of elevators saying, "The reception for the Secretary of Agriculture is in the main ballroom on the third floor."

Mac and Andre continued holding hands, walking slow, just looking, neither were socialites.

Two other couples stood waiting for the next elevator, one older and one older still. The men were pale, balding, and had tuxedoes tailored to fit their bulging bellies. Their wives were age-appropriate, dressed in sparkly evening gowns, and wore conflicting perfumes that were battling for dominance.

Mac and Andre, holding their noses and giggling, bolted past the couples when the elevator door opened on the third floor. They quick-stepped down the hallway, entered the ballroom, and began searching for their first priority— the bar.

She spotted it first. "Over there."

They strolled past the other attendees in the room, which seemed about half full. Most stood in groups near round tables set for dinner, others were milling about shaking hands, and some were at the bar keeping the waitstaff busy.

Mac didn't expect to meet anyone he knew. He'd been at the DOA less than a year, and although his title, Senior Agricultural Economist, sounded important, it was like his position at the New York bank. He was just an obscure accountant. He was at this government function not because of his supervisor or his supervisor's supervisor. He and Andre were there because of an invitation arranged by a man who had not yet arrived, Edward Clark.

"Two martinis." Mac waved at a bartender who nodded without looking at him.

The popular drink had been pre-mixed into pitchers and two drinks arrived at light speed.

"To you." Mac raised his glass. "And, you look beautiful."

Andre returned the gesture and sipped. "Thank you, but I have to say, in that tux, you look like the toy man on top of a wedding cake."

He grinned. "I do, don't I?"

She used her free hand to smooth the fabric of her dress. It was simple, long, black, had a slit up the hip side, and a revealing neckline. "I feel way underdressed here."

"No one will be looking at the dress, honey." Mac leaned back and did an exaggerated once over. "You have some magnificent breasts."

She actually blushed. "It's the benefit of having babies, big tits."

They polished off their drinks, and he signaled the bartender for a refill.

"Jesus H Christ, if it isn't Malcolm Wallace."

He recognized her voice immediately, and his blood turned to ice water. He took a short breath and turned around. "Hello Josefa."

She had a big smile, a tall drink, and a dress with a neckline that rivaled Andre's, minus baby boobs.

"Wallace," she gave him a quick once over, "you look like a toy man on a wedding cake."

Andre spit out some of her drink and broke up laughing. "I haven't met your friend before, but I like her already."

Josefa didn't wait for an introduction from Mac. "And you must be the amazing Andre I've heard so much about. My name

114

is Josefa. Perhaps you know my brother, Senator Lyndon Johnson?" She put on a Cheshire grin, and stuck out her hand.

"You're right, I am amazing." Andre took her hand. "And, I haven't met your brother, the Senator, although my husband apparently works for him. He has also told me... absolutely nothing about you. However, you seem to be very familiar with my wedding cake husband."

Josefa did a vaudevillian shocked look. "Mr. Wallace, how could you have not told your fabulous wife about your fabulous friend?"

Andre glared at Mac. "Yes, tell us how?"

He didn't get a chance to answer, not that he had one.

"Because he's a typical man— a barbarian." Josefa took Andre's elbow and pulled her forward. "Come, let's sit at a table. I'll tell you all about me, you can tell me all about you, and we'll talk shit about everyone else."

The pair started for a table near the front of the auditorium with Mac, in terror-shock, following behind.

Josefa selected a table, then sat between them. "So," Josefa addressed Andre paying no attention to Mac, "I met your man years ago, when he was attending the University of Texas. He was working with that little prick, Horace Busby."

Andre looked at Mac who just shrugged and tried to grin, because there was no hole to climb into and no bridge to jump off.

Josefa finished her drink and raised a hand, flagging a waiter who almost sprinted to her. "Another Manhattan for me, and two Martinis for my friends." She hesitated a second then changed the order. "No wait, make that two Manhattans, and four Martinis." When the waiter left, she smiled at Andre. "That should make this more fun, don't you think?"

Andre smiled and, unlike Mac, appeared to be relaxed by their new host's candor.

"Indeed, it always does. Please continue… you were saying, you met my husband years ago?"

"Yes. It was when he was with the crew from UT that was working for my asshole brother. Right Mac?"

Mac managed to creak out, "Correct."

Josefa picked a cigarette from a silver case and held it to her lips, unlit. "At the time, I considered bedding him," she rolled the cigarette in her fingers, "but I didn't want to suffer the wrath of Lyndon, so I moved on to other people not associated with the crew."

"Oh my God." Mac felt like hiding under the table.

Without looking at him, Josefa pointed toward Mac. "Although… the temptation was hard to resist. He is a handsome bastard, isn't he?"

"Yes, he is, and he's a great fuck too, but then you wouldn't know that… would you?"

Josefa shot right back without hesitation. "No, I wouldn't, and look at you with that mouth. You have nothing in common with all these other Washington, tight-ass bitches, do you?"

"Not a fucking thing, but I may have a thing or two in common with you."

Josefa laughed loudly, then struck a match and lit her cigarette. She paused as if she were considering something, then exhaled slowly. She gazed at Andre with mischievous eyes. "I think this is the beginning of a beautiful friendship."

Andre smiled and responded, equally as playful. "My favorite movie."

Mac didn't know why he was scared, but he was.

His wife turned to him and partially relieved his angst. "I really like your friend."

Feedback squealed from a microphone, followed by a fanfare played by a small orchestra. "Ladies and gentleman, if you would find your seats."

Josefa leaned toward them. "We don't have to stay for

dinner. I had planned on going to a party in Georgetown after. You should come."

Andre responded enthusiastically. "Absolutely, that sounds terrific."

Mac grumbled and grunted.

Josefa looked at him with disdain. "Uh oh. Not a unanimous vote."

Andre adopted the same look. "What?"

"I have to meet Ed Clark."

Josefa immediately straightened her back as if she had a sudden muscle spasm.

Andre seemed startled by her reaction.

Josefa leaned over close to Andre's ear and whispered. "That man is evil."

Andre pulled back and stared blankly at Josefa, then turned to Mac.

He knew the sister of Lyndon Johnson had just confirmed all of his wife's fears.

Josefa continued to press. "So, how 'bout that party? Are we going together or am I going stag?"

Both women stared at him waiting for an answer.

He manned up. "I can't leave before I see him. It shouldn't take long." He glanced back and forth at the unforgiving faces. "We could go... right after."

Andre shook her head, "Figures." She turned to Josefa and, exasperated, said, "I have to use the bathroom."

"Me too." Josefa grabbed her drink and her cigarettes.

Mac started to get up when the ladies rose.

"Don't bother." Andre waved off the attempted chivalry.

As he watched them go, he finished off the first of the two Martinis.

While they were gone, two couples sat down at the table. Mac shook hands, introduced himself and immediately forgot their names. The couples chatted while Mac drank his other Martini. A few minutes passed, then a few more.

Would she tell Andre about Houston?

A line of waiters carrying trays appeared, and began serving dinner to every place setting. He picked up his fork but not knowing whether or not to wait till the pair returned, he put it back down. More time passed. The other couples were eating, so he started.

"Thanks for waiting." His concentration was on what he believed to be chicken and didn't see the pair return.

Andre and Josefa sat down and addressed their dinners.

"Typical," Josefa said, confidently picking up a slice of zucchini, "rubber chicken and soggy vegetables. It's a government event. All flash, no substance."

A man's voice from behind ended her culinary review. "You have a bad attitude, Josefa."

Without turning around to face the voice, Josefa dropped her fork. It clattered on the plate. She stood, keeping her back to Edward Clark and walked away.

Andre looked at Mac for an explanation.

Mac stood up briskly. "Edward Clark, please let me introduce my wife, Andre. Andre this is Edward Clark."

"Pleasure." Clark held out his hand.

Andre hesitated at first, just looking at his hand, but then slowly accepted his greeting.

Clark showed some teeth when he grinned. "Are you enjoying yourself?"

"I was, but our entertainment just left."

Clark ignored the comment but kept the toothy smile. "May I steal your husband for a minute?"

"Sure, he's all yours." Andre flicked her wrist, and picked up a fork.

Mac put his hand on Andre's shoulder. "I'll be back as soon as I can."

"Don't rush." She poked at the chicken while looking around for Josefa.

Mac followed behind Clark, walking out of the ballroom, and down the hall in silence. It was unoccupied, and at its end Clark opened a panel door and gestured Mac to enter. It was an empty storage room with rectangular tables, folded in half, ready for transport, and columns of chairs stacked, one on another. They pulled up two loose chairs and sat opposite each other.

"First, Malcolm, we are very happy with the information you're retrieving."

Mac grinned, enthusiastically. "Thank you, and there's plenty more available. I have access to just about everything. At the DOA, nothing happens without a budget which I'm either formulating or part of a review. So, I see everything sooner or later."

"Yes, we know." Clark dismissed Mac's enthusiasm. "That kind of access is good, and might be helpful someday, but for the moment we're only interested in information concerning Texas. Recently, you've been sending intelligence we haven't asked for which we fear might cause you to be vulnerable to discovery. We don't want you to be exposed, and then connected to me or the Senator in any way. So please limit yourself to just Texas. And above all be careful."

"Got it, just cotton, wheat, corn, or oil and gas."

"Correct, we need to know about any sudden problems, reports, investigations, permit issues. Anything like that."

"Don't worry, I'm careful, but the department is so big, and so complicated, I think I could walk out of there with half the office furniture and no one would notice."

"Good... great." Clark hesitated then brushed imaginary dust from his lapel. "Nothing about cotton recently?"

Mac thought a minute. "No, sir, but I heard there is some legislation on the hill that will make cotton futures something to watch."

Clark immediately reacted. "Good... good work. And remember, just Texas."

"Of course. Is that all you need sir?"

Clark stood up, smiling. "Yes, that's it."

They started to leave.

"Wait a second, Mac." Clark stopped and looked like he was pondering his next remark. "You seem to have developed a friendship with the Senator's sister."

"Josefa? No sir, not a friend, not really. She just happened to be here tonight." Then he told the lie. "I haven't seen her since that party in D.C."

Clark went from friendly to serious instantly. "That's not what I heard. You need to be very careful not to endanger your career by getting caught up with her, and her... proclivities."

Mac nodded.

As they walked into the hall, Clark gave him the tooth grin. "Please extend my gratitude to your lovely wife for allowing me to interrupt your time at the party."

"Yes sir, I will."

Clark started to step away.

Mac suddenly spoke out of turn. "Can I ask you a question?"

Clark turned and grunted. "Yes."

"Who told you I had seen Josefa after the party in D.C.?"

Clark took a long moment, staring stone-faced at Mac, then walked away without answering.

CHAPTER 17

AUG 10, 1950

MAC ONLY HEARD the sound of his own footsteps echoing in the Great Hall. It was deathly quiet at 5:42 in the morning. He thought he was alone but couldn't be certain, the building was too big and he was too small.

Arriving early for a government job had its benefits. One of which was he had no problem parking on the street even though the building was only a few blocks from a tourist mecca, the Jefferson Memorial. The DOA was like every other government building in Washington D.C. Built in Romanesque style, it had an exterior dominated by massive pillars, supporting an immense portico. Huge entry doors opened into a three-story lobby, curved marble stairs, and tall windows that faced other equally impressive facades.

The journey to his office was proving to be a difficult assent. The elevators weren't working yet, so he needed to take the stairs to the third floor. Three hours sleep, three packs of cigarettes, and a lot of whisky resulted in, a desert-dry mouth, a shortness of breath, and a headache that worsened by the minute. Aspirin had little effect so far, neither had coffee. What he needed was sleep, which wasn't going to happen anytime soon.

Clark had set the time of the morning's call through his man in the office. At precisely 6:00 a.m., Mac was to dial the number he was given. He'd never called Clark from the DOA before—this was a first. In the past, security had always been paramount. He was to complete tasks assigned with no connection to Edward Clark or the Senator. Even the man in Clark's office, who made arrangements, called him from outside lines. Mac made his calls from public phone booths. All of his correspondence was addressed to several different PO boxes, and never had a return address. Today was different. It was a special project and had taken a great deal of research. He had written summaries but he might have to refer to files that would be difficult to transport out of the building. Mac's excitement about the call dampened as the effects of the great quantity of alcohol he had consumed the night before hadn't worn off.

He bent over at the top of the stairs, gasping for breath, but pleased he made it. It took a minute but he recovered. Before moving on, he checked the hall once more and only saw a janitor slowly pushing a cart. Satisfied he was alone, he walked down a corridor to a door marked 612.

His office was decorated in government minimal, with a metal desk, a phone and a bookcase. The only remembrance of his outside life was a silver-framed picture of Andre centered on two large filing cabinets. Mac plopped in his chair and laid his head back willing the headache to subside. He'd spent two days preparing for any questions, carefully arranging documents in files now piled neatly on his desk.

He sighed. He was ready but he worried the hangover would affect his performance. Mac opened a drawer, removed a pint bottle, opened the cap, and took a long draw of whisky.

The phone rang and he almost dropped the bottle. He capped it as quick as he could manage, dropped it back into the drawer, and picked up the receiver on the third ring, a little breathless from the effort.

There was no salutation. "You ready?"

Mac coughed from the sting of the booze. "Yes, sir."

"You sound out of breath."

"I went to the bathroom, heard the phone ringing, and ran to answer."

"Ah, huh." Ed Clark paused a bit before continuing. "Mac, this is a conference call. I want you to know there are other people listening, and you need to keep your responses confined only to my questions. Understood?"

"Yes, sir."

"Good, we are all aware of the subject matter but start at the beginning, and explain it as if we know nothing."

"Okay… I mean, yes, sir." Mac thought for a brief second about taking another drink but passed on the idea.

"Let's begin."

Mac opened the top file and withdrew a summary. "What I have researched is a possible result of the combination of a program enacted under Roosevelt's New Deal, and the federal government's infrastructure projects that rely on eminent domain." Mac took a beat, no one asked for clarification. "The federal government, in a post-war effort to stabilize cotton and sorghum prices, offered subsidies to qualified farmers for limiting production of those crops. Basically, farmers were paid to limit the number of acres planted for an annual per-acre fee."

Clark asked, "For how long?"

"Sir?"

Clark shot back quickly. "How long will the subsidies continue?"

"The program is structured like the oil depletion allowance. It was left undefined."

"So, indefinitely."

"Yes, sir. It would take an act of Congress to end it."

Static crackled over the phone.

"Okay, now explain how the eminent domain issue is connected."

Mac removed another file from the pile and opened to its summary. "This is a bit more complicated but I assure you what I'm about to tell you is accurate."

There was another bit of static crackle but Mac continued. "The government has the ability to exercise eminent domain which, as I'm sure you know, is the process by which private property can be seized for public use, with proper compensation, but without the owner's consent. This occurs when projects, for example— a new highway, an airport, or a reservoir — is approved for construction by the authorities."

"The subsidy and infrastructure are connected?" Clark's voice now sounded curious.

"Taking property for short money is usually devastating to small farmers, who are, historically, just making ends meet. Even though they get paid for the land, it's usually not enough to buy replacement acreage and, even if they could, the new property is rarely near the homestead. The farmers are unable to replace the acreage so the subsidy allotments go away with the property."

"Where is the advantage?"

"The key is the subsidy is transferable. For example, Mister X buys a couple of thousand unfarmable, undevelopable acres in Texas for next to nothing. He then finds farmers, subjected to a taking by eminent domain. They could be from Texas or any state really. Mister X then convinces the farmers to buy an equal amount of taken property from him and transfer the subsidy they can no longer use. The farmers purchase Mister X's property with a mortgage that has no payments for a year, then leases it back to Mister X for a monthly payment. The farmer never makes one mortgage payment, and defaults on the loan. The property reverts to Mister X ... but the subsidy stays with the property. The farmer gets a better deal. He gets paid for property taken for eminent domain, and then receives a lease payment every month for a year, maybe two. The deal costs Mister X some cash up front, but on the back end, he gets a government subsidy for every acre he buys for the foreseeable future."

"The farmers will go along with this?"

"Probably not the big planters, but the small ones, and there are thousands of them, absolutely. They really don't have any other options."

A different voice said, "Is it legal?"

Clark answered for Mac. "Technically, no. The original sale and mortgage were a pretext rather than a genuine sale. However, the question is not if it is legal, it's what is the enforcement at the DOA?"

Mac paused, but only for a moment. "Unless something changes, there would be no way to find the irregularity, unless, of course, Mister X gets greedy or a Texas investigator somehow got wind."

"In Texas." A different voice laughed.

Clark took control. "That's all. Thank you."

The crackle on the phone stopped and the line went silent.

Mac adjusted the files to sit neatly on the corner of the desk, then leaned back in the chair, a long stream of air escaping from deep in his lungs.

His performance was good, organized and informed. He knew that to be true, because he watched it happen. Part of him was removed and he could hear himself acting dedicated and professional. He was simultaneously, functional and numb.

He took the bottle from the drawer and had another drink, the whisky having no affect.

Air breezed through a vent in the ceiling. A door closed somewhere down the hall. On the cabinet, Andre, in portrait pose, was wearing a prom night smile.

The envelope in his jacket pocket poked his chest. He pulled it free and set it down, centered on the desk pad. It was thick, legal, and had *Mr. Malcolm Wallace* typed in black ink under *Notice for Divorce.*

Raising the bottle to her, he took a long swallow, then gripped its neck, and threw it straight and strong.

It shattered the glass in the silver frame.

CHAPTER 18

SEPTEMBER 1950. AUSTIN, TEXAS

ANDRE cautiously bent forward and peered down the alley, both hands clutching her purse. It was narrow, dark with foreboding stone walls. At the far end there was a set of wooden steps, lit by a single streetlight. She looked up and down the sidewalk wondering if this was another bad idea. Next to her, mounted side-by-side on the front wall of the theater, notices of upcoming performances featured Austin Community Theater Group. The one closest to the entrance advertised the recent hit Broadway play *Arsenic and Old Lace* which was opening in three weeks. She stepped into the alley, gingerly at first, then picked up her pace, her decision made.

Andre took the steps quickly, relieved when the backstage door was unlocked and opened into a well-lit hall. Her attention was drawn to voices which became more distinguishable as she walked down the corridor. A rehearsal was in progress. At its end, a series of curtains hung from ceiling-to-floor near three closed doors marked: Costumes, Make-up, Dressing Room. She stopped, not knowing where to go next.

"You lost?"

"Ohhh." She jumped, startled and frightened.

"Sorry, didn't mean to scare you." The man who had emerged from the Dressing Room wore a double-breasted suit, and a warm smile.

"That's okay," she said without conviction. "I'm looking for Josefa Johnson."

The smile got a little wider. "Ah… you must be Andre. Please allow me to introduce myself, I'm Douglas Kinser. Josefa mentioned you might stop by."

Andre rarely stumbled for a response but, "She did?" was all that came out.

"She's this way." He grabbed her hand, and guided her through the space between two of the hanging backdrops then down a set of stage-right stairs.

Josefa exclaimed from the darkened audience seats. "You came."

Andre saw her coming down the aisle, with an enthusiasm she hadn't expected.

Josefa had arms out and bare feet. "So glad to see you." She embraced Andre, hugging her close. She pushed back to arms-length, maintaining a grip on Andre's shoulders then nodded to Andre's escort. "Thank you, Douglas. I'll take her off your hands… for now."

"Nice meeting you." The actor bowed slightly then headed back up the stairs to the stage.

Taking her by the hand, Josefa led Andre up the slanted aisle. "Best seat in the theater, half way up the aisle, middle of the house. One can see the entire stage without turning one's head."

The commotion caused by her arrival hadn't interrupted the rehearsal, which now was in the middle of a scene. Andre had never been to a Broadway show, so she had nothing for comparison, however, the set was pretty impressive. There were walls with windows, old furniture, a set of stairs leading to a door on a second floor, and it looked like a living room in an old house.

"Obviously, this isn't Broadway but it's damn good, and that's considering we only get to put on a couple of plays a year. The cast volunteers... nobody gets paid. Ticket sales, concessions, everything goes to renting the theater, the sets, and the costumes, with the balance to a worthy charity. We've been together for a few years and we are a wild bunch." Josefa squeezed Andre's knee, smiled and added devilishly, "The cast parties are historic."

They sat quietly for a while. The actors were in costume but had no makeup. Two women played the parts of elderly good-natured murderers and looked to be in their thirties, the lead male about the same. Andre's escort, who didn't have many lines, just looked fine.

"Kids?" Josefa asked abruptly.

"With my mother, the sole benefit of moving back home."

"Just the two, right?"

"Yes." Andre responded, feeling a little cross-examined.

Josefa looked at her with concern while laying her hand back on Andre's knee. "How are you making out?"

"The divorce is still pending,"

Josefa grinned. "I know the process, been there, but have no fear, it'll happen."

Andre shrugged. "Mac is good about sending money. The kids are adjusting."

Josefa continued to probe. "That's not what I asked. I asked you... how are you doing?"

Andre took a beat, sighed, and let down her guard. "Okay, I guess, bored, but okay."

"Hmmm." Josefa gave her leg a reassuring pat. "Well, let's see if we can move your, just okay, up a couple of rows to, fucking great."

Andre pulled back and turned in her seat to face Josefa. "Why?"

"Excuse me. Why what?"

"I haven't seen or heard from you since the party in D.C. months ago, then suddenly out of the blue you call and invite me here... so I have to ask, why?"

Josefa smiled and looked Andre right in the eyes. "Remember what you said when I asked you if you had anything in common with the rest of the tight-assed bitches in Washington?"

"No, not really, something fresh, no doubt."

"You said, 'not a fucking thing, but I may have a thing or two in common with you.'" Josefa chuckled. "I remember it word for word."

Andre laughed, a little embarrassed. "Right, sounds like me."

"Indeed, and you are correct." Josefa looked back to the stage, her voice no longer in charge. "We are a lot alike. You see, I too have very little in common with most women... or men, for that matter. When I do run across a like-minded soul, I feel compelled to not let that opportunity pass me by." She looked back at Andre. "I don't like having regrets."

"I get it now," she lowered her eyes, "I thought you called me because of what happened in the bathroom."

Josefa laughed loud, then quickly lowered her voice. "Remember, at the party, when I said, 'this could be the—"

"Start of a beautiful friendship. I said it was from Casablanca."

Josefa gained Andre's eyes again. "Well, like the song says, a kiss is just a kiss."

Andre blushed again, a feeling she was not used to, and that made her more and more uncomfortable. "I was drunk."

A moment went past. Josefa leaned back in the seat. "No, you weren't."

The two women on stage started giggling as a part of the play, one louder than the other.

Josefa pointed to the two actresses. "What do you make of them?"

Andre, relieved at the change of subject, gave the pair a once over. "They look like a couple of Bible-beating, church-going, hairdos."

Josefa's laugh finally drew the attention of the director who shushed her.

Josefa waved compliance, then continued in a lower voice. "Your radar is way off, my dear. The lead," she pointed, "The one who looks like a preacher's wife?"

"I see her."

"She likes to dance topless on tables at cast parties. She's a total freak." Josefa changed subjects without any transition. "What did you think of Doug?"

Andre, caught off guard again, stammered, "Ah... I... ah... he's very handsome, I guess."

"Indeed."

Andre took Josefa's tactic and changed the subject, quickly. "What exactly do you do here?"

"I handle PR, fundraising, and the group's relationship with the other theater companies around the state."

"Around the state? I don't understand."

"This group is part of a network of Texas theater groups. We share sets, backdrops, and costumes, sometimes even actors. My contact with the other groups was the primary reason why I was involved in my brother's campaign. The association is small, but can be an influential political ally in a close race. There are dozens of companies supported by hundreds of people. Believe me, Lyndon and that bastard Clark would not have come near me unless they absolutely had to." She became animated. "And now after, Landslide Lyndon, who won by what, eighty-seven votes, won't even return my phone call. So, fuck him, Clark, Carter, and all the horses they came in on." Her voice had progressively gotten louder.

"Would you two ladies like some coffee? I'm buying." Doug Kinser hustled up the aisle, obviously sent by the director.

Andre put her hand on Josefa's knee. "I could use a cup, you?"

Josefa nodded, put on her shoes, and they walked up and out into the lobby.

Kinser offered, "There's a diner on the corner."

"There's a bar across the street." Josefa didn't wait for consent.

Andre and Kinser followed.

The place was empty save a rummy hunched on a stool at the far end of the bar. It might be someplace that got better when crowded but at the moment it smelled of old beer, and old food.

Andre smiled. "My kind of place."

Kinser chuckled.

A salty bartender, cigarette in mouth, paused his half-hearted bar wiping. "What to drink?"

"Three shots of the best bourbon you have, and three beers." Josefa then added. "In bottles, no glasses."

The bartender, not appearing offended, got busy.

"Good call." Kinser took a minute to survey, then pointed. "Over there looks okay."

They walked to a booth, followed shortly by the bartender whose service was surprisingly quick.

"Bring six more shots." Josefa said, taking the beers from a tray. "One check."

Josefa sat alone in the booth opposite Andre and Kinser. It was tight and Andre caught a whiff of Kinser's aftershave.

They passed the shots around and held them up for a toast.

Kinser asked. "What should we toast?"

Josefa rubbed her knee against Andre's. "The start of a beautiful friendship."

"We need to see a new movie." Andre laughed, her leg touching Kinser's thigh.

Josefa downed her shot. "I have a few movies we could watch."

Andre downed hers and Kinser his.

The next round of bourbon arrived just in time.

CHAPTER 19
OCTOBER 19, 1951. WASHINGTON D.C.

IT WAS COLDER than a usual October morning, not that Mac noticed or cared. He lay flat on his back, wearing a winkled suit jacket with matching pants, an incorrectly buttoned shirt, and only one tied shoe. The paper bag at his feet, once held the empty bottle he clutched to his chest.

Pain, from a few unconscious hours on the wooden bench, woke him. He groaned and struggled against stiff muscles to sit up. Looking around, he remembered walking to the park after the bar closed. The sun was up, but with no alcohol to numb the cold, he began to shiver.

Standing was painful but he managed. Erect and seeing the bottle was empty, he dropped it. It broke on the sidewalk, joining the paper bag and the rest of the trash strewn around the park. He pushed himself to begin the trek back to his apartment. One step at a time but, after only ten, he threw up.

Anacostia Park was at the end of Pennsylvania Avenue, a brisk walk from the Capital. He had seen the building lit in all its splendor from the bench, where he passed out the night before.

The park had tall trees, green grass, and bordered the Potomac, but it was on the wrong side of the river. Less than a mile from the hub of the government was one of the poorest neighborhoods in the District of Columbia, and the apartment of Malcolm Wallace.

Recovered, he began walking again, taking long breaths, trying to regain stability. The cold morning air helped to clear the cobwebs. While brushing off his jacket, he suddenly gripped his back pocket checking for his wallet. Finding it still there, he deduced he hadn't been mugged despite his body feeling like it had been beaten with a stick.

The deli on the corner of his street was open, and he spent about half of the money in his pocket on coffee. He held the hot paper cup with both hands as he walked up the sidewalk.

A car door slammed as he reached the steps to the three-story walkup where he lived.

"Wallace, you look like you got hit by a truck."

Mac turned around. Even though he heard his name he wasn't sure the person was speaking to him. He blinked, trying to clear his vision.

"Jesus, you look terrible. When was the last time you ate... or took a shower?"

Mac saw the man wave his hand in front of his nose then step back.

"Mr. Carter?"

"Wallace, let's get you inside and cleaned up. I need to talk to you."

The apartment, which didn't have much, had hot water. While Mac showered, Carter sat on the only chair in a kitchen that looked like more of a home to roaches than a human.

Mac emerged from the bathroom in boxer shorts and a t-shirt. "Why are you here?"

"You can't guess?"

Mac propped himself against the countertop near the sink. "I assume it's because I haven't been reporting in recently."

Carter raised his voice. "You haven't been to work in almost a month... didn't call into the DOA to tell them what was going on with you... and yes, you also haven't reported in to us."

Mac started pacing around, head down. "Yeah, I'm sorry about that. I've been out of sorts since Andre left. I had to move here. I couldn't afford the old apartment in Arlington, and send money. She's at her mother's but with two she can't work, and—"

"Enough, I don't want to hear about it." Cliff Carter held up both hands.

"But—"

"Stop. Don't want to and don't care." Carter stood up and waved him away. "Go put some clothes on. We'll get you something to eat."

Mac stood for a moment staring at him, then complied.

Carter ate eggs, bacon, home fried potatoes, and toast with coffee and orange juice.

Mac had coffee and dry toast.

"You need to eat something. You must have lost twenty pounds."

"Why are you here? I've never dealt with you before. It's always been Mr. Clark." Mac looked at him with no expression on his face.

"Fair question. The truth is, he didn't want to see you, and didn't want me to come here, either. But I convinced him that you've been valuable to us in the past, and you're worth a second chance."

"Bullshit." Mac didn't flinch, his face dark, showing no emotion.

Carter looked down as he calmly stirred his coffee. "Okay, you're right. That's not the reason."

Mac nodded.

"You've done things for us. Things you can never talk about."

Mac nodded, again.

"There's been a discussion about your drinking, and about how you might, inadvertently, talk about things you shouldn't."

Mac's jaws clenched, his expression harder.

Carter became a little less sure of himself. "But… I went to bat for you."

Mac flattened his hands on the table. "More bullshit."

Carter took a beat. "Alright, Mac, I'll get right to it."

"Good idea." He rolled his fingers, clenching fists.

Carter appeared jittery and spoke quickly. "There is a situation in Austin, and we think you might be the best person to handle it. We know all about your relationship with the Senator's sister, Josefa. You know, as well as we do, about her… wild streak."

"Ah uh." Mac showed his first sign of interest.

Carter, seeing the small reaction, pushed forward. "Well, the problem is that she's involved with a community theater in Austin where she developed a relationship with a man named Douglas Kinser." He drew out the word relationship. "Recently, Josefa has been beating down the doors to speak to her brother about getting a loan for this guy's small golf course."

"And, this involves me how?"

Carter didn't answer that question. "Josefa is smart, and knows the loan would be beyond appropriate for a US Senator, but she pushed for it anyway. She is strange and unpredictable, but this was very odd, even for her. We did some digging and we found out Kinser has been threatening Josefa about making her sex life public. He told her the loan would help him, basically forget all about her... adventures." Carter became very animated. "Naturally, we are looking to avoid a scandal. I think you know what would happen if the press got a hold of this. Mac, there were men... and women... even multiple people, like group sex. Well," he sighed and held up his hand, "that kind of publicity would damage the Senator, ruin Josefa, and would be bad for you, too."

Mac remained impassionate. "Exactly how is this bad for me?"

Carter continued again not answering. "There hasn't been an actual crime committed, and even if there was, we would never involve the police or lawyers. We really can't trust anybody, but I talked to Carter and convinced him that since you... are familiar with the parties involved, you would be able to talk to this guy, Kinser, and straighten him out. You could get him to understand trying to blackmail a Senator and using his sister is a real bad idea."

"And Josefa, she agrees that I could help?"

"She's not happy about this either, and understands she put her brother in a bad situation, but she said there's nothing she can do to stop Kinser."

"So, you want me... to go to Austin... just to talk to this guy?"

"Yes, we do. The guy is a golf pro, not a marine like you. We think if you put some pressure on him, he'll fold." Carter put on a weak smile.

Almost a full minute went by— Mac just staring straight ahead.

Finally, Mac took his hands off the table and put them on the seat, preparing to leave.

Carter panicked. "Will you do it?"

"No."

"No?" Carter's face colored red as panic rose.

"Correct. I won't do it. You have a lot of other resources, use one of them." Mac started to push out of the booth.

"This is your last chance, Mac. Either you do this or you're out."

Mac leaned forward. "In case you haven't noticed, I'm already out." He stood up fast and started to walk away.

Carter tried to get out of the booth. "Wait, Mac. Your… Andre… is involved."

Mac froze in place, his back to Carter.

"This is bigger than just Josefa and the golf pro."

Mac backed up and sat down.

"Josefa apparently befriended her when Andre moved back to Austin. Josefa hooked her up with this theater group. From what we can determine, this group is where all the trouble began." Carter continued, his voice firm. "Andre will be part of the story because she is involved with Douglas Kinser. They've been seeing each other for months. Josefa is also intimate with Kinser."

Mac remained silent but his hands were now gripped in tight fists.

Carter gave a quick glance around. "There are pictures, Mac, of the three of them… together."

Mac's head fell forward, eyes closed, motionless. After a minute of silence, he got up to leave.

Carter raised his voice. "Will you do it?"

Without turning around Mac answered. "Yes."

CHAPTER 20

OCTOBER 21, 1951

DRIVING OUT OF D.C., the first leg of the journey, took every bit of concentration Mac could muster. He knew where he was going, getting there was the problem. The lights and the traffic were distractions he had to push aside to let his instincts take control. His mind was on fire, and if he didn't let go, he wouldn't make it.

Now hours later and somewhere between Richmond and civilization, the white lines on the road gave the part of him that took over operating the car a confining boundary. The robot driver reacted to conditions, speed limits, and traffic lights, but little else.

Rational thought wasn't possible. His mind and body split. The physical being separated from a mind that was processing like he was tuning a radio in his car. There is static at first, then a song comes out of a speaker, scratchy at first, clearing as the signal strengthen, eventually dissolving back to static. After turning west past Richmond, the road he traveled was devoid of traffic, and Mac experienced many long patches of white noise. He was in the depths of psychosis with no way out.

His brain was not in sync with the body driving the car, but the need to urinate caused nature to win the battle. A dimly lit Texaco gas station sign appeared and he pulled into the parking lot. He stopped in front of two red star gas pumps that stood idle in front of a small general store. Mac pushed the car door open and slowly unbent himself, leaning backwards then side-to-side, recirculating blood and recognizing fatigue. He glanced at the store, which was dark inside and appeared closed. He took a couple of steps and peered through plate glass windows laden with stickers advertising new tires and oil changes.

"I was just gonna put the coffee up." A man had emerged from the side of the building.

Mac undaunted by the surprise of the man's appearance, saw the light in the window of the small house on the far side of the parking lot that he had not noticed.

"I'd be grateful." His voice was flat and had no inflection.

The man pulled on his coverall strap. "Be needin' a fill up?"

"Yes, sir."

"I'll turn the pumps on."

The man disappeared into the dark store, which lit to fluorescent life a few seconds later.

Mac walked to the side of the building where a Men sign hung from the wall, went in, and hit the light switch. He was confronted with his image in the mirror over the sink, a face he didn't recognize.

When Mac returned, he found the man at the pump filling the Ford.

He was old, worn, with straggly grey hair and a scrubby beard. He looked up at Mac and nodded toward the license plate, "Virginia?"

Mac shook his head. "The car is. I'm a Texan."

The handle clicked. "That'll be two dollars and eighty-six cents for the gas and the coffee. Should be ready by now. I'll put it in a cup for ya. How you want it?"

"Black."

Mac looked into the back of the car while he waited. A hastily packed suitcase rested on the back seat. In the cargo area of the station wagon, a tote bag with a picture of the Washington Zoo lay on its side, a stuffed hippopotamus next to it, a forgotten toy.

"Here ya go."

Mac took the coffee and handed the man three singles. "Keep it."

"Thanks, mister. Your trip, business or pleasure?"

"Personal, very personal."

The road sign read Texarkana 12 miles. He had driven this route a couple of times, and knew there were six more hours ahead. A few hundred feet of black tar was lit by headlights, the black of a moonless night hid everything else. The sound of the wheels churning up miles combined in a chorus with the hum of the engine. It was monotonous and hypnotic. Mile, after mile, after mile, with nothing but white noise.

Part of him was gripping the wheel, fixated on the triangle of light in front of the car.

The other part saw her appear. Andre was there, beside him, sitting in the passenger seat.

"Where did you go?" Her head was cocked to one side, with a displeasured expression.

"I don't... understand." Mac stuttered.

"It's Nora, isn't it?" Her expression turned angry.

"No... what Nora?" Mac was confused then angry. "Wait, you left me."

The vision became scratchy, fading in and out.

He whipped his head back and forth from the road to the vision.

Her lips parted. "There's nothing you can do."

A horn blasted as it sped by.

She was gone.

He banged the steering wheel, fumbled around on the seat for a pack of cigarettes, then pushed in the lighter. Seeing the ashtray was full, he tried to remove it and dump the mess out the window. It resisted, then popped free, its contents spraying the front seat with ashes and butts.

"Son of a bitch," he screamed.

He yanked the wheel and the car to the side of the road. He got out, his anger rising up, possessing him. He pulled the passenger door open and brushed out what he could, then sat and pushed the lighter in again. Sitting sideways, his feet were on the runner, a cigarette was hanging from his lips, and his hands were holding up his head.

This was fate. His dreams of greatness in college were never to be. Star quarterback, university student body president, Master's degree... all meant nothing. Andre was wrong. Nora. was a part of this life that was never meant to be.

I am a soldier, no need for why.

He flicked the butt to the road shoulder.

It only took an hour for the static to return. The same sound, the same dark night, the same vision.

"Mac." She was right beside him.

He didn't answer, forcing himself to stare out the windshield.

She whispered in his ear. "I'm waiting for you."

He swung his head. She wasn't there.

He felt her breath close to his face.

"You left me." His eyes were wide, but he couldn't see.

"I want you." She whispered in his ear.

The car drifted and he pulled it back across the line.

"Where are you?" Her voice was distant and fading.

Sweat poured from his forehead. He could feel his blood pumping heat through his body.

He rolled down the window, letting the silence in.

Dawn lit the road ahead. He was headed due south on Route 79, two hours out of Austin. The car stunk of body odor and smoke. It was almost twenty hours on the road and he hadn't slept in thirty. The suitcase, now on the passenger seat, lay open, its contents half in and half out. One hand held the wheel, the other a bottle of White Horse whisky. Before leaving Washington, he had wrapped the bottle of liquor in a towel and carefully placed it in the suitcase next to an automatic pistol.

He wasn't drunk, he was numb.

A car went by, then another. He was getting closer every mile.

A billboard caught his attention.

IF YOU DIE TONIGHT
IS IT
HEAVEN OR HELL?

CHURCH OF GOD – SUNDAY

Mac put the bottle to his lips.

There is no God.

144

The sun glared through the windshield that was covered with dust and dead bugs. The Ford shuttered when he turned the engine off. He'd reached his destination and his fate. His eyes were bleary and instantly watered. He knocked the empty whisky bottle to the floor when he grabbed a shirt from the open suitcase to wipe his eyes. He threw the shirt across the seat and reached into the case again, hand searching, eyes still straight ahead. When he felt the metal, his heart began racing.

He pushed open the car door and got out. Everything he saw was foreign, but the business expected new customers, and had clear signage leading to the office of the Butler Park Pitch and Putt. His vision was narrow and every sound he heard was delayed. The car door closing, his footsteps on the gravel, even the metal clicking when he pushed the slide to load the pistol, was like a foreign movie when the picture didn't match the dialogue.

The screen door opened with ease and slapped its frame when it closed behind him. The office was more of a shed, having a low ceiling and bare painted stud walls. A rack of golf clubs and a barrel of golf balls were between him and a counter, where a man was writing in a book and talking on the phone.

Mac approached.

The man, without looking up, made a one second gesture with his hand.

Mac was three steps away.

The man spoke as he hung up the phone. "Good morning. Nine holes?"

Mac read the name embroidered on the man's shirt at the same moment as Douglas Kinser saw the gun.

"Oh my—."

The first shot hit him in the chest, knocking him backwards.

Both hands gripped his shirt, his mouth fell open, sucking air. The next shot was to his head. He fell on his back, legs and arms spread.

Mac stepped to the edge of the counter, leaned over, and shot him twice more, in the groin.

Mac's ears were ringing so loud he didn't hear the sound of the screen door closing behind him. The sun blasted his face and he blocked it, holding his gun hand up to cover his eyes.

He didn't see the first witness standing ten feet away, and backpedaling toward the protection of a live oak tree. Mac also didn't see the other three witnesses, who had just finished playing golf and had paused on the walkway when they heard the shots.

Mac walked slowly toward the car, gun still in his hand. He got in, started the car, and drove away.

He wasn't in a hurry because he had no place to go.

CHAPTER 21

OCTOBER 23, 1951. THE RANCH

LYNDON JOHNSON SLAMMED the office door so hard it loosened the hinges. He leaned on the wall and rubbed his face with both hands. He reached to his shirt pocket for his pack of cigarettes, then cursed when he remembered Bird took it from him at breakfast. He stomped to his desk and started pulling drawers open looking for a stray.

The phone's receiver lay where he dropped it on the desk, a distant voice talking to dead air. "Lyndon. Pick up."

Johnson's search unsuccessful, he grabbed the phone, then plopped hard into the chair. "Clark, how could you be so fucking stupid?"

"Actually, it was Cliff, Lyndon. He took an initiative, something we hadn't discussed."

"Initiative," Johnson screamed, "you call shooting this guy, in broad daylight, in front of multiple witnesses... initiative?"

Clark's voice remained calm. "I was reluctant to call you prior to me having everything handled, but I wanted you to know before the story hit the papers. Obviously—"

"Too late. It's on the front page in the *Austin American* and the *Houston Chronicle*."

"I—"

Johnson shouted him down. "If this doesn't get handled right, everything, and I mean everything, will go to shit."

"I'm aware, sir. I'll handle it. Trust me."

Lyndon lost his mind. "Trust you? Trust you? If you don't fix this boy, I'll bury you."

The door squeaking went unnoticed.

He slammed the phone down so hard he hurt his hand. "Goddamn it."

"Lyndon." Bird spoke like his disappointed mother. "You might be able talk that way in the halls of Congress, but not in this house."

He started to speak but stopped, because explaining the reason would make his wife an accessory after the fact.

Austin, Texas

Edward Clark pushed the button on top of the speaker, disconnecting the call with Lyndon. For a moment both he and Cliff Carter sat in silence.

Cliff, looking like a condemned prisoner about to mount thirteen steps, spoke first.

"What do we do?"

Clark's response was quick. "We? No, not we... me. I'm going to fix this. You need to stay out of it, and far away from Wallace, and especially, the Senator."

Carter ducked his head, seemingly pleased his sentence for stupidity was being reduced from termination to suspension.

Ed Clark glared. "How could you not have seen this coming?"

Carter remained silent.

Clark shook his head in frustration. "I can't believe you told Wallace that Kinser was screwing his wife."

"They were separated for almost a—"

"His wife, man. His wife." Clark shook his head in frustration. "Never mind, forget it. The reason doesn't matter now." He took a breath, then stood. "What's important is, I have to do whatever is necessary to keep this away from LBJ." He took another breath and leaned back in his chair. "First, I've already called John Cofer—"

"Johnson's lawyer? The one who handled the Box 13 thing in the Supreme Court?"

Without acknowledging the questions, Clark continued. "He's clearing his calendar and will be here to handle the arraignment. In the meantime, Polk Sheldon will assess Wallace's condition and formulate a plan for bail."

"Bail? On first degree murder… in Texas?"

Clark held up his hand. "Cliff, don't worry about it. I want you to find M. E. Ruby and Bill Carrol and get them on the phone."

Cliff sat still, his expression changing from stunned surprise to curious suspicion.

"When you locate them, don't mention Wallace. I'll talk to them…" Clark drifted off into thought, then added, "they will post bail."

Ed Clark used one hand to motion Cliff to leave, then picked up a newspaper and began reading the headline.

Austin American-Statesman
Cops Hunt Motive
In Kinser Slaying

23 October 1951
City Detectives Tuesday sought a
motive in Monday's slaying of
Douglas "Doug" Kinser, popular
Austin golf professional.
Kinser, 33, was shot to death
about 3 p.m. on Monday in the club-
house of his pitch and putt golf
course just east of South Lamar
Boulevard.
Being questioned in the case was
Malcolm Everett Wallace, 30, who
Is an economist with the US Dept of
Agriculture in Washington D.C.

The rest of the article contained the details of the interview of two of the witnesses. There was a picture of the Pitch and Putt building with a police car parked in front. The rest was a quote at the bottom of the page from a detective who said Wallace was being held on suspicion of murder but hadn't spoken, and refused a lie detector test.

Carter pushed the door open slowly and leaned in. "Polk, line two."

Clark nodded and motioned to shut the door as he picked up the phone. "M.E.?"

"You got'em, friend. What can I do you for?"

"I'm going to need you to do a favor for our friend."

Travis County Jail

The stone walled headquarters of the Austin Police, complete with three-story towers at each end, had a passing resemblance to a medieval castle. It wasn't far from the truth. In this building there was definitely a hierarchy, men with vast authority over others held in the dungeon below.

It wasn't the first time Mac had been in the building. Back in his college days, he applied for a parade permit for a political rally upstairs in the county clerk's office. It was when he was an idealistic, young rebel, pushing the limit of society. Today, now very much in the present, he was a prisoner in the dungeon.

He woke up cold, hunched up in a fetal position, covered with a thin blanket. His head hurt, his body ached, and he was so dehydrated his tongue felt too big for his mouth. Standing and shivering, he grabbed the blanket off the bed and wrapped it around his shoulders. As he pulled it tight, he saw dried blood on his arms. He remembered his clothes being stripped off and placed in a bag marked EVIDENCE. The orange jumpsuit marked PRISONER was too small, his arms sticking out from the sleeves. He remembered washing his hands and face but missed the dried blood on his arms.

I need a drink.

He walked to the thick steel bars of his cage. He had been unconscious and lost sense of time. There was no window in the concrete walled cell, so he had no idea if it was day or night. He gripped the bars and pushed his face sideways, one way then the other, looking for something or somebody that could help him reclaim time.

His head pounded; stomach growled. He convulsed and threw up, half in the hall, half dripping from the bars.

"Hey, you're gonna clean that up, boy." A bald man wearing a too-small khaki shirt, black shining combat boots, and a badge appeared at the cell. He wasn't happy.

Mac's voice cracked when he spoke. "Sorry."

"Sorry don't cut it, boy."

"Can I have some water please?"

"There's a spigot next to the toilet, back there." He pointed to a stainless john in the shadow at the back of the cell. "I'll get you a bucket to clean up the puke."

Mac stood there looking at the guard who stood, hands on hips, looking back defiantly.

"You got something to say, boy?"

From somewhere inside, an instinct took over. Mac shook his head. "I got nothing to say."

The guard walked away.

Mac staggered back to the cot and sat. He looked to the toilet and saw the handle of a spigot sticking out of the wall. He tried to get up again but failed, his body suddenly racked with pain.

I need a drink.

He stuck out his hands, fingers outstretched, shaking uncontrollably. His ears started ringing again. He remembered the explosion of the gun. He remembered the body hitting the floor.

He remembered to keep his mouth shut.

Two Days Later

Edward Clark showed deference to Polk Sheldon's position in the legal community by sitting at a small conference table in his office instead of behind his desk.

Sheldon was short, thin, and looked like an old father figure, mostly because he had prematurely grey hair. He wore steel-rimmed glasses, had an intellectual air, and was extremely effective in the courtroom.

They sat across from each other waiting for LBJ's voice to come over the speaker on the telephone.

"Is Wallace talking?" Johnson came on without any salutation.

Polk spoke in a quiet, monotone voice, with no accent and little inflection. "Talking? He's almost catatonic. Not a word, except—"

Johnson didn't let him finish. "Except? Except what?"

"When Wallace was arrested, he said something to the detective who was putting on the cuffs." He paused a second. "Wallace said, 'I work for Johnson ... I need to get back to Washington.'"

Neither Johnson nor Clark spoke.

Polk continued. "I know the cop. His name is Detective Marion Lee, and he hasn't reported the statement."

Clark's voice trembled just a little. "You said you know him?"

"Yes, cousin of my wife."

Johnson sounded cautious. "And?"

Polk in the same monotone voice said, "Don't worry."

Clark grumbled and his voice regained its prowess. "Good, what else Polk?"

"It took two days but I got a habeas corpus and a $30,000 bond. There will be a Grand Jury on the 30th followed by an arraignment on November 2 where he will, without a doubt, be indicted."

Lyndon without acknowledging the unbelievable asked, "Will Cofer be there?"

Clark looked at Polk who seemed to have no reaction and answered, "Yes, he freed up his calendar and he'll sit first chair with Polk in support."

"Good, he's a pompous ass but he's the best. And what's Wallace's condition?"

"We'll have him detoxed and ready." Clark paused, still unsure about including an important detail.

"Anything else?"

"We think it will be essential to have his wife, Andre, sitting in the court behind him. Maybe her mother too."

"Why?"

Clark looked at Polk who nodded, got up, and walked out of the office.

"The prosecutor is Bob Long. Remember him?"

"Ah, huh. Ran for office a couple of years, lost."

"Right. He's going to try the case on the facts, witness testimony, gun powder residue, bloody clothes that match the victim—"

"No mention of—"

"Josefa, No."

"And?"

"That's it's, just the facts of the case. Nothing else."

"Wallace?"

"If its handled right, it might be something we can work with in the future."

Clark moved on. "We will press for a quick trial, and try to keep Wallace from doing anything stupid."

"You'd better."

The phone slammed in Clark's ear. He had held it away from his head, anticipating Johnson's reaction.

CHAPTER 22
FEBRUARY 26, 1952

TODAY WAS AN IMPORTANT DAY, a pivotal moment in a life when direction was irrevocably altered. A day when one would assume a person, knowing the gravitas of the coming events, would appear nervous, jumpy, and generally out of sorts. Mac, however, exhibited none of those emotions. To the casual observer, he looked as calm as one would be standing in line at a grocery store or waiting for a train. He strolled into the courtroom, looked around, observed the crowd, and thought the county could make some money if they charged for admission, surely the proceedings scheduled that morning would have rendered a high price. The lawyers were going to give their summations.

Over three days, the jury heard specific details, each one disputed and argued. In most trials, testimony presented was always fragmented and unconnected. However, on the last day, the pieces would come together with each side carefully structuring a story line combining all pertinent information into one believable event. Today, each lawyer would be bringing his A game, telling a story that had to be sold to a jury of twelve.

The attendees filed in as soon as the doors opened. Reporters with Press tags hanging around their necks, men in ties, and women with their Sunday hats, all competing for the best seats.

Mac saw Andre the moment she entered the courtroom. Subdued as instructed, she dressed plainly, wore short heels with no stockings, and no makeup. She did do something disruptive though, she had cut her hair. It was now short, hanging straight, and mannish, like a 1920's flapper. He smiled, she didn't. Arm-in-arm with her mother, Andre navigated the aisle, and found their reserved seats in the row directly behind the defense table. She looked down and away from her husband, avoiding all eye contact. The mother-in-law had no trouble staring at him.

Mac, seated next to Polk Sheldon, waited for the illustrious lead attorney's always dramatic entrance. For the past three days, John Cofer tried to time his entrance to occur moments before the court clerk announced the Judge's coming to the bench. Today he hit it perfect. The door flew open, and he strutted in wearing pomposity like a new suit. His attitude was his moniker, a trademark, and the persona he'd cultivated for years. Physically unimpressive, he was not tall, but not short. Not fat, but not thin, basically a non-descript man. However, when he stood in front of a jury, he was a giant. The character he portrayed was effective most of the time. The case against Malcolm Wallace was one of those exceptions. His prowess in the courtroom had been useless. His client was guilty, and nothing in heaven or earth would change that reality. But like all great performances, the show must go on.

Cofer purchased new ties and new shirts before the trial began. Every day, he appeared with a fresh look, shoes shined and cufflinks gleaming. He paraded, puffed, strutted when standing and guffawed, coughed, and grunted while seated. Nothing he did, however, diminished the attention of the jury from the prosecution's case. He objected frequently, trying every nuance of law learned over thirty years in practice. The effort was for naught, he knew it, the judge knew it, and the prosecution reveled in it. He would make his final argument this day, but in spite of his best efforts, he had no doubt the jury would find Mac Wallace guilty.

Judge Charles O'Betts entered, sat, and called the court to order with a single strike of his gavel. He motioned to the clerk. "Bring in the jury."

Twelve of Malcolm Wallace's peers, all middle-aged men, all white, and all from Austin, came in single file and were seated in a slightly elevated railed-in section.

O'Betts looked at the D.A. "Mr. Long, is the prosecution ready for its summation?"

Bob Long rose, stood straight, chin up, and looked confident. "We are your honor." The District Attorney was a tall, handsome man, whose only flaw in personal appearance this day was a crease in his hair caused by a cowboy hat he wore everywhere except the courtroom.

"Very well, please address the jury, Mr. Long."

The D.A. rose and walked to the jury box; hands folded like he was praying in church. "Ladies and Gentlemen, I don't plan to stand here and waste your time rehashing every piece of evidence introduced over the past three days. I won't do that because, I know, that would be an insult to you." He then spoke like an evangelist. "You are an intelligent jury. One that is more than capable of assessing the evidence that has been presented. And you will return a verdict of guilty as charged."

He paused and looked over at the defense table where John Cofer was writing on a pad, Polk Sheldon seemed worried, and Mac looked bored.

The prosecutor raised his hand, and pointed his finger at the defendant. "On October 21, 1951, that man, Malcolm Everett Wallace, shot and killed John Douglas Kinser in cold blood." He took a beat. "Gentlemen, as sure as I'm standing here in this courtroom, Malcolm Wallace committed this heinous crime." He started moving back and forth in front of the jury, like a lion in a cage. "Every piece of evidence presented in this court points to him. The four eye-witnesses all testified they saw the defendant walk out of the Butler Park Pitch and Putt office, moments after they heard shots from inside the office. There was gunshot residue on his hands and he was arrested a few blocks away, covered with the victim's blood. You heard from Joseph Schott, a former FBI agent, and friend of Mr. Wallace, who testified he gave a .25 caliber Schmeisser automatic pistol to the defendant as a present in 1946. The same caliber as the bullets found in the victim's body. The facts are: Malcolm Wallace pulled into the Butler Park Pitch and Putt, shot Doug Kinser four times, killing him, then calmly drove away. It is also a fact he was apprehended a few blocks away, driving the car identified by the witnesses leaving the crime scene minutes before." He took a breath slowing his pace. "Gentlemen, the defense has failed to present a single piece of exculpatory evidence or any testimony whatsoever that disputes these facts."

Long placed both hands on the railing, then looked into the eyes of each juror one-by-one as he spoke. "It is your obligation, your duty, to follow the law. The law says, the cold-blooded murder committed by the defendant requires a guilty verdict, and the ultimate penalty... death." He slapped the rail, startling a few of the jurors. "That man shot and killed John Douglas Kinser. Gentleme'n, you must follow the law, and find Malcolm Wallace guilty."

The courtroom was church quiet.

Mac inhaled a long breath, and tried to appear as if he wasn't affected by the D.A.'s closing. During the trial, the testimony from the witnesses, doctors, and cops at the scene was boring and easier to ignore. However, the D.A.'s summation, all of it put together in a story form, brought him to where he could no longer block the memory. He remembered the night in Washington when Cliff Carter asked him to talk to Kinser. To get him to back Kinser off of trying to use Josefa to bribe Johnson. He told Carter he wouldn't do it, he was done, out, he wasn't going to do anything for him, or Johnson or even Josefa. The job, the distant cities, the time he spent away from Andre, had cost him his marriage, his children, and his future. Cliff's conversation was clear, and he could now playback the moment when Carter told him about Andre and Kinser. He could see himself leaving D.C., his body polluted with alcohol, and his mind drifting into a fog which deepened with each passing mile. He could now grasp the reality of the state-of-mind that was about to cost him his life.

Mac turned to look at his wife. She glanced at him for a second. It was a cold, penetrating look of disgust. He turned back and stared straight ahead.

A single gavel strike echoed in the courtroom, breaking the silence. "Is the defense ready?"

"We are, Your Honor." Cofer jumped to his feet, his look either confident or pompous— it was hard to determine.

The attorney put his thumbs in the side pockets of his vest, and strutted toward the jury. "Gentleman, that was a powerful summation given by the estimable prosecutor. Indeed..." He gazed at the floor, then suddenly snapped straight, "but he was wrong. He said you must follow the law and he is right about that, but he failed to add these most important words. Those words are... beyond a reasonable doubt." He lowered his voice. "Gentleman, there is reasonable doubt. What is it you ask? It is several points of evidence. Like, for example, the four so-called eye witnesses had different physical descriptions of the man they saw emerging from the Pitch and Putt, two said he was about medium height, two said he was average. My client is six foot tall and definitely not average. Also missing from the prosecution's case was the murder weapon. My client was stopped and placed into custody minutes after the alleged shooting and no gun was found. I ask you, where is it? Yes, it's true, he was given a gun three years ago which was the same caliber, but this is Texas, gentlemen, how many guns do you own?"

He paused a second preparing for his coup de gras. "The prosecution has put on a convincing case. However, they are missing a key part of securing the truth. Motive. Why? They have a circumstantial case, that… might… point at my client but they haven't said why a man who is as accomplished as he, a man with no criminal record, would drive to Texas, and murder a stranger for no reason."

He looked at the jury searching for the one juror he could convince. He only needed one. "The fact is, Malcolm Wallace drove to Texas to see his children. His wife and mother-in-law are here, seated right behind him, showing their support."

All eyes turned to Andre whose face looked drawn and serious.

Cofer focused on a middle-aged man seated in the center of the box, who had looked for Andre, then at Malcolm, then back to Andre. "My client arrived and needed to get some exercise after a long drive. He saw the golf course, stopped, went in, and found the victim already dead on the floor. He ran to assist him, getting blood on his shirt, and then, thinking whoever killed this stranger might still be in the building, simply panicked, ran to his car and drove away."

Cofer stared at the one juror. "That is reasonable doubt. What the prosecution presented is what they think, mind you, *think*, happened. What I just told you, also could have happened. That is reasonable doubt. Gentlemen, you must find Malcolm Wallace not guilty. It's the law."

Bob Long was smiling and shaking his head.

Cofer strutted back to his seat.

The audience was mumbling.

The judge banged his gavel. "Order. Order in the court." He then addressed the jury. "Gentlemen, I will now read the jury instructions, then you'll be taken to the jury room, where you will consider your verdict."

Cofer thumbed his vest and Mac became the nervous, jumpy, and generally out of sorts person that was expected of a man on trial for murder in the first degree.

Polk Sheldon deposited papers and files into his briefcase. When finished, and without looking, he patted Mac's arm. "Good luck." He then stood and left.

Mac looked over at Cofer who was still basking in the glory of his summation. "Is he leaving?"

"It's almost 5 o'clock. The judge will send them home in about an hour and bring them back to start fresh in the morning." He thumbed his vest. "Given the reasonable doubt I just put into their heads, it might take quite a while."

Mac nodded and turned and saw Andre in the crowd headed for the door.

A few reporters tried to approach the defense table but were intercepted by court security officers.

"What should I do now?" He looked to Cofer for guidance.

The attorney leaned over and lowered his voice. "Go back to the motel. There are people who want to talk to you."

CHAPTER 23

FEBRUARY 27, 1952

THE FIRST THING that Jedidiah Duggan, the custodian of the Travis County Courthouse for thirty-five years, did when he arrived at 6:45 AM was open the windows in the courtroom. Early in the month, it had rained almost every day, followed by two weeks that were unseasonably hot. The combination provided perfect conditions for the year's first hatching of stink bugs. They entered Jedidiah's coveted domain along with the spectators observing the trial of Malcolm Wallace.

Despite their demon-like appearance, most Texans knew not to squash the little buggers. The insects didn't bite or sting. However, if they were mashed under foot, they released a foul odor. Yesterday, several hundred stink bugs were trampled and cleaning up their remains became the morning's first task. Jedidiah opened all the windows, then rhythmically worked a long-handled mop cleaning the bug parts and airing out the room. He was working against the clock to finish his work before court went into session. Despite predictions of another hot day, the windows needed to be shut tight by sunup to avoid another visit from the stinky creatures of the park.

At first, Jedidiah hadn't noticed that Judge Charles O'Betts was seated in the big chair behind the bench. He was almost hidden behind several thick law books piled one upon another. "Morin' your honor, didn't see you there."

Judge O'Betts paused his work. "Good morning, Jedidiah."

"Will I be botherin' you if'n I keep plugging along?"

O'Betts put down his pen. "No indeed. You keep doing what you're doing." He chuckled. "I think you're the only one who is accomplishing anything worthwhile today."

"Thank you, Your Honor."

The judge sighed, leaned back, and crossed his arms. "Jedidiah, I have a question."

"Your Honor?"

"It seems to me that no matter where I am, here seated at the bench, walking in the hallway, or even on the sidewalk outside, you always call me Your Honor. Why is that?"

Jedidiah propped a hand on top of the mop. "Respect."

"You don't know me, and I'd venture you don't follow the proceedings in this room, so how is it that I've managed to obtain your respect?"

"Well, I'll tell you plain. Since the day you became a judge; you always called me Jedidiah. You never called me by any other name… and believe me, I've been called plenty of names. You always use my proper name, and treat me with respect. I do the same. I call you Your Honor because of the chair you in. As long as you wearing the robe, you're Your Honor to me."

O'Betts sat back in his chair.

Jedidiah resumed mopping then said, "You in here before the cock crowing too, just like me. Must be somethin' important."

O'Betts picked up his pen and looked down to the case law he was studying. "Yes, Jedidiah, just like you, I'm cleaning up stuff that stinks."

Mac shaved, showered, then put on a clean white shirt, grey tie, and his suit. He was tying his shoes when he heard a knock on the motel door.

"Good morning." Edward Clark stood in the doorway blocking the morning sun.

"Come in." Mac stepped aside.

Clark, with a disapproving look, kept his hands close to his chest as he surveyed the room. "Have you had anything to drink?"

Mac was immediately on the defensive. "No, I haven't had a drink since—"

"Since you were arrested for murder?"

Mac stuttered. "Ah… yes. I mean no, sir, I haven't had anything to drink."

"Good." He stopped searching and faced Mac. "Today, after the trial ends, leave quickly, and don't say anything to anyone. Come back here, and I'll give you details on what's next."

Mac was stunned. "I… I don't understand. Don't they have to—?"

"Yes, they do." Clark became professorial. "Assuming you're freed, leave quietly, make no comments to anyone, and return here. Understand?"

Mac stammered, "Yes, I come back here."

"Good." Clark turned and walked out the door. He left it open.

Mac wandered back to the bed, sat, and finished tying his shoes.

Andre was in her assigned position next to her mother, directly behind the defense table. There were five rows of spectators, and almost every reporter in the area crowded into a standing room only area. John Cofer sat in the first chair of the defense table. The next seat, usually occupied by Polk Sheldon, was empty.

Mac, sitting at the end of the table, leaned over to Cofer. "Is Sheldon coming?"

The attorney, without looking, responded curtly. "No."

"Why?"

"All rise."

Attention turned to the clerk.

Judge O'Betts, in a black robe, entered quickly and took his seat behind the bench. Wasting no time, he immediately addressed the spectators. "Ladies and gentlemen, the jury has notified the court that they have reached a verdict. In a moment, I will bring them in and their decision will be read." He pointed his gavel at the audience. "I caution you all, especially the reporters I've allowed in the courtroom today, I will not tolerate any demonstrations or disruptions to these proceedings. If the defendant is found guilty, the jury will be asked if they've reached a decision on a sentence. This is a capital crime with the maximum penalty being death. I remind you again, I will find anyone causing a disruption in contempt of court." O'Betts scowled at the crowd then pointed to the clerk. "Bring them in."

Twelve jurors walked, single file, to their seats.

Mac's heart was racing, and even his hands were sweating.

Cofer was reading a document, not paying attention.

O'Betts addressed the jury. "Mr. Foreman, has the jury reached a verdict?"

A short man, obviously nervous, rose. "We have, Your Honor."

"Is the verdict unanimous?"

"It is."

"Please hand it to the clerk."

The clerk gave a folded paper to the judge, he read it, then handed it back to the clerk who returned it to the foreman.

The judge looked at Mac. "The defendant will rise to hear the verdict."

Cofer stood first. Mac, white faced, wobbled a bit, but got up.

The judge looked to the jury box. "Please read the verdict."

The foreman unfolded the paper and read the form. "In the matter of Texas versus Malcolm Everett Wallace on the sole count of murder in the first degree with malice and forethought, we the jury find the defendant… guilty."

The audience reacted with quiet mumbling over a couple of low-volume cheers.

The District Attorney grinned and began packing papers into his briefcase.

O'Betts banged his gavel. "Order." The judge turned back to the foreman. "Having found the defendant guilty, has the jury rendered a decision on sentence?"

The foreman hesitated.

The spectators became silent.

"Your Honor, we do not have a unanimous decision on sentencing."

O'Betts asked, "What is the vote count?"

"There are eleven votes for the death penalty, and one vote for life in prison."

The audience remained silent, every eye on the judge.

Bob Long, still smiling, picked up his briefcase, got up, and started down the aisle toward the door. The other attorney on the prosecution team seemed confused, remained seated, but looked unsure if he should follow his boss.

O'Betts took a moment. Looking down, he tapped his fingers on the bench several times. He cleared his throat, then addressed the jury. "Gentlemen of the jury, the court thanks you for your service in this trial. You're dismissed. The clerk will see you out."

Mac didn't know if he should continue to stand or sit. He looked to Cofer for guidance and found he was already seated. Mac turned to sit, and glanced at Andre. She had a tear on her cheek.

It took a few minutes until the last juror left the courtroom.

The spectators were still quiet, save an occasional click of a camera shutter.

The judge folded his hands on the desk, then with a determined expression addressed Mac. "The defendant will rise to hear the sentence of this court."

Mac stood, his hands shaking, and his shirt soaked with sweat.

Cofer remained in his chair.

"According to the Texas Code of Criminal Proceedings, Title 1, Chapter 37, Article 7 paragraph a, and Article 9 paragraph c; in a felony criminal trial, both the jury's verdict, and the sentence recommendation, must be unanimous. If the verdict is not unanimous, a mistrial is automatically triggered. In this case, the jury unanimously found the defendant guilty of murder in the first degree with malice and aforethought. That verdict stands as rendered. However, the jury was not unanimous on sentence. Therefore, according to Texas law, the decision falls to the court." The judge took a breath, glanced around the court, then spoke quickly. "This court finds the prosecution failed to establish a motive for this crime, which is essential in a first-degree felony trial. This court determines that the jury's verdict will likely be overturned on appeal. In order to save the taxpayers and the court system a lengthy appeal process, which will succeed, this court sentences the defendant... to five years in the state penitentiary and I'm also suspending the sentence."

A gasp turned into loud objections. The Kinser family, who to this point, had remained quiet during the three days of trial, began shouting.

O'Betts directed his final words on the case to Mac. "Mr.

Wallace your bail bond is abandoned and you're free to go. This court is adjourned."

Cofer grabbed Mac's arm. "Let's go."

Mac, moving like a robot, followed his attorney into the center aisle. Spectators from both sides of the court pushed toward the pair. Reporters, blocking the exit, were yelled questions. The Kinser family were red-faced and irate, some shaking fists, some crying. Two police officers pushed through and took Mac by either arm and led him back down the aisle, past the bench, and out the jury door. Cofer shuffled behind. The police hustled them down a corridor leading to a door marked exit. One cop kicked open the door and the other gave Mac a shove.

Mac stumbled into hot air and bright sun.

Cofer pointed toward the parking lot. "This is fortunate; my car is just over there."

It only took a minute, but the reporters figured out the escape route and came around the corner of the building in a swarm.

Secure in the car, Cofer pointed it toward the street and drove.

Mac was still dazed and very confused.

Cofer had his eyes fixed on the road ahead.

Mac cleared his throat. "What should I do now?"

Cofer, eyes still straight ahead, said, "Disappear."

The phone rang and Lyndon Johnson hurried to his desk to answer. "What happened?"

"Guilty of murder but got five years, suspended. He's out. Also, Lyndon, it wasn't said in court but if he isn't arrested for anything else for five years his record will be expunged."

"Good, good." Lyndon took a breath and sat down in his

chair. "To be clear, there was no mention of Josefa or me during the trial?"

"Long never brought it up. Not one mention in the entire trial, and according to my sources, our boy said nothing while he was in jail."

"Our boy?"

"Lyndon, we talked about this."

Johnson paused to re-consider their previous decision, then moved on. "Is he set up with TEMCO?"

"Yes, same position he held in New York and at the DOA, senior accounting. He'll be happy."

Johnson roared. "Happy... he should be French kissing your bunghole."

Clark grumbled. "I'll get him organized and on his way to Dallas by morning."

"How about the wife? What are we doing about her? She can't stay in Austin."

"You're right, she was as much a part of this as Josefa. We can't have her talking to the press either. It shouldn't be difficult to get her out of town, her husband was just convicted of first-degree murder. I'm sure she'll go too."

Johnson grunted. "You think Dallas is far enough from this? Maybe we should think about California."

"Lyndon, stop worrying." Clark sounded confident when he spoke. "The story's been reported in Dallas, but never made the front page. Even if it gets better coverage tomorrow, it'll die quickly."

"Ed, I hope you're right about all this."

There was a long pause.

Clark eased LBJ to the next level. "He did whatever we told him to do before, and never once asked why. Now, after this... what we did... we own him."

PART THREE

THE END. 1953 - 1971

CHAPTER 24

NOVEMBER, 1958

HE COULDN'T HAVE FELT MORE out of place. His best suit, best tie, and newest shoes, didn't matter. Wealth surrounded him at a level he'd never witnessed. Mac was seated in the French Room of the Adolphus Hotel, which was, although his experience was limited, the most luxurious hotel in the south. The menu was leather-bound, and the list of dishes had no prices. The plates were real china, the silverware ornate, and the tablecloth was a better fabric than his suit. The room had a dozen tables, and a like number of guests, none of whom gave him a glance.

He looked at his watch. *She always does this to me.*

A waiter appeared and refilled the water glass. "Monsieur, you wish to wait for your guest, oui?"

For a moment he was tempted to order a drink, but was fearful of its cost. "Yes, thank you, I'll wait." As the man walked away, Mac wondered who was more out of place, the French waiter, or the blue-collar accountant.

Josefa arrived with the flair he remembered. Still thin, still beautiful, still dressed to the nines, and this was lunch. She wore dark trousers with perfect pleats, and a white silk blouse with no bra, her top offering little warmth to the air-conditioned restaurant.

Mac half-raised an arm and waved.

She pushed past the maitre d'.

He stood when she got close and pulled out her chair. There was something different. She smiled, but it wasn't happy.

"You look exactly the same." She leaned to kiss his cheek.

"You look as always," he grinned, remembering what she looked like naked, "amazing."

It's her eyes.

"How's your delicious wife, these days?"

He hit the ditch immediately. "Divorced again."

She mocked a shock look. "How many is that, two or three?"

He chuckled, "Two, but believe it or not we started dating again."

She took a cigarette case from a small purse. "I'm not surprised. I couldn't keep my hands off her either." She flicked a lighter.

"Still a wild woman, I see."

She inhaled deeply, turned her head to the side, and blew a stream of grey smoke, all the while staring at him. Her expression emotionless.

The waiter arrived abruptly with a water pitcher. "Bonne apres-midi, madam. Would you care for some refreshment?"

She didn't hesitate. "Martini dry," she nodded at Mac, "and a Manhattan rocks."

"Oui, madam. Tout suite." He disappeared.

"I hate the French," looking down she flicked an ash, "little dicks."

"Haven't changed a bit."

"Sure, I have... I had to, self-preservation. If I had kept up that pace, I'd be dead by now."

Mac smiled. "It was fun."

She smiled back, and reached across the table putting her hand on top of his. "Yes… it was."

The waiter arrived, balancing a tray. With an elaborate production, he placed the drinks in front of Josefa and Mac, then posed— movie character obnoxious.

Josefa looked up at the waiter, smiled, then picked up the glass and downed it. "Another round, tout fucking suite."

The waiter was shocked, and Mac laughed.

After several drinks, small talk about his kids, her second divorce, and two Salada Nicoise, she suggested they take coffee on the veranda.

The Adolphus for many years was the tallest building in the Dallas skyline, but the title was taken away by two garish structures that lacked grace, or flair. This building had grand style, beautiful architectural appointments, and a balcony, where they sat alone, high above the bustling minions.

She sipped the coffee while gazing at the skyline. "You are in danger." Her voice was low.

Mac reacted with surprise. "What?"

"I know about what's been going on since they got you out of that mess in Austin."

He saw it in her eyes, again.

"I really didn't think…" She ducked her head a little, totally out of character. "We were all just having a good time. I never thought—."

"You didn't have anything to do with what I did. I was alone in D.C. for almost a year. I started drinking heavy. I stopped showing up at work… stopped reporting to them. I was so angry and frustrated… and drunk. I wanted out, I wanted to get away from the whole thing. So, when Cliff came to me and told me what they wanted me to do, I said I wouldn't do it."

"Do what?"

"Talk to Kinser."

She looked stunned.

"When I said no, Carter got pissed and told me about Andre having an affair with him… and you. He said Kinser had pictures of the three of you and—."

"Carter? Cliff Carter told you there were pictures?"

"Yes. He said Kinser was using them to blackmail you and your brother."

"Mother—." She slapped the table, her face flushed red. "Mac, there weren't any pictures. I'm not saying the three of us weren't… fooling around. We were."

Mac's face was blank.

"But it wasn't anything, just fun. Mac, Doug wasn't a bad guy. There were no pictures and he wasn't blackmailing anybody."

"A complete lie?"

"Not all of it. I did ask Lyndon to see about a loan for Doug's business, and I did put a lot of pressure on him to do it. I had never asked him for anything, ever." She calmed down a bit, her cheeks less red. "I think my prick brother didn't want anything to do with me or my friends. But I wouldn't stop, so they wanted you to make it stop."

"And I said no—."

"So, Carter told you a fucking story that wasn't true. Honeyboy, they used you."

Traffic noise from the street, and the sound of the wind blowing past the twentieth floor, was the only sound for several minutes.

"What did you mean when you said that I was in danger?"

She pushed back in her chair and lit a cigarette. Her eyes gazing off to the distance. "After the trial, they got you a job, and moved you and your family, correct?"

"With TEMCO, they're an aeronautics company, here in Dallas."

"They're a defense contractor. D.H. Byrd, my brother's Dallas oil buddy, owns a big piece of them."

Mac's voice went low. "I know."

She reached across the table and gripped both his hands. "You need to listen to me."

He nodded.

"Clark and Carter have an arrangement with my brother. They make deals, using Lyndon's influence, and make a lot of money. Lyndon is the majority leader in the Senate and wields that power over everything, especially things in Texas. Think about it. My brother went to Congress in '37 with one suit and only one pair of shoes that didn't have holes. Today after collecting only a congressional salary for twenty years, he's got millions."

"I thought the TV stations—."

She laughed. "Sure, Lady Bird... on her own... bought a bunch of radio stations, then got licensed by the FCC for television, with almost no competition, and became a Texas communication giant, all with just an apron and a smile."

"Well—"

Josefa wasn't done. "Then there's the other scams. Cash from Billy Sol Estes and Bobby Baker show up in duffle bags. They are working deals in defense contracts, oil, casinos in the Dominican Republic, even cotton futures. His reach is anything he can touch."

The French waiter pushed open the glass door. "Madam, Monsieur, will there be anything else?"

She answered. "The coffee stinks. Bring four more drinks, two Martinis and two Manhattans."

Showing great offense, the waiter stalked off.

She smiled. "I really like doing that."

"I can tell."

She shook her almost empty glass. "Are you still a drunk, like me?"

"I... ah—."

"I heard while you were on parole you got arrested twice for DUI, and showed up drunk in court."

He nodded, sheepishly.

"Ever wonder why that didn't violate your parole?"

"No, not really, but, Polk Sheldon, one of the lawyers who represented me, has petitioned for my record to be expunged. They want me to get Top Secret clearance again."

"Listen to what you're saying, Honeyboy. This is Texas. Nobody... ever... has gotten a suspended sentence for first-degree murder, then got their record cleaned. They got you, Mac. They got you, and they will use you till they can't. Then you'll be," her eyes hit the table and she took in a small breath, "just like me."

The waiter returned with a tray, the drinks, and a check. He stalked off again, this time with no niceties.

His presence invigorated her spirit. "The French are so pompous."

"So... why did you say I'd be like you?"

She pursed her lips, grimaced, and her eyes welled. "I don't have much of a future."

"What? What do you mean?"

Her expression changed back to aloof. "I'm not here about me. I'm here about you, and I'll tell you why, but first a question."

He nodded.

"Since... Austin, they've asked you to do some things, yes?"

He nodded again.

"Things that are not legal."

He nodded.

"Things you need to drink before?"

"And after."

"Money?"

"No... no. They give me cash, once in a while, but mostly it's to cover expenses. They got me this job, and I get paid pretty good but once in a while I have to do them... favors." He felt small.

"The men I mentioned before, Estes and Baker. You know them?"

"I don't know anything about Baker, but I've heard about Estes. He's a big wheeler dealer here in Texas."

"Baker is the same, but works out of D.C."

"Both are involved with Clark and Carter?"

"And my brother." She paused to sip then leaned forward, her voice lower. "There's going to be trouble. The kind of trouble that will be hard to duck, even for a majority leader. They are operating under the delusion they can get away with anything and are becoming sloppy. Lyndon's attention isn't on what these guys are doing, just how much they're making. He's not a puppet, but when he sees big bucks, he jumps on board. Honey-boy, I've met these guys, and I believe they'll bring him down."

"Really?"

"Mac, these are powerful men. You of all people should know that."

"I do." He grabbed his drink.

She suddenly broke into a loud laugh. "You have to stop saying that."

"Stop saying what?"

"I do." She laughed again. "Really, three times, same woman? And they call me crazy."

He choked, spraying some of his Manhattan.

She shook her head a little. "I really do miss you, and Andre."

Mac recalled the past. "We did have some fun, you and I."

She looked at him and twirled the olive toothpick in her glass.

"I know that look." Mac finished his drink.

"You're right, it is a look... but I don't do that anymore." The fear in her eyes was replaced with a sparkle.

"What, sleep with men?"

"No, silly boy, I'm still… flexible. When I said I don't do that anymore, I meant I've adopted a new rule— no more fucking in the afternoon. I'm strictly a night owl."

He started to smile but her sparkle suddenly disappeared.

"Listen Mac, I'm serious. The two of us have a lot in common. We are rooted deep in this and can't get out. You know, as well as I do, if either one of us gets chatty or tries to leave… bad things will happen."

"Not to you, me maybe, but not you, you're his sister."

She finished her drink.

"These men become monsters when threatened. We are caught in the whirlpool, and it's impossible to get out."

"I don't understand. You haven't done anything."

"I'm an embarrassment, especially to somebody with absolutely relentless ambition. Mac, you must do what they want you to do." She sipped her drink then finished the sentence. "And I'll do what I have to do."

Josefa opened the folder and examined the check. Drawing bills from her purse, she looked at Mac and grinned. "About my new rule."

"What about it?"

The look was back. "Rules are meant to be broken."

He grinned. "This is a hotel."

"With big beds and cool sheets."

CHAPTER 25

DECEMBER, 1958

THE ROOM HAD FRESH TOWELS, white porcelain fixtures, and a wall phone. The bathroom, adjoined to the Senate Majority leader's office, also had a door but it was seldom closed.

Everett Dirksen, the raspy voiced Senate Minority Leader, stood a few feet away from the open door and listened to Lyndon Johnson rant while he sat on the toilet.

"I'm telling you, if you go up against me on this, if you deny me approval on the budget because one of your Republican brethren attached a bullshit amendment, I'll do everything in my power to handcuff whatever your party brings to the floor in the next session."

"Lyndon—."

"Don't fucking Lyndon me. You assholes stuck this on my budget at the last minute hoping I wouldn't put up a stink. Well, you can walk in here and smell the stink I'm gonna' generate."

Dirksen was overpowered and outmanned. The Republicans hadn't had a majority in the Senate in twenty-six years and the likelihood of that changing anytime soon was slim. The only way to get a bill to the President for signature was through Lyndon Johnson.

LBJ pulled toilet paper from a roll and, while wiping, looked at Dirksen who stood silent, facing forward but looking away. Johnson stood, pulled up his pants, then washed his hands, still fixing a hard glare at the minority leader in the mirror.

He turned and came out, towel in hand, but with a calmer voice. "Listen Everette, we need to get this to the President for a signature, now. I can't have a fight over the budget before recess. You need to go along with me, and I'll do my best to get this amendment taken care of when we reconvene." He stuck out his hand. "Everett, I gotta have ya. Are you with me or not?"

Dirksen took Johnson's hand, which was still wet. "Okay Ly—."

Johnson didn't let him finish. "Marion, get Joe Martin on the phone." He put a hand on Dirksen's back, and guided him towards the door. "Everett, close the door will ya? And give Louella Lady Bird's and my best." He spun and walked toward his desk, and Edward Clark, who was seated on a couch across the room.

The door clicked, and the desk phone rang. Marion's voice came over the intercom. "The House Minority leader on two, sir."

LBJ grabbed the phone. "Joe, we're almost out of here, and I don't want any problems on your end of the budget vote, ya hear me? Dirksen is on board. You'll drop the amendment, and we'll pick it up sometime in the next session." He got loud. "No more fucking problems. Right?" He paused and listened for two seconds. "Good, thanks Joe, and give your mother, Elisabeth, Lady Bird's and my best."

Johnson hung up the phone. "That boy has a lot in common with J. Edgar; still lives with his mother." He clucked. "At least he doesn't have a Clyde hiding in the closet."

"I'll never get over how you can remember all the names."

Johnson didn't hear it. He walked to the picture window behind his desk. "I think he's gonna run."

"Who?"

"Kennedy."

"Lyndon, it's too soon to be thinking about who you'll run against."

Lyndon looked hard at his advisor. "Anticipate every move your enemy will make, or you'll lose before you begin."

Clark capitulated. "I think it's Humphrey."

Johnson harrumphed. "Hubert will run, but I can beat him every day and twice on

Sunday. He's an empty shirt."

Clark thumbed his vest when he spoke. "If Hubert is just a suit, then Kennedy is just a haircut with a funny accent."

Lyndon glared at Clark. "He's a fucking war hero with a billionaire father, who will do anything to get a son in the White House."

"Okay, Joe Kennedy is rich but, the kid, a war hero? His plywood powerboat got run over in the fog, not exactly Admiral Halsey."

Johnson pointed at Clark. "Maybe you're right. The only bill Jack got passed was the Cape Cod National Sea Shore Act. I just don't want to underestimate the Kennedys. Don't forget the old man got the younger brother, Robert, appointed Chief Counsel to the McClellan Committee. He was the driving force behind the hearings on the teamsters and Jimmy Hoffa."

Clark scratched his head. "I agree. That did surprise a lot of people; a Democrat going after labor."

"Especially the boys in Chicago, but a problem with the unions will make it harder if he runs." He got up close and leaned into Clark. "And he will run. We need to prepare."

"Okay... okay. When do you want to start rallying the troops?"

Lyndon backed off and walked to the window. "This is a

great view, but," he paused a second, "the view from 1600 Pennsylvania is better." He turned around and plopped into his chair. "Let's start with the Suite 8F bunch and the Dallas group. See if you can put something together for me over the holidays."

Clark was drumming the arms of his chair and looking at the ceiling.

"What?"

"I'm hesitating to mention this."

Lyndon growled.

"There are some rumblings coming out of the DOA about the cotton deal."

Lyndon leaned back.

"I don't think it's serious, yet. But you know how... rambunctious... Billy Sol can be."

Johnson's face got red. "No, I don't."

Clark raised both hands. "You're right, we only see the results not how he does it." He pointed to a black canvas bag on a chair near the door. "However, he is making a lot of money, for us."

Johnson looked at the bag, then at Clark. "What rumblings?"

"I have a source who told me there are some people who are starting to get interested in cotton allotments."

Lyndon put his Sunday go-to-meeting fingers together. "Get me names and their positions at the DOA. Let's see if we can improve their lives with new positions at Transportation or Commerce."

Clark grinned a little. "All promotions, of course?"

"Will that do it?"

Clark nodded tentatively. "Probably."

Lyndon put a hand flat on the desk, and pointed at Carter with the other. "You get into this, and keep that little prick on a leash. I have big plans, Ed, and Billy Sol Estes isn't going to fuck that up."

CHAPTER 26

APRIL 16, 1960

THE PEDERNALES RIVER meandered peacefully in front of LBJ's ranch. On both banks, green grass surrounded groups of tall and wide Blackjack Oaks. The Yellow Trumpet trees Bird had planted, just started to bloom, making the view from the front porch of the sprawling ranch house a site to behold. It was quiet, tranquil, and a far cry from the turbulence happening inside.

Ten men were grouped in the dining room, drinks in hand, discussing politics in full voice. They were expressing righteous indignation over government hacks' never-ending efforts to tax them into poverty. They were the wealthiest men in Texas, and one of them was probably the richest man in the United States. They had been invited to the ranch to hear how Lyndon Johnson's win of the Presidency would further enrich their lives.

LBJ had a leg up on the railing of the back porch, finishing a cigarette he'd acquired from one of the group's many bodyguards. Edward Clark and Cliff Carter stood silently beside him waiting instruction. Unlike the visitors, who even without suits and ties looked formal, Johnson wore jeans, a western style khaki shirt, and his signature hat. He took a last drag, crushed it out on the post, then tossed the butt into a bush. "Let's go in."

When the group saw him coming, they started moving toward chairs. H.L. Hunt and Clint Murchison were already in the center seats.

"Gentlemen, thank you for taking time to be here today. Bird and I—."

"Stop with the small talk, what's in this for us?" Hunt either grunted or exhaled, it was difficult to determine.

LBJ wasn't intimidated. "H.L., you are one arrogant prick."

For a moment it seemed like even the river stopped flowing.

Hunt chuckled. "You're right, I am."

The others in the room, with the exception of Murchison, looked impressed.

Hunt's expression returned to stone. "I speak for all of us when I say you should begin with exactly how you propose to win the nomination. Four days ago, Kennedy won Illinois with 65 percent of the vote. Humphrey was next, in a field of seven, with only 8 percent. Kennedy is building steam, so please explain why you haven't declared, and why your name is not on the ballots."

"You're correct. Kennedy did well, and that was a surprise... but there are only sixteen primaries and if he wins them all, which is not possible, he'll still be short hundreds of votes on the first ballot. Seven governors are on their own state's ballots, and will win as favorite sons. They'll control all electoral votes of their home states at the convention. It's the way it's always been done and is politics as usual."

Morgan Davis chimed in. "Lyndon, you know Humble Oil has always backed you—"

"But?" Lyndon asked gruffly.

"But Kennedy is getting a lot of good press. Your name is not coming up as a nominee, and some of us don't understand how you can beat him."

"Morgan, the primaries are just a small part of what's needed to secure the nomination. I'm working the governors and leaders of the party in every state, especially the ones with a lot of electoral votes. California, where Pat Brown controls thirty-two votes, is a state where Kennedy isn't even on the ballot. I'll announce before the convention, go in strong with my pledged votes, and it'll be a dogfight for the top spot."

Davis seemed satisfied.

Johnson leaned toward the group, hands on hips, aggressive. "You all know me. Do you really believe a freshman Senator from the Northeast will stand a chance against the Majority Leader of the party? Jack Kennedy may get some popular votes because he has a damn good-looking wife and a rich father, but I'm the favorite son of this party."

Carter started to applaud and Clark stopped him.

"I don't like what you're doing with the niggers." Murchison spit spray when he talked.

LBJ crossed the room and leaned over Murchison's chair. "Clint, I put up with that bullshit from you for years, and I'm here to tell you... I'm done with it. I don't give a rat fuck what you think about integration, but you should give a rat fuck about how my political strategy has survived and flourished. How I have amassed enough political power to be the most influential man in Congress, and how I'll use the same strategy, which by the way has made everybody in this room a shitload of money, to get into the White House."

Murchison, maybe for the first time in his life, remained silent.

Johnson stepped away and addressed the group. "I'm not taking away any of y'all's business savvy, but you're not the only smart people around. And some of those smart people are looking to take what you've worked to accumulate for years. But what you have, that they don't have, is... me."

He lowered his tone, knowing he had the crowd. "You need

to trust my strategy, and support me. Help me get to the White House and, I promise you, it'll be the best investment you ever made."

Clark and Carter both looked like they were holding their breath. They stood motionless as if their futures would be determined in the next few seconds.

Murchison spoke first. "Lyndon. I don't want to have anything to do with this civil rights nonsense," he shifted around in his chair, trying to stand, "but... I can't argue with success."

Lyndon moved to help him up.

The others stood, a few patting Lyndon on his back, others just standing smiling; but all seemed to be onboard.

Carter stepped forward. "Gentlemen, if you care to move out to the back patio, you'll find the best barbeque in the state of Texas waiting for you."

The men moved past Johnson, shaking hands one by one. As the last one left, he turned to his lawyer and bag man. "There's nothing between me and the White House now."

The boys were paired off, H.L. Hunt and Hugh Cullen were in a conversation, away from the other groups.

"Look at him." Clark pointed toward the two oil magnets.

Carter glanced over. "Which one?"

"Hunt."

"What about him?"

"He had seven children with his first wife, who died a few years ago but," he turned and grinned at Carter, "at the same time, he also had another wife in Florida. He had four children with her, got found out, then bought his way out of a bigamy suit."

"Really?"

"Really but," Clark held up a finger, "he wasn't done yet. He then married another woman in '57 and had four more children, fifteen in all." He paused. "It's also rumored he has another wife in New York."

"Get the—"

"This man adamantly professes Christian values and morality, and funds the far-right wing, Minutemen, and the John Birch Society."

"Do as I say not as I do."

"He's the richest man in the country— a billionaire." LBJ had come up unseen from behind. "And if he heard what you just said, you'd be pickin' highway trash on a Texas road gang."

Clark flushed, caught in the act. "Sorry, sir."

"Never mind that, let's take a drive."

Clark objected. "Sir? What about—"

"They'll be fine. Let's go."

Johnson took point and walked toward the garage. Clark got in the passenger side of Johnson's Cadillac convertible, and Carter climbed in the back. A second after the door shut, LBJ was off, leaving a rooster tail of dust behind.

He drove along a dirt tractor road, around a field, then bounced across a dry creek bed. Black Angus steers, munching grass in a pasture, took off running when Johnson braked hard, sliding to a stop.

Clark and Carter coughed and waved their hands to clear the dust.

LBJ, unfazed, had his cowboy hat still firmly in place. "Tell me what's happening at the DOA."

Carter leaned over the seat. "We have a source, in the Pecos office, who told us there is still a man pursuing the cotton allotments. His name is Henry Marshall."

Clark added, "He's been there for twenty-four years and is a senior inspector. Over the past couple of years, he approved 138 applications Estes made. But our source also says he's having second thoughts about the allotment program, and is now pushing to interview the farmers. If he does, the results will not be good for Estes... or us."

"What's being done?"

"Like we talked about before, two of the people have been promoted impairing Marshall from moving forward. In addition, some other roadblocks were put in place to slow him down, but we don't think he's getting the message."

LBJ tipped the brim of his hat down to his nose and rested his head on the back of the seat while he thought.

Clark and Carter waited patiently.

"Have you tried to move him?"

"No sir. That seems too obvious and might arouse suspicion."

Johnson snapped around. "I'm running for President. I can't have a story like this breaking in the middle of my campaign." He pointed at Clark. "Find a way to vacate a seat at DOA in Washington. Make him one of the Assistant Secretaries or something." He turned to Carter. "Make him listen. One way... or another."

Carter froze and looked down.

Johnson started the car and drove like a madman again, leaving a trail of flying dirt and debris.

CHAPTER 27

JULY 16, 1960

HE HATED LOS ANGELES, and the smog. He hated the people, their west coast accent, and their Hollywood politics. The entire state was high on his list as well, but what he hated more than anything in the world was losing— and he had lost. Lyndon Johnson awoke, after a fitful night's sleep, as the Democratic Party's nominated candidate for Vice President.

The phone was ringing. He rolled over and looked at the clock, exactly 9:00 a.m. His no-phone call restriction had just expired. On the other side of the hotel nightstand, the matching bed was empty. He assumed Bird had risen early, and left for her morning constitutional, which was actually a stroll through the nearest flower garden. At least he didn't have to listen to her sing the praises of her husband being the running mate of the newest icon of American politics, John F. Kennedy. He couldn't understand how she, of all people, had found a liking for the Haircut— Jackie he got, but JFK?

LBJ had added Jack Kennedy to the hate list last night, when balloons fell from the ceiling celebrating JFK's nomination for President. It was supposed to be him.

His knees hurt from standing all night, and his hands were bruised from the constant glad-handing. He was sore, hoarse, and to make matters even worse, he stubbed his toe on the dresser when he got up to piss.

The phone stopped ringing, then immediately started again. It continued to ring while he was finishing his bathroom business. It stopped, then started again. He hobbled back to the bed. "What?"

"Clark here, sir."

"What is it?" He rubbed his foot, getting angrier by the second.

"You had the phone blocked. They couldn't get through, so they called me. It was Hoover."

"What does that little fag want, now?"

"He's insisting you return the file he gave you. He said it should be kept in a safe place."

"Yeah, back in Washington, with the rest of his blackmail files." He sat down on the bed. "Call for coffee, then come up."

A few minutes later, Clark knocked.

Johnson pulled open the door, then started for the bathroom. He wore a bathrobe— untied.

Clark followed, looking down and away.

"Get with the Kennedy people, and find out what they want from me: press interviews, speaking dates. You know the drill. Oh, and tell them I'll send copies of my speeches." Johnson pulled a cigarette from a pack in his bathrobe pocket.

Clark looked up and down quickly. "Ah… they already contacted Busby."

"And?"

"He was told they would write all your speeches, and handle all the campaign events. They told him you should go back to Washington and wait for instructions. The Senator was going to Hyannis Port to rest, and they'd be in touch when they need you."

Johnson bristled. "It's Bobby's retribution for my deal with Jack."

"Sir?"

"Before the first ballot, I knew I didn't have the votes. I had to make a deal, or I'd be shut out."

"I'm sorry I wasn't here for you, but I needed to be in Austin—"

Johnson stopped him with a raised palm. "No need, I heard why. Anne is okay?"

Clark nodded. "Recovering."

"Good, good." Johnson sat on the bed. "As you know, Kennedy came to the convention with 620 committed votes. I had 520, and 761 votes were needed to win the nomination. I got Humphrey to agree to endorse me, but it wasn't enough. Before the first ballot, Bobby makes a deal with Stuart Symington, to give his 150 votes to Jack. In return, Jack makes Symington the VP. The deal gives Jack the—"

"Nomination."

"Right." He grinned slyly. "But... I went to see Jack when his brother, Bobby, was in Stuart's room helping him write his acceptance speech."

"But if Jack already gave the—"

"He did but it hadn't been announced and, after my meeting, he had to take it back."

Clark looked stunned. "How did you do it?"

"First, I told Jack that I was the only man in the Democratic Party that could carry the south. Symington is a good man, but he's from Minnesota, which to anybody south of the Mason Dixon is a foreign country." Johnson lit the cigarette. "He already knew I had the southern vote, so I had to add a persuader. I told him that he had a real enemy in J. Edgar. I told Jack, Hoover thought he would be forced into mandatory retirement if he was elected." Johnson took a draw, blew out the smoke, then squinted. "I hemmed and hawed a bit, then I told

Jack that Hoover gave me a file containing a lot of damaging information about certain sexual escapades. I told him that Edger said if I didn't want to use it, to give it to Nixon. Of course, I said I refused to do that."

"What did he say?" Clark looked fascinated by the story.

"He did the Kennedy shuffle a bit, right up to when I dropped the file on the table. As Jack opened it, I said, 'If you put me on the ticket as VP, you'll win on the first ballot, and I'll keep Hoover under control.'"

"He agreed without talking to Bobby?"

"Yep. We shook hands, I grabbed the file, and left. Twenty minutes later Bobby shows up, absolutely irate. He was off the chart pissed."

"What did you say?"

"I told him to talk to his brother... who will be the next President of the United States when I get him the south."

Lyndon dropped the robe and started to dress.

"I do have another question."

Johnson nodded.

"Why would you give up being majority leader to be a Vice President?"

He pulled up his pants. "Well, I'll tell you. I ran for President in '56 and lost. That was one. I ran this time, and lost again. That's two. No one has ever won on a third attempt. Besides, I can't keep up the pace necessary to run for office again. I had a heart attack five years ago that almost killed me. Another run? No, I can't do it."

"But VP?"

The phone rang again.

Johnson nodded at Clark. "Get that."

Clark answered, then extended the receiver. "It's Clare Boothe Luce, she wants to congratulate you."

"I think she's shilling for Vanity Fair— wants a story." LBJ beckoned for the phone. "Clare." He listened for a moment.

"Thanks, and tell Henry, Lady Bird and I send our best." He paused again, listening. "Why VP?" Johnson looked at Clark and grinned. "Clare, I looked it up: one out of every four Presidents has died in office. I'm a gambling man, darlin', and this is the only chance I got."

Johnson hung up the phone, walked back into the bathroom.

There was a knock at the door. "Room service."

Clark took the tray from the busboy. He set it on a table and poured himself a cup.

Johnson yelled. "Have somebody get me and Bird on the next flight out. I want to go to the ranch."

Clark looked like he had something important to say, but didn't.

CHAPTER 28

FEBRUARY 2, 1961

IT WASN'T a homecoming he had dreamed while attending the University of Texas. He believed he would be returning as a Master's graduate, a former cock-of-the-walk, campus leader, with a smoking hot wife who was the embodiment of every youthful fantasy. Instead, his homecoming to Austin was to the Travis County Jail, where his reputation was considerably different— convicted murderer.

Mac Wallace had a three-day beard, soiled clothes, and he thought the vomit on his shoes was probably his, but he wasn't certain. The last time he was locked up, he was isolated in a single cell, with round-the-clock guards. It was a bit different today. He was in group holding, with four other drunks, a couple of kids who vandalized a graveyard, and a husband who'd been arrested for domestic abuse. Mac couldn't remember why he'd been arrested but he was aware of the other prisoners' charges because they were constantly complaining and would not shut the fuck up. His head was pounding, and his stomach was doing cartwheels.

"Wallace." A guard appeared at the cage door and rattled keys.

Mac got up from the bench, and felt the pain of his injuries.

The guard pointed then beckoned. "Let's go."

The other detainees began shouting demands for their release.

Wallace exited and, without being told, turned around to be handcuffed. He followed the guard up old stone stairs into a room filled with bright light and sharply dressed cops. Several officers were processing suspects, others at desks talked on the phone, and a few were standing by a coffee pot sharing war stories.

Polk Sheldon stood at a counter, behind which was a man who looked like he was the general of all cops. He was big, balding, and had the face of a boxer who lost a lot.

Sheldon stepped forward and took Mac by the arm. "Officer, cuffs please."

The guard looked at the general, who nodded, and the cuffs came off.

His lawyer got in Mac's face. "Don't talk. I'll answer all questions."

"Name?" The general's voice matched his face.

The lawyer stepped to the window and pushed a paper across the counter. "Malcolm Wallace, slip 62587A, released on his own recognizance."

The general shuffled a few apparently well-organized papers. "Sign here. Initial here. Sign here."

Mac stepped up and did as he was instructed.

The general seemed long past comment or judgment. He pulled the papers back, and handed Mac a brown envelope with his wallet, watch and keys, then pointed without looking up. "Leave."

The daylight made Mac's eyes water.

Sheldon looked at him, and curious, wagged a finger at the tears. "Grateful to be out?"

"Blinded by the light." Mac wiped them, which made dirt streaks. "I could use coffee."

"You could use a shower."

It was the same motel that he holed up in during the trial years before. It was cheap and smelled of mold, but he smelled much worse. He stripped, tore open all the little soap packs, and got in the shower. The water ran over black and blue bruises, and cuts he'd incurred sometime over the past several days. He remembered the fight at the bar, although he couldn't remember who it was with, or what it was about. His memory flashed momentarily on a second fight, but site and circumstance of that confrontation were completely lost in the fog.

While scrubbing down, he heard the motel door open and slam shut.

Mac leaned his forehead against the tile, and let the hot water soak his head. He took in a couple of deep breaths of steam that helped clear his lungs. He got out of the shower, and while drying off, looked into the mirror over the sink. There was a cut on his forehead, and his cheek, and red and purple skin blossomed under his eye. When he raised his hand to inspect the wounds, he saw his knuckles were bruised and swollen.

He put the towel around his waist, and came out of the bathroom finding his lawyer gone, and Cliff Carter seated in a chair.

Carter spoke dispassionately. "This makes four."

Mac paused, but wasn't surprised. "Actually, three."

"Three in Dallas, and this one, in Austin, makes four DUI arrests."

"Oh. Sorry, I thought you were talking about the divorces."

Carter's tone changed almost imperceptibly, but it did. "Right, I know." He looked at Mac, clearly curious. "Didn't you two just get re-married?"

"Yep, made it fourteen months this time."

Carter, his moment of humanity apparently gone, stood, and got back on mission. "Wallace, we've bailed you out of trouble, time and time again. You have no idea how difficult it is to keep the court from violating you back to prison." He pointed at Mac. "You have to know, if they did, you would be subject to the original sentence, life without parole."

Mac stared straight ahead, impassive.

Carter walked over to where two suitcases lay open on the bed. Clothes were lying about, nothing in drawers. The only thing in the room that seemed positioned were two framed pictures, one of Andre, who Carter had met, and the other, of Mac's children, whom he had not.

Mac, still in the towel, got up, walked to the bed, and started searching in the pile for clean clothes.

"In Washington, you told me you didn't want to do things to help us out anymore. I get it." He corrected himself. "I mean… we get it, and we've come up with a way for that to happen."

Mac found underwear and dropped the towel.

"We know a man named James Ling, he's a friend and has been a big help to the campaigns over the years. He owns Ling Electronics in Anaheim, California. They're a pretty big company and have several contracts with the DOD." Carter took a moment then continued. "Like you, he does favors for us, and we do favors for him. The short story is we asked a favor of him, and basically, we can get you a new job, a new start, and a way for you to be able to support those beautiful children." Clark pointed to the picture on the dresser.

Mac turned to Carter with the same blank expression. "If?"

Carter sputtered a bit. "We need a favor."

Mac pulled on a pair of jeans. "Which is?"

Carter took out an envelope and put it on the table. "There is a man who works at the Department of Agriculture in Pecos. His name is Henry Marshall, and he's causing some problems for a friend of ours, Billy Sol Estes."

Mac's brain immediately fired up, remembering Josefa's warning.

"We want you to go there, and speak to him. You'll pick someplace private, then ask him to stop investigating cotton allotments." He tapped the envelope. "The details are in here. Just convince him not to talk, that's it."

"And if he refuses?"

Carter waved his hand. "I know you can be very persuasive."

Mac went into soldier mode. "When?"

"It needs to be done before the middle of June, latest. There is a hearing, where he's supposed to testify and that can't happen. So, go, do some recon, find a place where you'll be alone with him, then... do it."

There was a part of him that wanted to run. The other part said, "Understood."

Carter smiled, then tapped the table again. "Good. There's cash in here, for expenses."

Mac nodded.

Carter got up, walked to the door, opened it, then turned around. "Stop drinking Mac, you're killing yourself." The door snapped shut like a jail cell.

Mac looked into the mirror above the picture of his kids. "Not fast enough."

CHAPTER 29

JUNE 3, 1961

HE BECAME aware of his surroundings like he'd just awakened from a deep sleep, although he'd only drifted for a minute. However, instead of adjusting a pillow or pulling up a blanket, Mac was standing on a dirt road in the middle of the night. He was alone, surrounded by prairie, fenced-in with barbed wire.

A part of him, the one in control years ago, would have been shocked about why he was there, certainly confused, but the part of him that had control now felt comfortable in the dark.

Getting to that place, that zone, was a battle. The rational part of him tried hard to rationalize, compartmentalize— all the ize crap he learned in college, but he found the only way to empty his brain of anger was to empty a bottle— in that he excelled.

Malcolm.

He could see her face, hovering just a few unreachable feet away.

Malcolm.

He closed his eyes and shook his head.

She disappeared.

He had driven from Dallas, arrived just before sunset, and pulled off the two-lane blacktop onto a dirt tractor road where a post held a small, weather-beaten, wood sign. The black letters burnt into the wood spelled *MARSHALL*. Mac had to drive slowly on the rutted road, maneuvering his car about a quarter of a mile. He had stopped where the road ended.

He lit a cigarette, and started walking back up a slight incline toward where he'd left his car. The road dead-ended at a widened turnaround that was flanked with a wooden shed, and a tractor covered with a tarp. The old building had no windows, a double door, and a rusted tin roof that was bowed in the middle. Across the circle of dirt was a gate that opened to a pasture that was small for a Texas ranch, but was still big on view. He sat on the hood, and looked at the night sky that was full of stars and touched the horizon in every direction.

Malcolm.

He slid off and got into the car, where his comfort lay waiting.

Cramped muscles woke him. Drool ran down the car window, and his cheek had left a mark. Panic, adrenaline, or maybe fear, bolted through his body, causing him to jerk upright, his knee banging into the steering wheel. He quickly searched the area through all the car windows. Nothing was moving. He glanced at his watch, 4:30.

Heart still pounding, he blindly reached for the bottle he'd left on the passenger seat. About two fingers of liquid remained. He unscrewed the cap and downed what was left. The fire gave him energy, stimulated his cramped-up body, which now had to urinate.

Mac got out and relieved himself in the middle of the driveway. The air still crisp with the night's chill brought a flash of childhood memories: his grandfather's farm, in the backcountry near Austin, its old red barn, and peace. It was fleeting, a second, a moment of his youth. A distant memory of a different life.

He walked to the gate and leaned on the top rail. On the other side of the fence, there was a standing faucet, slowly dripping water into a galvanized trough. The dirt around it muddy from use. Three other troughs, stacked end-to-end, were empty. Also surrounded with torn up turf, they were the reason why Henry Marshall came here every day. He had to feed the stock.

The sky was clear, and billions of stars, together with a half-moon, provided enough light for Mac to see cattle slowly moving toward the gate looking for their morning feed. They'd spent the night, like every other night of their lives, grouped together in a pasture, providing herd protection from coyotes.

He walked over to the shed. Double doors had a chain and lock, but there was enough give in them to see bags of feed stacked inside. He leaned against the shed and thought about what came next.

Mac got in the car, and backed it into a space between the tractor and the shed. It was tight, but it fit. He squeezed out the door, then walked down the road toward the highway. He went about fifty feet, and turned around. The car was hidden. He walked back, and didn't see the glimmer of glass from the windshield until he was almost in front of the shed.

While standing in the road, he heard hooves thumping on the ground behind him. Two horses had suddenly appeared at the fence. They whinnied and snorted, demanding their morning meal. The cattle were still making their way, apparently not as impatient. Mac walked up to the fence line and tried to stroke the nose of the tall bay that was leaning its front quarter into the gate. The horse shook his head, not letting Mac touch him, but it didn't run away. The other horse, black with a longungroomed mane, was prancing around, nervous, and not as brave as his companion. He took a cigarette from a pack, lit it, then blew a stream of smoke. The horse backed up a few more steps.

Mac heard a car. He turned quickly, and saw two headlights in the distance, pulling off the road, and starting to bounce up the driveway. He quickly stubbed his cigarette, tossed it, and walked across the turnaround, to the far side of the shed.

An old Chevy Fleetside pickup moved back and forth on the road, skillfully maneuvering the pot holes. He recognized the model; his grandfather had the same truck. Mac stopped watching for a moment, leaned his back against the wall, and let out a long breath.

Do it.

Mac watched as the lights got closer and closer, stopping short of the shed.

The man who was driving got out, leaving the car running and the headlights on, even though the morning sun was taking over quickly. He put his hands in his back pockets, stretched a bit, looked around a little, then walked toward the gate.

Mac heard more hooves pounding on the ground. The cattle that had been just meandering were now running toward the troughs, and the man at the fence.

He wasn't big, but wasn't small either. He stood straight, and wore a broke-in hat. The man was doing what dozens of other Texans who didn't live on their small ranches did every day: feed their stock before going to work in the city.

Mac wasn't certain it was him until he saw the man's face, and his bookkeeper glasses. It was the picture Carter gave him. He was Henry Marshall.

Mac watched as both horses leaned their heads together over the gate, getting their muzzles stroked. Marshall then patted them on their necks. "Okay, that's enough, gotta' get to work." He spun around, took three or four steps, then froze.

Mac thought he was made.

Marshall raised his nose in the air, moved his head slowly from side to side. He stopped and took quick steps to the back of the truck, out of the glare of the headlights.

Mac retreated back against the wall. *Fucking cigarettes.*

Marshall put both hands on his hips. "Who's there?"

Mac stepped out from the side of the shed.

Marshall saw him and squinted, bobbing his head as if different light would help recognition.

Mac continued moving forward.

"Who are you, Mister, and what do you want?"

Mac's mind went numb, empty, no thoughts. Everything was blocked. He knew his feet were moving, and he could see the man talking, but he couldn't hear anything.

Marshall didn't retreat even a step. Mac was a foot taller and fifty pounds heavier but the rancher had a John Wayne attitude and stood firm.

Mac hit him with a right cross.

Marshall came off the ground, flying backwards, slamming into the truck's bumper. He fell to the ground in a heap, and didn't move.

Mac had been there, watching. He saw it, felt it, but couldn't stop it from happening.

A noise, the sound of lungs sucking air, came from the heap on the ground.

Mac cautiously rolled Marshall over. There was a red mark where his fist hit Marshall's face. There was also a round crater where the back of Marshall's head hit the bumper.

The body lay still, the truck's tailpipe spitting exhaust on his face.

Mac opened the truck's passenger door, sat down, put his feet on the truck's runner, and stared out into the rising sun.

Suddenly, the heap groaned, Marshall's head moved a little and one arm started to reach to his wounds.

Shit.

The heap groaned again; a leg moved.

Mac leaned back on the seat and his head hit something hard. He turned and saw Marshall's rifle, mounted in a gun rack across the back window. He took it down, got out, and used the bolt action to chamber a bullet. He walked up to the heap, and shot it in the chest. He cranked another bullet, and shot again. He did it again, and again, and again. He stopped because there wasn't a sixth bullet in the magazine.

Henry Marshall stopped moving.

Mac dropped the gun on the ground next to the body.

The horses had run away after the first shot, but that was thirty minutes ago. They'd come back and were thumping the ground, again. The cattle were still far away.

Mac, sitting in the truck, heard the commotion. He leaned in and removed the keys from the ignition, walked to the shed, and opened the lock. He shouldered a bag of oats, then walked past the truck and the heap. He pushed the gate open and headed to the trough. The horses backed off, but only a few steps. Mac dropped the sack on the ground and removed his pocket knife from his jeans. He slit the top of the bag, poured the feed out, then stepped back.

The horses pawed the ground, reluctant, but then shuffled forward and stuck their noses into their morning meal.

Mac tried to pat the bay but both horses immediately bolted, standing away, not letting him get close.

He walked, past the body still lying where it fell, eased his car out, then drove down the dirt road, back to Dallas.

The morning had been unlike any other he'd ever seen, and he'd been working at this gas station for almost nine years. Nolan

Griffin saw three county police cars running down the highway, all in a big hurry. Then he saw an ambulance, then a couple minutes later, his father's hunting buddy Doctor Lee Farmer, driving a car marked Coroner. He figured something big happened somewhere close by.

Hours later, when a police cruiser pulled in, he came out of the office and headed to the pumps. But Sheriff Howard Stegall didn't pull in to get gas. He got out, put on his hat, and walked up to Nolan, all official like.

"Morning Sheriff."

The Sheriff took off his sunglasses and looked at Griffin with an intense stare. "Did you see any strangers round these parts? Anybody new pull in to get gas, yesterday or today?"

Griffin nodded immediately. "Yes sir, sure was. I took notice of a man, before we closed up last night, cause almost nobody but local folk stop here."

Stegall got interested. "Can you describe him?"

"Absolutely. He was about thirty, maybe a little older, had black hair," Nolan stuck an open palm up flat over his head, "a pretty big guy. Oh, and he had on these black-rimmed glasses. You know like Clark Kent wears on TV." Nolan grinned.

Stegall didn't grin back. "I need you to come in to the station. We'll need a sketch of who you saw."

Griffin got excited. "Sure, no problem. What's going on?"

The Sheriff didn't answer the question. "Did the man say anything to you?"

"Yes sir." Griffin thought a second. "He asked where the Marshall place was."

The sheriff looked up at the attendant, this time with his head tilted to one side. "You sure about that?"

"Yep. I'm certain." Griffin smiled, and nodded immediately. "Say, what's going on Sheriff?"

Stegall put his sunglasses back on. "Henry Marshall didn't

show up for work. Somebody went up to his place looking and they found him up at the ranch, dead."

"Holy Moley… dead?"

"Doc Farmer came up, examined the body, and ruled it a suicide."

"Gee, that's a shame. He was always nice to me." Nolan scratched his head a bit. "You still need me to come in for the picture?"

"Yep."

"Does the stranger asking for directions mean anything?"

"Probably nothing, and doesn't matter. Doc Farmer already ruled it self-inflicted, but you come in anyway."

Nolan smiled, happy today was different than yesterday.

CHAPTER 30

SEPTEMBER, 1961

"LET ME SEE THAT." LBJ beckoned to Ed Clark who hesitated. Johnson's expression became intense and menacing. "Give it to me."

Clark reached across the desk and handed him the three-page document, then looked at Cliff Carter who was sitting next to him in a matching leather chair.

Johnson quickly glanced at the closed office door, assuring himself they were alone. He flipped to the third page, read a few lines, then turned back to page two. When he found what he was looking for he squinted through his reading glasses.

Clark looked surprised at LBJ's concentration. His usual casual glance, followed by 'just tell me what it says' didn't happen. The Vice President read every word.

When finished, Johnson removed his glasses, sighed, and ducked his chin to his chest. Slow words came next. "You two are the dumbest fuckups on the face of this earth."

Both of the subjects of his wrath remained silent.

LBJ put his glasses back on, and read out loud. "External

injuries - there were lacerations and a bruise on the right cheek and a fracture of the occipital bone."

"Back of the skull." Clark clarified.

LBJ growled and continued. "Internal injuries - the lungs contained 15% carbon monoxide which, prior to death, might have been 30%. There were five entrance wounds in the lower chest and abdomen, with corresponding exit wounds in the lower back. The wounds were consistent with the 22-caliber rifle found at the scene."

LBJ turned the final page to read the coroner's conclusion. "Medical Diagnosis – Suicide. The condition of the body and supporting evidence collected at the scene are conclusive. Cause of death – self-inflicted, carbon monoxide poisoning."

The silence that followed was broken by the intercom. "Mr. Vice President, the majority leader has arrived."

Johnson hit the intercom. "I'll be right there. Get Senator Mansfield some coffee."

Clark coughed then volunteered an answer to an unasked question. "A conversation took place with the coroner prior to his final determination."

LBJ just stared at him.

Clark continued. "The family is upset, but I think we have that handled."

Carter coughed nervously.

LBJ wielded his death stare in Cliff's direction. "You have something to add?"

Carter shook his head.

LBJ leaned back in his chair then spun around to face the window. A full minute went by before he spoke. "Fucking Bobby."

Carter and Clark looked at each other, puzzled.

LBJ kept staring out the window at the trees between his office in the Eisenhower Executive Office Building and the White House. "Where is the mastermind who handled this?"

"California." Clark responded quickly. "We got him in with Ling Electronics in Anaheim."

Johnson turned the chair around slowly. "And?"

Carter chimed in with the good news. "The investigation has stalled. It's not over, there are a few more involved, but it definitely slowed."

LBJ just shook his head, and took another long minute. "Bobby never wanted me anywhere near the Presidency. He hates me for how I got the nod from his brother." Suddenly, he threw the papers at Clark. "This is exactly what he's looking for to get me off the ticket."

Clark leaned forward and whispered. "We'll clean this up."

LBJ pointed a crooked finger. "What about—"

"Estes?"

Johnson nodded once.

"I think he gets the picture, now. He knows what will happen."

Clark whispered again. "We'll handle this—"

LBJ jumped up. "You'd better, but for God sakes, leave your Mr. California out of it."

"Understood."

Johnson walked to the door, stopping before turning the handle. "Everything needs to be settled soon." He turned around. "Everything."

It was another sunny day, like every other day, warm and full of sunshine— depressing. At least the walk from the parking lot to the office building's front doors were traffic free. Ling Electronics was like prison. Mac had the same job he had since the New York bank, an accountant, although he no longer put figures in columns. He watched other people put numbers in columns.

He slowly walked up the fire stairs instead of taking the elevator. It wasn't for exercise. It was because there was never anybody in the concrete stairwell, just him, and his echo.

"Good morning." The bright, young, enterprising receptionist greeted him with a smile.

He grunted.

"Mister Wallace, there are two men waiting for you in your office."

That stopped him. Nobody but his two subordinates and one superior ever wanted to see him. "Who are they and why are they in my office?"

"I don't know," she stumbled, realizing her mistake. "And, they... they said they had an appointment."

He grunted again, then walked down the corridor, his fingers white knuckling the handle of his briefcase.

He stopped short of the glass-paneled door. Two black suits, under two short haircuts, sat with their backs to him, not talking, staring straight ahead.

"Do I know you?" Mac came in fast, walked around his desk, and remained standing.

Both men reached into their jacket breast pockets. They expertly flipped open their badges and IDs. The man on Mac's right glared. "Naval Intelligence."

"What do you want?" Mac sat down behind the desk.

The two men looked at each other.

The one on Mac's right spoke. "Normally, people we speak to are surprised, when two officers from law enforcement show up in their offices first thing in the morning. You appear calm, and not at all curious. Don't you think that's strange?"

"Do you ask everyone you meet, first thing in the morning, questions about other people's reactions?"

The men seemed unfazed. "We're here because the Office of

Naval Intelligence has been charged to investigate your Top-Secret Clearance."

Mac reflected their stone-faced demeaner. "And?"

"And. There are questions about how a convicted felon, even though the record has been expunged, continues to hold a TSC."

Mac reacted with surprise. "Expunged?"

"Yes." The speaker flipped open a notepad. "Attorney Polk Sheldon, appearing for Malcolm Wallace in Travis County Court, successfully had the felony conviction and subsequent sentence removed from the official record."

Mac gathered himself.

Speaker held out the notebook. "How is that possible? Since the trial you've been in constant trouble with the law. You've had four, no, five drunk driving arrests in Texas and one here in California. Not to mention the indecent exposure arrest."

"Good lawyer." Mac's moment of weakness had disappeared.

"Don't you think that's strange?"

"What I think seems irrelevant." Mac leaned forward a little. "You're not asking questions. Please don't tell me Naval Intelligence came all the way to California just for my take on the Texas legal system."

Speaker flipped the notebook closed. "We're here out of courtesy—"

"No, you're not."

"Right." Speaker smiled a little. "No, we're not. Your case was brought to our attention by a Texas Ranger, Clint Peoples. Apparently, he couldn't get anybody's attention in... Texas... so he came to us. Do you know him?"

"Finally, a direct question. No, I do not know anyone named Clint Peoples."

"Do you know Henry Marshall?"

"No." Mac's stomach rolled over.

"Right." Speaker paused and both men rose simultaneously.

"After we're done in California, we'll be paying a visit to your wife."

"Ex-wife."

"Mary DuBois, of Dallas, Texas."

"Andre."

"Pardon?"

"Andre DuBois Wallace."

Speaker seemed confused and started to pull out the notebook.

Mac stood and pointed to the door. "You'll figure it out."

After the door closed on the two, Mac sat back down hard in the chair.

Motherfuckers. Expunged.

CHAPTER 31

DECEMBER 24, 1961

THE PHONE RINGING didn't bother him, even though it was early on Sunday morning. He sat up in bed and just looked it, sitting on the nightstand.

It wasn't the hour of the call, or even the day, it was that his phone rang at all.

Mac gripped the handle and slowly raised it to his ear. "Hello."

There was a slight rustling on the other end. "Honeyboy."

Mac smiled. "Hi, Josefa."

"Hi yourself."

"I know better than to ask how you got my number."

"I dialed information."

"Oh, right, that makes sense."

"You should get an unlisted number, if you don't want any calls."

"Don't need one. Nobody ever calls me."

"I just did."

"Yes, you did."

There was a moment of quiet.

"So, why did you call? Just miss me... wait," Mac's voice got a little energized. "Are you here, in California?"

"Oh... listen to you, getting all excited about little old me... but, sadly, I'm not in the sunshine state."

"I thought that was Florida."

"Don't get fresh with me... I... I..." Her voice trailed off.

"Josefa?"

"I just called to say Merry Christmas." Her voice sounded distant.

"No, you didn't. I haven't heard from you in a year or better. What's wrong?"

More quiet.

"I can get a plane ticket." Mac offered even though he was insincere about the offer.

"No... no. That won't help." Her voice jumped up. "But, wait... that is so sweet of you to offer."

"But?"

"But... things are not going well here. I've become quite the anchor for my brother, and his band of cutthroats."

Mac chuckled. "You back to your old tricks again?"

Her voice seemed weak. "No, sadly, no. I'm just—"

"Just what, Josefa? Come on now, I've never heard you talk like this. Usually, it's me that's all down in the dumps."

"You know you're right." She recovered. "How is it there?"

"Here? It's terrible. I've been expelled from Texas and subjected to constant sunshine, and fair weather. I have the most boring job I've ever had in my life. I'm under investigation by Naval Intelligence, and there is no decent barb-a-que anywhere."

"Yes, but are you getting fucked?"

"Only by Clark, Carter, and your brother."

The air went out of the balloon.

"Me too." She said, low and slow.

He tried to brighten the conversation. "Are you coming here anytime soon? Maybe we could meet and share war stories."

"Mr. Moss might object."

"Oh, excuse me, I forgot you got married again."

"I did, but it didn't help, which is the problem I guess."

"Still a wild woman."

He could almost see her throw her shoulders back when she spoke. "You bet your ass."

Moments went by again.

"Josefa?"

"I'm here. I miss it."

"Me too. It was great back then, wasn't it?"

She giggled. "We had a lot of fun. Maybe too much."

"Ah... you know me, Honeyboy... never enough... never enough."

He heard a rustling noise, like the phone was dropped then picked up.

"I have to go. You have a nice Christmas."

"You too."

He started to hang up.

"Be careful."

"What?"

"Just..." she stopped.

He heard her breathe into the receiver.

"It's nothing... never mind." Her voice suddenly sparkled. "But listen, Honeyboy."

"I'm listening."

"I hope you have an absolutely filthy dream about me tonight."

He laughed out loud, but she was gone.

Austin Chronicle
MRS. MOSS, 49
DIES; SISTER OF
VICE PRESIDENT
Fredericksburg, Texas. Dec 25
(UPI) – Mrs Josefa Moss, 49
younger sister of Vice President
Lyndon B. Johnson, died in her
sleep last night of a cerebral
hemorrhage.
Mrs. Moss died after spending
the evening with the entire
Johnson clan around the
Christmas tree at the LBJ ranch
east of Fredericksburg.
She was buried at the ranch
on the same day as she died.
No autopsy was performed.

CHAPTER 32

MARCH 29, 1962

EDWARD CLARK WALKED QUICKLY, which was odd for him, and his body responded negatively. He wasn't in danger, or late for a meeting, he was merely in a hurry to get to his office. He was breathing heavy, and sweat had formed on his brow. A search of his pockets failed to find a handkerchief; the end of his tie filled the need. He had to call the Vice President and assure him he was handling the arrest of Billy Sol Estes.

His downtown destination just off Commerce Avenue had a brick front, a solid oak door, and a bronze plaque engraved with the name of the number one law firm in Austin Texas, Looney and Clark – Attorneys at Law. The door squeaked open as he entered and the momentary relief of the building's air-conditioning evaporated when he saw Clint Murchison's bodyguard seated outside his office door.

Clark's secretary shrugged her shoulders, a helpless look on her face.

He acknowledged her distress with a small shake of his head and breezed past the giant bulk of a man without a greeting.

Clint Murchison was seated in the high-backed leather chair opposite Clark's desk.

Clark approached but knew better than to sit behind his desk, because it would appear a superior position. He opted, instead, to sit in the matching client chair, next to the billionaire.

"Good afternoon." Murchison dripped sarcasm as he glanced at his watch.

"Thank you, and a very pleasant 9:10 in the morning to you."

The soft, round-faced, thin-haired man signaled his displeasure at Clark's response with a snort and an impatient tap of his cane on the floor.

Clark, needing to recover, took a breath. "What can I do for my best client, on this fine day?"

Murchison waved his walking stick. "I read in the morning paper your attempt to pick up loose change with this cotton deal has backfired in a big way. Estes is in jail, and, you know, that other idiot, Baker, is next."

Clark nonchalantly rocked his head up and down, then smiled. "It's not going to be a problem..." his voice became a percentage point more aggressive, "and it wasn't loose change. Everyone, including you, saw profit from the cotton, storage tanks, and fertilizer deals."

The client got red-faced. "Loose change, dammit. You idiots... your boss included, were sticking your noses in the pig trough for extra swill instead of looking out for your benefactors. Y'all wasted time with these small-time con men, when you should have been stopping this Goddamn commie president from taking away our depletion allowance." He banged the cane, hard. "That's hundreds of millions of dollars a year to oil."

"Believe me." Clark stayed calm and enunciated each word. "That... will... never... ever... happen."

Murchison reluctantly nodded agreement. "That may be so, for now," his voice calmer, "but this mess in the papers has made your boss vulnerable. You know as well as I do, the brother, that other liberal prick, wants Lyndon off the reelection ticket. Then who knows what will happen."

Clark just nodded without commenting, instinctually knowing not to interrupt his wealthiest client.

"Estes and Baker are amateurs. They were sloppy, got caught, and the newspapers are already saying they're guilty. Lyndon's name was even mentioned in an article about who's responsible for letting them get away with bilking the government. What happens if they go telling tales?"

Clark raised stop sign hands. "Estes is well aware of what can happen if that road is taken."

Murchison narrowed his eyes. "You mean because of that DOA man... the suicide?"

Clark didn't nod, didn't blink, didn't breathe.

"How 'bout the other one, Baker? I've been told the hammer's gonna' drop on that idiot, very soon."

Clark again raised the stop sign. "They both know what to... and, what not to say."

Murchison slid forward in the chair, exerting effort, and made guttural sounds as he tried to get up.

Clark didn't move to help.

The round old man stood then sturdied himself with his cane. He took a few steps, then leaned on the back of the chair. He gazed down at the seat, his balding head shining in the florescent light. "The two of them have made a lot of serious enemies."

"Estes and Baker?" Clark asked, surprised.

Clint shook his head, his face wrinkled with frustration that Clark failed to follow his thinking. "No... no, the Kennedys. Serious men seriously hate them. They must think their daddy's money makes them invincible."

Clark caught up. "Joe Kennedy is very rich, but hate? He's only been in office for fourteen months."

Murchison scoffed. "I'm gonna' give you a little history lesson, because you need to understand a few things."

Clark settled in.

"Their first mistake was breaking a promise made by the father to Sam Giancana. If elected, he guaranteed the sons would lay off the mob in Chicago. So, Giancana used his influence with the unions to get the vote to fall for Kennedy. He beat Nixon by less than one percent. Chicago won Illinois, and Illinois put him in the White House."

Murchison coughed clearing his throat, then continued. "The Kennedy adminstration deported Carlos Marcello who ran gaming in New Orleans and the mob's interests in Cuba." He stared hard at Clark. "Marcello and their other target, Santo Trafficante, controlled seven hotel/casinos that ceased to exist when Castro took over. It cost the Mafia a fortune."

Clark continued to listen carefully, although much of it he already knew.

"Also, Marcello was working with the CIA to assassinate Castro."

He didn't know that.

Murchison staggered a bit, and seemed weak legged, but continued talking as he took his seat again. "The mob wanted Cuba back and developed a relationship with the exiled Cubans, and a lot of patriots who wanted Castro dead. So... an alliance formed and together with the CIA the Bay of Pigs invasion happened. It was disaster, because Kennedy, who signed off, refused to send air support." He took a long breath. "Kennedy blamed the CIA, and he fired Allen Dulles, who is now more dangerous than he was in office."

Clark nodded politely.

The man shook his head. "I still can't believe he said... in public... he wanted to 'splinter the CIA into a thousand pieces and scatter it to the winds.' The FBI, Mossad, MI-6, even the KGB, are nothing compared to the power behind the CIA."

Murchison, recovered from his stroll around the chair, continued. "Now, he's aiming at the DOD. He's cutting huge, multi-billion-dollar contracts and wants to cut Defense to the bone to advance domestic programs. And... he won't commit to Vietnam."

Clark interrupted. "You know that Lyndon is fully behind sending troops."

The man just waved his hand. "Lyndon has no influence on that subject."

Clark nodded slightly.

He pointed his cane. "Then... there's what he's doing to us— oil. He's already passed the Kennedy Act which costs us fifteen percent of all profits from foreign oil and...if he's reelected in '64, his first priority will be to repeal the oil depletion allowance." His face got red again. "Do you know how much that will cost us?"

Clark didn't get a chance to answer.

"Three hundred million a year. Three hundred million. That son of a bitch needs to die."

Clark's hands immediately went up. "Clint, stop. You shouldn't be saying things like that, people will get the wrong idea."

Murchison paused a second then grunted and looked away.

"Besides, he's a young man."

Murchison grunted again. "Doesn't matter... dead's dead."

"You're talking crazy— that can't happen here."

The man laughed out loud. "For a smart man, you're pretty fucking naive."

Clark, offended, didn't respond.

"Just since the end of the war, Presidents got dead in Guatemala, Nicaragua, and Panama." He started counting on fingers. "There were the heads of Jordan, Ethiopia, and the Dominican Republic and... Jesus Christ, Clark, the CIA just helped kill Lumumba in the Congo last year. Nobody knew and they didn't even tell the Haircut for months."

"Okay, maybe those things happened, but none of them happen—"

"Here, on US soil." Murchison went back to lecture mode. "You're right. The men who killed Lincoln, Garfield, and McKinley were all radicals." He took a long breath. "What's different is Kennedy's enemies are not crazy revolutionaries with a pistol." He leaned forward and whispered. "He will never see them coming."

Clark didn't know what to say. He knew this man, and the reach of the influence he and his allies wielded.

Murchison grunted again, trying to stand. When up, he tested his leg movement with his cane, then started for the door. "Clark… get your two problems under control. I'm not speaking just for myself." He came to a stop slowly, turned halfway, and stared.

Clark was repelled by what looked like pure hate.

"Anyone who comes to power makes enemies that try to take them down. Someone has— others want. It starts slow, building from within, and a coup d'état happens, not when someone says do it— it happens when no one stops it."

Cold ran up Clark's back.

"He's already dead." Murchison turned, and slowly shuffled toward the door.

It took twenty minutes for his call to go through to the Vice President. Clark sat in his chair, unable to concentrate on anything, his mind still reeling from the implications of what had just transpired. He had just witnessed a credible threat against a sitting president by what one of the richest men in the country called a conspiracy involving extremely powerful men.

He wanted a drink, and it was not even eleven o'clock in the morning.

"Mr. Clark, the Vice President."

He spun around and paused before picking up the phone, still not knowing what to say. "Mr. Vice President."

"Clark, are you on top of this? Did he make any statement?"

"Ah, no sir. No statement. I'm… ah." Clark hesitated to continue.

"Clark?"

"Mr. Vice President. I'm not sure I can talk about this over the phone."

Another pause.

Johnson's voice became agitated. "Well, what can you say?"

Clark started carefully. "Clint Murchison was waiting for me when I came in this morning."

"About this?"

"Yes, at first, and I think he's satisfied, for the moment. But that's not the issue that concerns me. He said some things—"

"Do I need to hear this?"

"I don't think there's a choice about that, Mr. Vice President."

"Can you come here, to Washington?"

"I can, but I don't think that would be wise. It's best this be unofficial."

Clark heard the chair in the Vice President's office squeaking. He'd seen LBJ rock back and forth when he was upset.

"I'll be at the ranch in three days. Can it wait?"

"It will have to."

The phone disconnected.

Clark leaned back in the chair and closed his eyes.

I hope it can wait.

CHAPTER 33

APRIL 1, 1962

HE CAME into the hotel covered with a fine coat of red and black dust. It was Texas dirt, hard and heavy and always tightly packed, giving plants little opportunity to root. Water ran off quick. And when the sun baked down, barren, rootless soil became a choking cloud when disturbed. LBJ dusted his shoulders as he walked next to the two Secret Service men flanking him. Two other men in black waited by the elevator and stood watching the entrance and balcony.

The door opened almost on cue and the Vice President went in, turned around, and saw a few onlookers who'd stopped in the Driskell Lobby seemingly excited to see such a famous person. He didn't wave, didn't smile, just waited, crossed armed, for the doors to close.

A suit opened the door and started to walk in his suite on the fifth floor.

"No. You boys wait here."

The apparent leader of the group stepped forward. "Can't do it, Mr. Vice President. Mr. Clark and Mr. Carter are waiting but only Mr. Clark has been cleared." He took a step.

Johnson blocked the advancing bodyguard. "This is my suite. They are my guests and you are not coming." He got an inch from the suit's nose and squinted. "Understood?"

The advance stopped.

Johnson closed the door in the suit's face.

"Good afternoon, Mr. Vice President." Cliff Carter stood almost at attention.

Clark added, "Good afternoon."

Johnson breezed past them. "I gotta take a shit." He walked to the bathroom and left the door wide open as was his habit. He dropped his pants and sat on the toilet. "I just came from the ranch. I took a ride in the Lincoln but it was hotter than a burnin' stump. In April, can you believe that?"

Neither Clark nor Carter responded.

Johnson looked at them curiously, grunted then reach for the toilet paper. "Okay, what's on your mind?"

Clark beckoned to Carter to move. "We'll wait for you out here, sir."

They sat on a couch and heard the water running.

Johnson walked out slowly drying his hands on a towel, focused on them.

"Mr. Vice President—"

"Cut the shit, Clark. What's up, and why did you bring Cliff along?"

"Sir," Clark began. "As I said on the phone Clint Murchison came to see me and said some disturbing things I think you should know about."

"He always says—"

"No sir. Not like this."

Clark never interrupted him. His lawyer had his attention.

"Basically, Mr. Murchison said there is a group of powerful men who are committed to see the President..." Clark didn't finish.

"See the President what?"

227

Clark looked around the room.

"It's secure. You can talk freely."

"Dead. They want to kill the President."

LBJ stopped drying, his hands falling to his sides, the towel dropping to the floor.

Carter stared at Clark, looking like it was a complete surprise to him.

LBJ looked at Clark. "You bring him along as a witness?"

"Wait, what?"

Johnson walked to the bar and poured three fingers of whisky. With his back to the men he asked, "You want some?"

Clark didn't respond but Carter eked out a "Yes, sir."

Johnson, watching the two men behind him in the mirror, slowly poured Carter a matching drink.

"I'm sorry to bring this—"

Johnson held up his hand and Clark stopped talking. He turned around, walked to the couch, and handed Carter the drink. He just stood there. Uncomfortable seconds went by.

Carter took a sip, then coughed a little.

Johnson chuckled. "Good, ain't it?" He ambled to a chair, sat, then swirled the brown liquid in the glass without drinking. He looked down at the glass then took a sip. Without looking at them, he said, "I know."

Clark sat back and Carter took another sip, this time not choking.

Johnson tilted the glass again. "Anyone who comes to power makes enemies that try to take them down. Someone has— others want."

Clark stuttered. "That's... exactly... what he said."

Johnson blew right past it. "The boys have pissed off and pissed on a bunch of bad people." He waved his hand dismissively. "Besides, every President has had enemies. Nature of the game."

Clark's surprise became resolve. "I do not believe this is that.

From what I heard this isn't just having enemies who make threats, it's about people who are going to act. Don't you think, I... I mean we, should advise the Secret Service?"

LBJ got very serious, leaned forward, and glared. "You're suggesting that we accuse one of the most powerful men in the country of being involved in a plot to assassinate the President of the United States?"

"I... ah..."

LBJ shouted. "I... ah... Come on boy. Spit it out. Are you suggesting that one of the most powerful men in the country is involved in a plot to assassinate the President of the United States?"

Clark sputtered, "Well he didn't actually say that. He just said he knew of people who—"

"Who what? People who wanted him dead? People want me dead. I'm sure that there are people who want you dead." He took another drink, then wiped his face with the back of his hand. "If you go around talking like this, I'm pretty sure it will happen."

Carter looked like he wanted to be anywhere but there.

Clark tried to regain high ground. "Sir, I just felt you should know."

LBJ sat back. "Well, now I know."

There was dead quiet in the room.

Finally, LBJ got up and went back to the bar for a refill. He did not offer them a refill.

"Ed, you've been a friend for a long, long time." He turned, full glass in hand. "We've done some things." He swirled the liquid. "There was the golf pro and DOA—"

"That was different and you know it... sir."

LBJ grinned a little. "You're right. That was just helping a friend... after the fact. It was something that happened that we didn't have anything to do with." He took a sip. "But it didn't hurt us any, did it?"

Carter looked at Clark.

LBJ walked back to his chair. "I'm not staying here tonight. Bird and I have guests coming for dinner. But I do have another appointment meeting me here."

Clark and Carter got up.

LBJ remained seated. "Clark, if a friend calls me and needs my help, I'm going to oblige him."

Clark stared at the Vice President.

"I've asked you this before and now I'm asking you again. Are you onboard?"

Clark didn't hesitate. "No sir. I'm not."

LBJ finished his drink. "Thank you, Ed." He held out his hand. "You've made huge contributions to my life and I won't forget that." He gave Ed Clark a two-handed shake.

They started for the door.

"Carter."

Cliff turned to face the Vice President of the United States. "Sir?"

"Is that boy from Austin still hiding out in California?"

Carter looked surprised by the question. "He is."

"Good to know… good to know. Now if you'll excuse me fellas, I gotta drain old jumbo. That whisky just runs right through me."

CHAPTER 34

SEPTEMBER, 1962

HE DIDN'T KNOW what was making him suddenly tense up, his stomach knotted and queasy. It was a day like any other, like every other. Mac glanced at his wristwatch. Arriving at the start of the workday had been problematic, but he was getting better — only late once this week, so it wasn't that. The angst lasted more than a moment, and he didn't understand why. He parked in the same lot, walked on the same sidewalk, everything was the same, and yet, something was off.

Mac came around the corner of the office building, heading for the front door of Ling Electronics. On the street in front, a black, four-door sedan with tinted windows, and very little chrome sat in a no-parking zone at the curb. The sight of it caused him to slow his step. There were no markings, no long radio antenna, and no spotlight mounted on the driver side of the car. In spite of not having the usual markings of a police vehicle, he knew the car belonged to some branch of law enforcement. His first instinct was to turn around, go back to his car, and drive away. However, he knew if they were looking for him, sooner or later, he'd be found.

Mac gutted up, ducked his head, and pushed forward, entering through the glass doors along with several others. The lobby was crowded with employees. White marble floor tiles acted as a percussion instrument being drummed in rhythm, by shoes walking in different directions. People sounds echoed off the glass and steel of an austere interior. A giant skylight at the peak of the three-story structure provided a tunnel of light to the black and white space. The only visible color belonged to a long, wide, white banner dangling from the ceiling, with LING ELECTRONICS written in bold red letters.

A while ago, a bird had somehow found its way into what was now an elaborate cage. It sailed and swooped every day, looking for handouts. The workers responded to the bird's plight, and as a result of their generosity, the imprisoned bird had deposited streaks of white bird shit on the company name.

Mac took the steps to the second floor, then walked down the corridor to his office. He stopped in the hall, and peeked through the glass panel before opening the door. Two broad-shouldered, black-suited men, with military haircuts, were seated with their backs to him in front of his desk. It was a déjà vu moment. He took a breath and turned the handle. They didn't turn around when he entered. Mac walked to his chair, placed his briefcase on the floor, sat, put both hands flat on the desk, and waited for them to speak.

"I'm Lieutenant Commander Brooks, and this is Lieutenant Green. We're investigators from the office of Naval Intelligence, Washington D.C."

Both men simultaneously produced and flipped open leather cases with their military IDs and gold badges.

Mac remained quiet.

Brooks continued. "You are Malcolm Everett Wallace?"

Mac nodded.

"Currently, you hold a Top-Secret Clearance classification,

which makes you a qualifier for defense department contracts obtained by this firm." Brooks stared at Mac.

"Is that a question or a statement?" Mac's voice was monotone.

Lieutenant Green handed Brooks a notebook.

Ignoring Mac's question, Brooks flipped it open, and began reading. "Your TS clearance is being investigated, again, because our office finds the issuance of a Top-Secret Clearance to a man convicted of first-degree murder to be… incomprehensible."

Mac was unfazed.

Brooks and Green both fixed their eyes on Mac.

Brooks leaned forward a little. "Earlier this month, a Grand Jury in Robertson County, Texas, reopened the case involving the death of a Department of Agriculture official, Mr. Henry Marshall."

Mac felt his stomach roll, but he maintained his composure, staring straight ahead at the space between the two men.

Brooks waited a moment, then continued. "You already know the details of the investigation, because Naval Intelligence interviewed you once before about the Marshall case."

Mac shrugged. "I'll tell you, like I told the other two NI agents, I don't know anything about that. So, why are you here?"

Brooks sat back. "You learned from the first investigation that Clint Peoples, the Texas Ranger, believes you may be responsible for Marshall's death."

Mac didn't react.

"This Grand Jury was impaneled because of questions concerning the accuracy of the autopsy, which led to a broader inquiry. That investigation uncovered new evidence that points to murder… not suicide."

Mac's vision went back to the space between the two men's shoulders.

Brooks continued. "Once murder was a possibility, we began

to try to determine why he would be killed." Brooks flipped a page and read. "The Department of Agriculture had instructed Mr. Marshall to investigate a case of suspected fraud by Billy Sol Estes. Marshall's notes indicated Estes received approximately twenty-one million dollars a year for growing and storing non-existing crops of cotton. On June 3, 1961, a few days before Marshall was to testify before a congressional committee, he was found dead at his ranch. The cause of death was ruled a suicide."

Mac had to fight to remain calm.

Brooks flipped to the next page. "Do you know the Texas Ranger, Peoples?"

"No. No idea who he is, never heard of him."

"The two officers from NI who interviewed you, a few months ago, didn't ask about him?"

For the first time, Mac twitched. "Yes, but no. I mean. Yes, they asked me but I told them I didn't know a Texas Ranger named Peoples."

Brooks looked at Green. "Do you have any idea why a Texas Ranger would make an allegation that you are somehow connected to the suicide of a man that you claim to have no connection with and never met?"

Mac just shook his head, learning from his mistake.

Brooks leaned forward slightly. "Can you explain the incomprehensible issuance of a Top-Secret Clearance to a convicted murderer?"

Mac didn't respond.

Brook grunted, then made a face of exasperation, but it was unconvincing. "The steps taken to gain approval for your TS clearance probably would have stayed buried in a file cabinet had it not been for the Marshall case. Your name gets mentioned, your file is pulled, and we find your issued Top Secret status even before your record is cleaned." Brooks took a breath. "The first NI investigation was dropped because the death of Mr. Marshall was affirmed as a suicide. However, questions about you remained open."

Mac glanced at Brooks waiting for the reason why they were here.

More note pages were turned. "Mr. Wallace, on March 29, Billy Sol Estes, along with his partners, Harold Orr and Coleman Wade, were indicted by a federal grand jury on fifty-seven counts of fraud."

Mac sat stiff, shoulders back, eyes front.

"Now get this, and this is also in the area of the incomprehensible," Brooks grinned slyly, "the day before those indictments came down, George Krutilek, the chief accountant for Estes was found dead from guess what... suicide."

Mac blinked, but continued to stare straight ahead.

"Also," Brooks laughed, "both Orr and Wade are dead. Cause of death... also apparent suicides. Beyond imagination...right?"

Without looking, Brooks held the notebook out to Lieutenant Green who took over. He had an accountant's attitude, and read facts like numbers in columns. "The case against Estes is being heard in federal court. It has caught the attention of The President of the United States. He asked the Attorney General, Robert Kennedy, to get involved. All the federal agencies are participating: the DOA, the FBI, and Naval Intelligence. He wants to know how a former Marine, convicted of first-degree murder, who inexplicably gained clearance to receive Top Secret information, is connected to the case."

Oh my God.

Mac turned his head toward Green. "I heard coincidence. What is the evidence?"

"Good question." He flipped a few more pages. "Mr. Wallace, because you're in California, and far from Robertson County, you probably haven't seen the local papers about details of the Marshall death."

Mac waited for the hammer to drop.

Green looked down, then slowly fixed a stare. "Do you know a young man named Nolan Griffin?"

Mac shook his head, confidently. "I do not."

"You may not know him but he knows you. You see, he's an attendant at a little country gas station near Mr. Marshall's ranch in Robertson County."

A vague recollection caused Mac's stomach to roll over.

"Mr. Griffin told the police that a man stopped for gas the evening before the body was discovered. He said the man had out-of-state plates, but didn't remember which one. He also said the man asked for directions to the Marshall ranch." Green closed the notebook and removed a piece of paper from his jacket. He looked at it, then slapped it down in front of Mac. "Does this man look familiar to you?"

Mac couldn't help but react. It was a crude, black and white, artist rendering of a man who looked exactly like him. He stared at it for a moment, then pushed it away, the paper sliding off the desk, to the floor.

Green looked at Brooks, apparently it was his turn again.

"Mr. Wallace." Brooks looked at the ceiling and scratched his chin, thoughtfully. "Marshall was shot five times, had a cracked skull, and carbon monoxide in his lungs. His death was no suicide." He pointed at Mac. "We know you're not connected to the fraud, you never met Estes, or his partners, but we know you're involved. Our question is... why? Why would you do it?"

Mac fought to regain his composure, but didn't answer.

Brooks changed subjects. "Do you remember the attorney who defended you in Austin?"

Mac looked down, a little confused. "Sheldon. Polk Sheldon."

"No not him, you had two attorneys."

"Yes, the other one was John Cofer."

"Good. Good." He looked at Green. "See, I told you he'd cooperate." He smiled at Mac. "Now, guess who represents Billy Sol Estes?"

Mac shook his head.

"Your guy, John Cofer."

Mac took a breath, again confused. "So?"

"So, the attorney who got you off on a first-degree murder charge is the same man who represents Billy Sol Estes in a case where the witness is murdered by a man who looks exactly like you."

Nobody spoke.

Brooks looked down, and spoke softly. "John Cofer also represented Lyndon Johnson when he was accused of voter fraud in his Senate election." He paused a second then added. "Do you know Edward Clark?"

Panic began to grip his being. He shook his head.

"For the record, that's a no?"

Mac didn't respond.

"Well, John Cofer works for Edward Clark. And, Edward Clark is the Vice President's business lawyer. Can you tell me why Edward Clark wrote a letter of recommendation to the DOA to get you a position in Arlington, Virginia in September of 1949?"

Mac didn't answer.

"Can you tell me why Edward Clark's associate, Cliff Carter, obtained your position at TEMCO, another defense contractor, shortly after you were convicted of shooting Douglas Kinser to death?"

A bead of sweat rolled down Mac's forehead.

Brooks put both hands on the desk. "Some people think Billy Sol Estes received protection in setting up the cotton fraud from Edward Clark, and from the then Senator from Texas, Lyndon Johnson."

Brooks became non-military, and almost whispered. "You're

in deep shit, life threatening shit. These are the most powerful men in the country, and you are shit, stuck in shit."

Mac made a noise but it wasn't a word.

Green started a lecture. "Wallace, there are five things that are needed to prosecute a case in court: who, what, why, where and when. The where and when are fact. The what is murder not suicide. We know who the players are but what's missing is the why. Of course, the fraud is about money, but why the murder, that's the real question."

Brooks went back to the whisper. "Is it possible that Lyndon Johnson, through Edward Clark and Cliff Carter, ordered you to murder Henry Marshall?"

Mac swallowed loud enough to be heard.

Brooks slapped both hands on the desk. "We need you to testify that Henry Marshall was murdered, because he was about to expose Billy Sol Estes of a fraud that involved the Vice President of the United States."

Mac couldn't speak even if he wanted to.

Brooks pressed. "Estes will be tried and convicted, that's an absolute. So far, he won't give anybody else up, but if he does, and believe me, sooner or later, he will, the whole house of cards falls… right on you."

Mac remained frozen stiff.

"We can put you at the scene. You have no alibi. You're connected to the fraud."

Mac felt words coming but Green didn't give it enough time.

"Look, if you cooperate, it will go a long way with the court. We can guarantee the prosecution will make you a deal that will get you out from whatever you're under right now."

Mac's mind's eye flashed on the twisted bodies of Marshall and Kinser. He closed his eyes and saw Josefa, ghost white, her eyes closed in death. In that moment, he knew his life was about to change.

"What do you say, Mr. Wallace? Will you cooperate?"

Mac pushed his chair back and slapped his hands on the desk. He looked squarely at both men. "You have drawn a conclusion from the fact that I was represented by one of the best defense attorneys in Texas, who also just happened to represent someone accused of fraud whom I've never met. You say you can put me at the scene because of a drawing that could be a sketch of Clark Kent. You point to a letter of recommendation written ten years ago by a fellow alumnus of the University I attended as if it were part of a plot." Mac glared at both men. "And somehow you have the balls to accuse the Vice President of the United States of being involved in a murder. Gentlemen, to use your word, this is incomprehensible." Mac tried to smile. "Fellas, you are missing a lot more than just an answer to... why."

Green reached to the floor, picked up the sketch, then stood up.

Brooks also rose saying, "I take it then, that's a no."

Mac remained in his chair. "I don't know anything about any of this."

The two men left without another word.

Mac's hands started shaking as the door closed. He reached down and felt his pants, he hadn't stood up because he thought he may have pissed himself. Suddenly, he reached for the waste can, doubled over, and heaved. After depositing his morning coffee in the bin, he wiped his face as best he could, and slumped back in the chair.

It took a few minutes to regain a normal heartbeat. After he recovered, he placed his briefcase on the desk, popped the lock, and sorted through the contents until he found his phone book. His hands were still shaking, making it difficult to turn the pages. Mac reached for the phone, hesitated because he wasn't ever supposed to call from his office, but dialed anyway.

"Good morning, Law offices of Looney, Clark. This is Margarete, how can I help you?"

"Edward Clark, please."

"May I tell him who's calling?"

"Malcolm Wallace."

"Hold please, Mr. Wallace."

A couple of minutes went by, which was not helping his nerves.

Margarete came back on the line. "Ah... Mr. Wallace. Mr. Clark is unavailable."

"When should I call back... or can I leave a number for him to call me?"

"Mr. Wallace...ah." The woman cleared her throat, then said firmly, "Mr. Wallace, Mr. Clark said to tell you he no longer represents you, and will not be able to assist you in any way."

Mac, stunned, didn't know what to say.

"He suggested you should try to reach a Mr. Carter. He said you would know who that is."

Mac still couldn't respond.

"Mr. Wallace, did you get that... Mr. Clark said to call Mr. Carter?"

"Yes, thank you."

"Have a good day." The line went dead.

He replaced the handset and slowly picked up his phone book to look for a number he knew he didn't have.

CHAPTER 35

JUNE 3, 1963

HIS HEART WAS THUMPING HARD. It felt like it was going to explode. He had just thrown up again, and the sweat pouring off his face was cold. His vision was clouded, body shaking, his mind disoriented and accompanied with the occasional hallucination. Mac knew why it was happening. Alcohol— not having any, was the cause.

Mac pushed himself up off the concrete floor and away from the toilet. He couldn't stand so he sat and looked up at the ceiling. His condition wasn't causing him regret, or remorse, or even motivating him to stop drinking. He knew he would recover as soon as he could get another drink. But that wasn't possible, because he was in jail— again.

There were two other men in the cell. One was old, fat, and had torn clothes marked with dried blood. The other prisoner was young, probably only 18 or 19. He sat on a cot, back to the wall, knees to his chin, whimpering. Mac didn't know what happened to them and didn't care. All he wanted was to get out of this filthy jail, and get a bottle.

The bang of a distant door was deafening. Footsteps in the

corridor sounded like an entire troop of soldiers in marching formation, but only two men appeared at the door of the cell.

"That's him." Cliff Carter pointed. "The one on the floor, in the corner."

The door swung open and clanged against the cage like a bell in a church tower. He grabbed his ears, rose up on his knees, then doubled up, his head finding the toilet. He wretched again and again. It ended when his eyes rolled back, and silence and darkness took over.

He woke up on a bed. There was a pillow, a blanket. He lifted his head and blinked the crust from his eyes. His mouth was a desert, and he smelled like a sewer.

"Get up. Take a shower."

He was in a motel room, darkened with a drawn shade. The only light came from the TV that Cliff Carter was watching.

"In there." Carter, without looking at Mac, pointed to the bathroom door. "There is soap, a razor, and fresh clothes from your luggage."

Mac tried to speak. A sound came out, but it was unrecognizable. He almost fell getting out of bed, and was halfway there before realizing he was bruised, had long scratches on both arms, and was naked.

He emerged, almost an hour later, clean shaven, wearing a white t-shirt and jeans. He looked almost human, but still felt like he was ready for the grave.

"Food." Carter, still staring at the TV, pointed to a counter. "Eat first, then you can have a drink."

Mac immediately began shuffling to a white paper bag. He pulled out a hamburger, and mashed it into his mouth. It took all the energy he had to eat and, when finished, he fell back onto the bed, exhausted.

Carter waited a minute before he got up and walked to a dresser. He opened a drawer, pulled out a bottle of whisky, and tossed it onto the bed.

Mac stretched his arm, grabbed the bottle, pulling it to his chest like a mother clutching a baby.

"Jesus." Carter shook his head in disgust, and plopped back into the chair.

Mac cracked the seal and took a long drink. The fire in his throat was glorious. He recapped the bottle, surrounded it with his arms, and closed his eyes.

Light shattered his sleep. Mac woke, this time, without dry-mouth. He slapped his hand around the bed, and breathed a sigh of relief when it landed on the bottle.

"Come on, get up." Carter pulled the drapes open, and daylight poured in.

"What time is it?" Mac raised a hand to shade his eyes.

"It's ten o'clock on Monday morning."

"Monday?"

"You were arrested on Friday, and spent three days in jail for drunk driving and reckless endangerment."

"Monday?"

"Are you deaf? Yes, it's Monday June 3rd. You were supposed to meet me in Dallas on Friday. What happened?"

Mac tried to clear the fog. "Uh… I remember the airplane, and picking up a car."

"And?"

"I drove out of the airport, but—"

"But… Let me guess. You stopped for a drink."

"I did." Mac nodded. "I remember. It was really hot, and the bar was cool. I started jugging and jawin' with the bartender and—."

"Enough," Carter demanded. "Why are you all the way out here in the middle of nowhere?"

Mac shrugged. "Uh... where am I?"

"Rusk County, fifty miles east of Dallas."

He shook his head a little, not recalling at first. "Wait, I remember. I went east instead of west on I-40. When I finally realized I was going the wrong way, I got off the highway... but—"

Carter interrupted again. "But...you stopped and had a few drinks."

Mac nodded, sheepishly.

"Well, shortly after your pitstop, you were arrested for getting on the interstate going the wrong way and into oncoming traffic. Fortunately, you jumped the median, and ran the car into a field before you hit anything or anybody."

Mac shook his head, not remembering that part of his journey, but knowing it was probably true.

Carter started pacing around the room with his head down.

"Wait." Mac had a moment of curiosity. "How did you know I'd been arrested?"

"How did you book the flight and the car?"

Mac became defensive. "I used the travel agent you told me to use."

"The police ran the plates on the car, saw it was a rental. They called the car rental company to make sure it wasn't stolen. The car people called the travel agent, and the travel agent called me." Carter raised his voice. "You just can't find enough ways to make my life difficult."

Mac ducked his head. "I'm sorry."

Carter turned his back to Mac. "Fucking asshole."

Mac felt for the bottle, but didn't uncap it. "Why am I here? I mean why am I here in Texas?"

"Like I told you on the phone, I wanted to see you to assess the next step."

"What next step?" Mac's frustration burst out. "I didn't hear from you for weeks after I called Clark when the Naval storm troopers tried to get me to testify. He refused to talk to me and had a secretary tell me to call you." His voice got even louder. "I didn't know what to do until you called me at Ling." His head started throbbing again.

"You called Clark at his office, you idiot." Carter's voice was louder than Mac's. "I had to wait to get in touch with you, because there can't be any connection between you and us." His voice came down a notch. "But now, after this... Jesus Christ, Wallace, every time I give you an opportunity, you shit the bed."

Mac ducked his head.

Carter sounded exasperated. "Look, you can stop worrying about the investigation. That's over. Last month, Estes got fifteen years, and he still isn't talking. Nobody is looking anymore... it's done. Over."

"That's good." Mac breathed a small sigh. "But, thanks for letting me sit out there waiting for somebody to slap handcuffs on me."

Carter dismissed him with a condescending wave-off. "It was necessary."

Mac flamed. "Really, necessary? I was something once. I had dreams, aspirations. I wanted to make a difference and I thought... doing the things I did... would get me somewhere, in Washington—"

"You're right, you might have made a difference but you cared more about women and booze than the man you should have served. We asked you to stay under the radar for a reason but you didn't stay out of the spotlight, did you?" He stepped forward backing Mac away. "We wanted you to talk to an asshole who was trying to blackmail a United States Senator. Instead, you shot him five times, in broad daylight in front of five witnesses."

"I… I."

Clark took another step forward, squared off in front of Mac and waited.

Mac ducked his head and cowered. "So, it's over."

"Yes, it's over." Carter turned around and lowered his voice.

Mac sat back down on the bed. The sting of being chastised made him want a drink but he held off.

Carter wielded around and held up a finger. "Tell me something. Did I hear right? Did you just get married, again?"

The question broke the tension. Mac laughed. "I did. Last month. She's a grad student, who was interning at Link."

"Isn't that like number four?"

"Four, but does marrying the same woman three times count as one, or three?"

Clark shook his head "I still don't understand that."

"Yeah, me neither." Mac picked up the bottle. "Victoria is the new one's name. We started going out, drank a lot, she got pregnant so… I didn't have any choice. She's actually due in a couple of weeks so… at least the kid will be legal."

Carter didn't comment further, just stared at him like he was debating some internal thought. He walked to the chair and sat down.

Mac got up from the bed and took two glasses from the counter. He held the whisky bottle up at Carter.

Carter nodded. "Why not? Sure, pour me a short one."

Mac handed the glass to Carter, then stood quiet for a moment. "Can I ever come back to Texas? I fucking hate California."

Carter took a swig. "Mac, you're not on the top of anybody's list. Some people never want to see you again."

Mac's mind flashed on Josefa, and his blood ran cold.

"You got carried away and fucked up... twice."

"I was drunk."

"Yeah, and obviously, that hasn't changed."

Mac held his head low.

"You did stupid things. But," Carter took another sip from his glass, "something is in motion now that might resolve a lot of problems, which also might be the opportunity you need to prove your value."

"Which means I can come back to Texas?"

"Maybe."

"That would be great." Mac drank more than a swig.

"However, we will need another favor to help make that change happen."

Mac took a step backwards. "No... no more. I don't want any more problems. I just want to come home. I don't want—"

Clark held up a hand. "It's not like that... nothing like before. Just remember, we never asked you to do what you did, but we were there to help even though you fucked up bad. Right?"

Expunged. You knew my conviction went away. You used me.

"Your job, since the beginning, was to do the thing we asked you to do, without knowing why. Correct?"

Mac nodded.

"Some time in the near future, if you agree: I'll call you, you'll quit your job, go where I tell you, and do what's asked, and only what's asked."

Mac stood firm. "Okay, but I won't—"

"Wallace, it's just a favor for a friend. That's all it will be."

"Why me? There must be others."

"We have sources, elsewhere, but you've been there since the beginning. You've done what we asked and never asked why. Frankly, that's rare. Mac, when you're not abusing alcohol, you're exactly what we need."

Mac stood silent. "I'm not sure I should believe you."

247

Carter stood up, his face angry, his tone final. "Then don't." He finished his drink and started for the door.

"Wait." Mac panicked.

Carter turned around slowly.

Mac stared at Carter. "Okay… I'll do what you ask."

"Will the new wife be a problem?"

"No problem." Mac shook his head.

"Go back to California, and wait for my call."

"What about this arrest?"

Carter grinned slyly, "What arrest?" He turned the handle, opened the door, and walked out into the heat of the Texas day.

CHAPTER 36

JUNE 10, 1963

BACK PAIN NECESSITATED a last-minute injection of procaine. Dr. Feelgood, as Jackie called him, also sprayed ethyl chloride and administered a cocktail of amphetamines, which gave the President the ability to appear as if he were pain free. It was far from the truth.

If the car he was in was a taxi, the travel time from the White House to American University would be about twenty to twenty-five minutes, depending on traffic. The ten-car motorcade, which required every intersection between the two points barricaded and manned with armed guards, travelled the distance in less than ten minutes. John F. Kennedy exited his Lincoln Continental limousine at the John M. Reeves Athletic Center, at American University, to give a commencement address. His audience was the graduating class, a sea of onlookers, and TV cameras which would record a speech for the ages.

Thousands of miles away there was a room where men, who were more concerned with the right-now than the future, were not looking forward to proclamations made that day with enthusiasm, but rather with malice and hate. They had feared the worst from this President, and to them, his speeches were filled with words that embodied every fear, and ideas that cemented their resolve for a change of leadership.

Clint Murchison sat in a high-backed leather chair. H. L. Hunt in the chair next to him. Several other members of the 8F group had gathered, along with the oil giants, at the Driscoll Hotel for a meeting on what was supposed to be ancillary issues, however, the speech from Washington was being broadcast on National TV, and their morbid curiosity refused to allow them the ability to ignore the words from a man they had come to loath with deep passion.

"Turn that up." Murchison waved his walking stick at a lower-level member of the group. "I can't hear over your meaningless chatter."

The man dressed in a very expensive suit obeyed without hesitation.

The announcer on the TV disappeared, and the Haircut took the stage. After the preliminary nonsense greetings were concluded, John F. Kennedy began delivering his message. "…I have, therefore, chosen this time, and this place, to discuss a topic on which ignorance too often abounds, and the truth too rarely perceived – and that is the most important topic on earth: Peace. What kind of a peace do I mean? What kind of a peace do we seek? Not a *Pax Americana* enforced on the world by American weapons of war. Not the peace of the grave or the security of the slave. I am talking about genuine peace, the kind of peace that makes life on earth worth living, the kind that enables men and nations to grow and to hope and build a better life for their children — not merely peace for Americans but peace for all men and women — not merely peace in our time but peace for all time."

Hunt choked on a sip of iced tea at the statement.

"In short, both the United States and its allies, and the Soviet Union and its allies, have a mutually deep interest in a just and genuine peace, and in halting the arms race. Today, the expenditure of billions of dollars every year on weapons acquired for the purpose of making sure we never need them is essential to the keeping of peace. But surely the acquisition of such stockpiles — which can only destroy and never create — is not the only, and much less the most efficient, means of peace. For we are both devoting massive sums of money to weapons that could better be devoted to combat ignorance, poverty, and disease. We are both caught in a vicious and dangerous cycle with suspicion on one side breeding suspicion on the other, and new weapons begetting counter weapons.

A "motherfucker" was heard from a member.

"Agreements to this end are in the interest of the Soviet Union, as well as ours, and even the most hostile nations can be relied upon to accept and keep those treaty obligations, and only those treaty obligations, which are in their interest. So, let us not be blind to our differences, but let us also direct attention to our common interests, and the means by which those differences can be resolved. And, if we cannot end now our differences, at least we can help make the world safe for diversity. For, in the final analysis, our most basic common link is that we all inhabit this small planet. We all breathe the same air. We all cherish our children's future, and we are all mortal."

Another voice from the back spoke. "That's right you commi loving cocksucker, you're gonna find out just how fucking mortal you are."

The others in the room erupted into a great clatter of conversation causing Hunt to rise. "I want quiet."

"While we proceed to safeguard our national interests, let us also safeguard human interests. And the elimination of war and arms is clearly in the interest of both. No treaty, however much it may be to the advantage of all, however tightly it may be worded, can provide absolute security against the risks of deception and evasion. But it can — if it is sufficiently effective in its enforcement, and if it is sufficiently in the interests of its signers — offer far more security and far fewer risks than an unabated, uncontrolled, unpredictable arms race. The United States, as the world knows, will never start a war. We do not want a war. We do not now expect a war. This generation of Americans has already had enough — more than enough — of war and hate and oppression. We shall be prepared if others wish it. We shall be alert to try to stop it. But we shall also do our part to build a world of peace where the weak are safe and the strong are just. We are not helpless before that task, or hopeless of its success. Confident and unafraid, we labor on — not toward a strategy of annihilation but toward a strategy of peace. Thank you."

The announcer came back on the screen just as H. L. Hunt threw his drink at the TV. A waiter, standing silent in the corner, seemed relieved he missed.

Murchison leaned towards the other mega wealthy oil man. "Word was passed to me from the Agency."

Hunt nodded. "Me too."

"And?"

"It's not up to us."

Murchison paused a second, nodded, then added. "Does he know?"

Hunt nodded.

"You really think he will go along?"

Hunt looked over to Murchison. "Henry Luce… you know him?"

"Owns Time, Fortune, and Life magazines."

"The managing editor running Life told him Robert Kennedy is feeding information to a reporter named Holland McComb about Lyndon."

"What?"

"I asked Edgar to confirm, and he did. He said McComb is

concentrating on Estes and Baker, trying to tie them and Lyndon to Giancana and Trafficante."

"That could be a real problem for us too."

Hunt waved him off. "Luce said the editor is looking to do a cover story in November. He also said he will stall it, maybe October even November, but if Life doesn't publish, the reporter will just walk it to the newspapers. You know Ben Bradlee at the Post is like another brother to Jack. He'd run with this in a heartbeat."

"Does the reporter have the story?"

"Luce said yes and it's so devastating that Kennedy will have everything he needs to take Lyndon off the ticket… maybe worse."

Murchison paused, looked at his shoes, then tapped his cane. "You didn't answer my question. Will Lyndon go along? The aftermath needs to be controlled."

"No. It shouldn't be controlled."

"What… why?'

"Confusion, misdirection, and controversy are essential."

"But, again… will he go along?"

"It's not up to him." Hunt started to get up. "And it's not up to us… to start it, or stop it." He pointed to the TV that had a camera on the President shaking hands with the gathered crowd.

"That man has a lot of enemies."

CHAPTER 37
NOVEMBER 21, 1963

MAC WALKED twelve blocks from the Baker Hotel to Griggs Park. The plane ride to Dallas had lasted five bumpy hours and he hadn't recovered, but the walk was helping. His mood was good, relaxed and his gait was brisk. The bellman had told him it was about a twenty-minute walk, but he'd done it in fifteen. The meeting was at six o'clock, and he wasn't late. In fact, he would be half an hour early. Dallas wasn't completely unknown to him, but he hadn't been to this park before and he wanted the lay of the land.

He'd come into the park from the south entrance, and now stood looking at a map posted on a wooden bulletin board. Griggs was elliptical in shape, had a six-lane highway bordering one side, industrial buildings secured with tall fences along the other, and three access points: top, middle, and where he stood. The map located the principal feature of the park, and the base-ball field where he was to meet Cliff Carter.

He'd passed only two people walking dogs on his way to the field, he'd expected more. He assumed, because it was surrounded by businesses, it would have been more popular at lunchtime. The park was wide open, with very few trees. However, it had a great view of the Dallas skyline. He came up on the field, walked past a concession stand, and entered onto the field between the dugout and the backstop. The field was well-kept, with close cut grass, and had remnants of chalked lines from a recent game. It was empty, no team was practicing, and no father and son duos were playing catch. He walked up the steps of the metal stands along first base and sat on the top row. From there he had a clear view of the park and all three entrances. It was late afternoon, and the Texas sun was still up, but low on the horizon. It was cool and calm with just an occasional whiff of fresh cut grass on a gentle breeze. It reminded him of his playing days, when, after practice, tired and sore, he felt he'd accomplished something. The end of the day then was a far cry from the sun setting today.

He hadn't heard from Carter for almost six months, not since he'd been arrested for the DUI. He hadn't talked to Edward Clark in more than a year. So, neither knew he'd stopped drinking. It was the hardest thing he'd ever done. He struggled every day, with no help, because his new wife took the baby and moved back to her parents. Her leaving was definitely for the best, the marriage of convenience never really had a chance. Every day that he white-knuckled his recovery gave him a little bit more clarity. He accepted responsibility for failing Andre, for falling victim to his ambition, and finally facing the truth of how he so totally fucked up his life. His last realization was he wasn't done yet.

In the distance, Mac saw a man with no dog approaching the field. He was tall, wore a long dark coat, had short black hair, and was definitely not Cliff Carter. Mac glanced north, then south, and saw two men of similar ilk, positioned near the other entrances. The man in the long coat disappeared for a moment, then came out from behind the backstop, and walked across the field to the stands.

This can't be good.

The man stopped, glanced up at Mac, and checked his flank before ascending.

CIA… FBI?

Trench Coat sat down near Mac, just out of arms reach. Looking forward, he spoke in a low voice. "A friend of ours has a problem and wants your help."

"Our friend? Who is that?"

His head whipped around and he glared at Mac. "Don't be stupid. Carter told us you'd cooperate. Was he wrong?"

Mac shrugged, a little scared, but feeling defiant. "Depends."

The man studied Mac's face. "This isn't a discussion. You have two options."

"Do what you want… or not?" Mac used sarcasm to fight being a little scared, elevating to full on panic.

"One of those is correct." The man's eyes were dark, face white, and his stare terrifying.

Mac lost the attitude. "What do I have to do?"

Trench Coat looked forward again. "Tonight, we need you to deliver instructions to a man, and tell him that everything is on track. Then tomorrow, pick him up at work, and deliver him to an address in Dallas."

Mac nodded, then said quickly, "Sounds simple enough, but before we get to the who, what, where thing…why me?"

"Cliff Carter told us you are smart, reliable, and that you can be very convincing."

"Bullshit."

The man didn't flinch. "He said that you can keep him on track."

"On track? What does, on track, mean?"

Trench Coat looked at Mac like he was deciding what to do next. "The man has been groomed for a task that will change the course of our country. It has taken months to set up, and he is now in a position to complete the assignment."

"However?"

"There is no however. We need to make contact, tonight as scheduled. We need someone not affiliated with any... of our associates, to deliver instructions." He hesitated, "And, tomorrow, give him a ride to a pickup point."

"Again... that's bullshit. I don't think I'm the only man on the face of the fucking earth that can do this... favor."

Trench Coat repeated himself. "Cliff Carter said you were the man for the job. You complete assignments, and don't ask why." He pointed at Mac. "Now, I'm telling you... don't ask why."

Mac slapped both hands on his knees, and stood up. "Well then, cowboy, he told you wrong. If you don't tell me why, I'm gone."

The man chuckled and shook his head. "No."

"Okay, bye, bye." Mac only got two steps down.

The man spoke low and slow. "There are two ways for you to leave here."

The wave of panic returned. Mac froze on the step. He put on the toughest face he could muster, and whipped around. "I'll ask one more time, why?"

The man looked at him for a long minute then chose. "Sit."

Mac obliged. He sat, but two rows away.

"The people you work with are about to be exposed in an investigation that will affect not only them, but also the men who put them in power. That can't happen. Cliff Carter asked you to do a favor that will protect not only them, but the people I work for as well."

"You mean Clint—"

"No names." Trench Coat quickly cut Mac off. "You know who I'm talking about. But it's not just them, and the investigation is not the only reason why this is going to happen. People of power have come together to change things."

Mac said nothing for a full minute. "I don't think I heard a reason why I am the only one available to carry this message?"

"You're not the only one, and I don't think this is a good idea. I think you are the worst possible choice, and you will definitely fuck this up."

"So do I." Mac looked down, thought for a second, then looked up. "But you still haven't answered the question... why me?"

The man's voice got hard and he pointed a finger at Mac's chest. "Because, my people are worried that your people will turn on them after the fact. My people want your people to have skin in the game."

"And I'm the skin?"

"Correct. You're their guy, so now, nobody can plead ignorance. Everybody's in."

"And this man, the one I'm to meet to give assurance and instruction? Is he somebody's guy?"

"No, far from it. He is just part of an illusion." He looked up. "Illusion is confusion."

"And that makes him...?"

The man shrugged. "Expendable."

Mac looked straight ahead.

Trench Coat got mean. "So... now you know why. You need to make a choice right here and right now. Will you do what is asked?"

The look on the man's face made Mac realize he was also non-essential personnel. He exhaled a long breath and nodded.

"His name is Lee Oswald. He is staying in a rooming house in south Dallas. He knows that someone will pick him up tonight, and take him to see his wife. She and their kids live with a couple about twenty minutes north. The couple and the wife are not involved. The wife is Russian and barely speaks English. The couple is some executive from Bell Helicopter, and his wife."

That got Mac's attention but he just continued to listen.

"Oswald will be waiting at the entrance of North Creek

Park at six o'clock." He looked at his watch. "That's two hours from now. He's 24, 5'9", and about 140 lbs. He'll be wearing a light-colored jacket. On the ride, you tell him that tomorrow you'll be parked outside where he works, the Texas School Book Depository, at noon. Tell him, when he comes out of the building, you're going to take him here." He drew a small purple ticket from his pocket that had Texas Theater printed across the top. "It's a movie house. Tell him, he should go inside and wait. As soon as its safe, we'll come get him, and take him to the port in Houston, where he'll board a boat to Cuba."

"Cuba?" That was a surprise.

The man looked straight ahead. "He knows about that, and thinks he'll be a god when he gets there."

Mac looked quizzical, but didn't take it further. "So… why did you wait till now to arrange for this ride?"

"I didn't and I told you, I didn't think this was a smart move. But I don't make decisions, I just do what I'm told." He pointed his finger at Mac's chest again. "Just like you need to do right now. Do what you're told. Got it?"

Mac was facing Trench Coat and, when he turned around, he saw that the two men who were at the park exits were now standing at the bottom of the stands.

"There are two ways out of here." Trench Coat's voice was low. "Pick one."

Mac slowed the car and pulled to the curb unseen by the man in the light jacket. Mac sat patiently watching the entrance to the park, and both sides of the street, looking for anyone else who might have an interest in this man. Mac lit a cigarette. The man was shifting around, his head bobbing back and forth, nervously looking up and down the street. He was not being very cautious and looked exactly like someone who was waiting for a ride.

Satisfied, he tossed the butt out the window, drove up to the entrance of the park, and stopped on the curb in front of Lee Oswald.

The man in the light-colored jacket took a few steps, and peered into the open passenger-side window. "You my ride?"

Mac waved his hand. "Get in." He did and Mac pulled away. "Where we headed?"

Oswald pointed straight ahead. "Irving, 2515 west 5th Street. Not that far. Do you know where that is?"

"I know where Irving is. I take the boulevard north, right?"

"Yep. Straight ahead."

A few minutes passed by and both men remained silent.

Mac glanced over. Oswald was drumming his fingers on his knee but seemed calm. "You live out here?"

"No. The wife does. I live in a rooming house back in Dallas."

"Oh." Mac let his silence ask why.

"We've been fighting." Oswald looked out the side window. "I was asked to leave."

"Sorry."

"Don't be. It was a mistake from the beginning. She's nice and all. A good person really, but she's a fish out of water. Get me?"

"Out of water."

"Right." His words were excited and rapid fire. "This is my time now, and I can't be dragging her around with me. You know what I'm talking about. Besides… they told me, if I want, they'll get her to me later on. I mean after it all calms down… you know?"

"Calm's down."

"Right. It's all set. I got a ride into work tomorrow and," he got excited again, "I'm all set for noon—"

"Noon."

"Right. It's all set up on the sixth floor. I got it done this afternoon when nobody was around. It's perfect."

"Sixth floor."

"Right. I take the shot when the car moves toward the overpass." He put his hand up. "Don't remind me again. I've been told a hundred times, don't shoot when it's coming toward me on Houston."

"Not on Houston."

"Right." He grinned a little. "I'm pretty good but if the shot goes high, it might ricochet and hit the cars behind."

"And hit—?"

Oswald screwed up his face. "Johnson."

"Right."

Oswald went back to looking out the window.

"Tomorrow, I'll be parked in this car on Houston. I'm to take you here." He handed Oswald the ticket to the movie. "Someone else will come and take you to the boat and—"

"Cuba." He grinned again. "Finally, I can do what I want, when I want... and I'll be a fuckin' hero."

Mac drove with his fingers white from gripping the wheel.

"Hey, are you picking up the other guy too?"

Mac turned and looked at him, trying his best to keep a straight face. "No. That must be someone else."

Oswald paused a second then said softly. "I hope they don't send him to Cuba too."

Mac didn't speak again until they got to 5th Street. "Outside, on the curb, this car, noon."

Oswald pulled his hand up and pretended to shoot with a finger. "Right."

Mac pulled away and headed back to Dallas.

They're going to kill the President.

His horror show was blowing up in his face. His stomach turned and he yanked the car to the curb, throwing up almost before he got the door open. He put the car in park and rolled out, laying on somebody's front lawn. He laid on his back looking up at the stars.

I can't stop it. At least two shooters.

He thought about making an anonymous tip which, no doubt, would be one of a hundred. If he gave the police a name or a place, the trench coat and his people would know it was him. And it wouldn't stop it. There's a second gun.

He lay there a while. Rerunning everything in his head. He went back to the beginning, replaying his life…Andre… Josefa. He thought about what he'd done and why he was where he was right now.

Simplifying provided an answer. He was useful to them in the beginning because he did little things, they needed to help them get where they wanted to be. They haven't asked for a favor in a year because they didn't need him anymore. Until now. But there was no future. Nothing ahead. They no longer needed an accountant.

Oswald is expendable… and so am I.

His focus changed. He wasn't thinking of the past anymore. He needed a plan.

What do I have and what do they need?

He sat up.

Top Secret and Sixth Floor.

CHAPTER 38

NOVEMBER 22, 1963

THE *DALLAS MORNING News* headline read *Storm of Political Controversy Swirls around Kennedy on Visit;* A subhead read *Split State Party Continues Feud.* Mac breezed through the articles – Johnson did this, and Connelly did that. A story about the current Texas Senator and the Vice President gained a below-the-fold headline. It read *Yarbrough snubs LBJ.* Mac had been in California for a long time, but the political gamesmanship in Texas hadn't changed a lick.

Another headline, further down the page, read *Love Field Braces for Thousands.* The articles surrounded a map of the route of the Presidential motorcade. Police were expecting crowds, not only at the airport, but also all along the route through down-town. Mac folded the paper and looked up and down the street, acting as if he were waiting for a bus. He was leaning on the brick of a building, on the corner of Houston and Elm Streets. The brick wall was directly across from the Texas School Book Depository but he wasn't waiting for a bus. He was waiting for Lee Harvey Oswald.

From this position, the front door and loading dock entrance were both visible. Everyone coming into or out of the building had to pass through one of those two doors. Mac looked at his watch: 11:30. Mac stood up straight and stretched. He started walking and saw a poster stapled onto a telephone pole next to a waste can. It had a picture of John F. Kennedy in the center and WANTED FOR TREASON printed in heavy black letters across the top. Mac threw his newspaper in the can.

He walked on the east side of Houston toward the loading dock then stood, again as if he were looking for the next bus. Mac continued north, past the building then crossed the road and walked around back to where the building intersected with a railroad yard. There was no movement, no running trains or people, just dust and stationary box cars. He continued on, past the back of the Depository, and stopped at a white fence that bordered Elm Street. The wood pickets blocked the way down to the road. The hill on the other side of the fence was high ground, shaded by live oaks. He rested both arms on top of the fence and thought people would gather on the hill to watch as the President drove past.

He looked at his watch: 11:45. He walked back across the train tracks, past the back of the building and out onto Houston Street. He headed South to Elm and, as he arrived, three black vans slid to the curb. A troop of men, three with dogs, got out. The Secret Service arrived in advance of the motorcade.

He hadn't had much sleep but he wasn't tired. Adrenalin was fueling his body along with a breakfast of ham, eggs, and real grits. He had savored the true Southern cooking and somehow, even knowing what was going to happen, he was calm.

He'd done what he needed to do last night after he returned to Dallas. It was even easier than he thought it would be, security in the Depository was non-existent. He had every confidence in his plan. No one would see it coming. They wouldn't have a clue until long after he was back in California, eating their horrible, healthy food. They wouldn't see it because in every battle plan, no matter how efficient or proficient— there is always an unanticipated factor and Mac Wallace was the wild card.

Unless, of course, he was wrong.

A stream of people flowed behind spectators that were now standing three deep at the curb. Mac moved off the wall and got into the flow, wandering slowly, appearing not to be in any particular hurry. It was now 12:06. He was back on the corner of Houston and Elm; the Depository was in front of him.

He looked up. The east window on the sixth floor was open about half way.

The voices of the people got louder as if a wave were approaching from a distance. Police had moved into the street and were standing in front of the crowd, but they too were looking for the motorcade.

Mac looked down Elm, looked up at the fence, looked at the open windows on the office buildings surrounding Dealey Plaza.

It's a turkey shoot.

A pair of motorcycles, with lights flashing, turned off Main Street onto Houston.

People started cheering and yelling "Jackie."

Two more motorcycles preceded the Lincoln. There was her pink suit — hands were waving as the convertible approached.

Mac was thirty feet away when the Presidential motorcade made its final turn.

He saw JFK brush his hair back off his forehead, then smile.

Ten seconds later there was a crack.

Five more seconds passed. A louder bang echoed around the Plaza.

The crowd stopped waving. Heads were turning. A woman near Mac screamed. More sounds.

Mac caught a puff of grey rising from behind the white picket fence.

Four seconds later, the President was dead.

People fell to the ground. Engines roared. There was more screaming. An officer dropped his motorcycle on its side and ran up the hill. Parents pushed their children to the ground and covered them with their bodies.

Some people were just standing, frozen, watching in a daze.

It was chaos.

The motorcade disappeared under the overpass. The car carrying the soon-to-be President of the United States followed close behind the bloody Lincoln Continental convertible.

Mac stood still, his back against the building.

The crowd was running in different directions. The police, not knowing where to go, stood pointing guns in every direction. Reporters jumped from cars in what was left of the motorcade and were jamming into storefronts looking for a working phone.

Mac's eyes were fixed on the loading dock exit.

Time was ticking slowly and, for a second, Mac thought maybe he didn't see Oswald leave. Maybe something unexpected happened, and Oswald wasn't going to come out of the building looking for a non-existent blue Ford.

His watch read: 12:38. Nine minutes since the first shot.

Then suddenly, there he was. He wore the same light-colored jacket. Oswald hurried down the loading dock steps, and out onto the sidewalk. He crossed to the other side of Houston, his head swiveling back and forth, searching for the blue Ford. He ran a few steps west. Stopped. Reversed his course, stopped, stood still, then threw his hands out in frustration. He mouthed something that Mac was much too far away to hear.

Mac's eyes stayed glued on Oswald who started walking north on Elm Street, away from the Plaza. Oswald attempted to mix in with some of the crowd fleeing the scene. He moved with the group going up Elm Street, away from the plaza, but when the crowd thinned, he picked up his pace.

Mac was on the other side of the street, staying about a half a block behind.

Seven blocks from the Depository, Oswald got onto a bus that had stopped for passengers.

Mac watched the bus drive slowly away.

Where Oswald was headed was of great interest to Mac, but he didn't quicken his step or look for a cab to follow. All the early morning wandering he'd done was paying off. He knew exactly where he was, and he headed east at the next block. His hotel and the blue Ford were a block away.

He also didn't have to hurry because he knew where Oswald was going.

When he reached his rental car, Mac pulled a street map from the glove compartment. Oswald's bus was headed southwest of Dealey Plaza and, naturally, traffic would be slow. He would have ample time to arrive before Lee Harvey Oswald reached the Theater.

Mac drove north, away from all the commotion. He made a wide loop, and eventually the heavy traffic cleared. He had taken a longer route but he got to Jefferson Boulevard confident he'd arrived in time. He parked on the street, then walked toward a neighborhood barbershop where, outside on the sidewalk, there was an old-fashioned shoeshine stand. It could not have been possible to find a spot that was more suitable to watch the show Mac knew was about to happen.

"Shine sir?"

"Indeed. Please." Mac climbed up two steps to the chair and put his feet on the two copper foot stands.

Perfect.

A black man dressed in a pressed white jacket sat on his well-worn stool and flipped open his shine box.

Mac folded his fingers in his lap.

The man looked up at his customer. His face was drawn, his eyes teared and sad. "The Lord took a great man from us today."

"I heard about the shooting. He's dead then?"

"Yes sir, they just announced it on the radio. Yes sir… a great man." He ducked his head, hiding his face.

Mac didn't respond, he just kept his focus on the building across the street.

The man in the white coat put polish crème on both shoes then proceeded to buff them. His head shifted back and forth; his face grimaced.

Mac looked down and saw a tear running down his cheek.

Suddenly, a police car pulled up to the Texas Theater across the street. Lights were on but there was no siren. Two officers got out and meandered to the ticket window. However, before they got there, the street exploded like the troops landing at Normandy. More police cars roared down the street, sirens blaring, horns blowing, some sliding to a stop. Uniforms burst out and ran into the theater, guns out and held high.

"I wonder what that's about?" Mac speculated, but he already knew.

A woman pulling a hand cart weaved through the cars and came up on the shoeshine man. "Lord, look what's going on, Alfred."

The man said, "Loretta, what's that all about?"

"I don't know, really." She shook her head. "Mable… the ticket girl… well, she saw a man go in without paying for a ticket. But then I heard one of the police say that man matched up to a man killed a policeman up on 10th street. I just don't know… I mean, the man just didn't pay for the movie."

"Uh ah. But maybe it be something else." The man had

stopped mid-shine, and stood staring at the feature performance happening across the street outside the Texas Theater.

Mac looked at his watch: 1:46.

Sixty-six minutes since the first shot.

The man turned and looked at Mac with a questioning face. "You think that's the man who did that terrible thing?" His voice trailed off.

Mac shrugged. "Could be."

"But then... how did they know he was there?"

Mac pointed a finger. "Sir, now that is a good question."

A few minutes later Lee Harvey Oswald emerged from the theater, in handcuffs, flanked by four uniforms.

Confusion is illusion.

The man who undoubtably killed the President of the United States was in custody.

CHAPTER 39

NOVEMBER 26, 1963

IT WAS TUESDAY MORNING, the day after John F. Kennedy's funeral, and the world was going back to work. Time had suddenly stood still three days before, work stopped, schools closed, and people all over the world waited for the next bit of news. Newspapers, radio, and television were the connection to millions quietly waiting for something, anything, that might give them answers. A crack of sound in Dallas on Friday afternoon became a roar of constant noise, which ended on Monday with the methodical rhythm of funeral parade drums and the heartbreaking sight of a boy saluting his father's casket.

The unfathomable events of the past three days were no longer being broadcast. The barricades along the route of the funeral procession were being disassembled. Street cleaners were busy collecting trash left by over a million people. They had crowded on the streets to watch a horse-drawn caisson, laden with the President's coffin, travel five miles to Arlington Cemetery.

Lyndon Johnson awoke at his home in Forest Hills knowing today, the first working day of his Presidency, would be the last day he and Bird would be in their Washington home. Tonight, they would sleep at the White House. Johnson sat at the kitchen table, dressed and ready for work, drinking coffee and reading the *New York Times*. Every article was about either, the assassination on Friday, the murder of Lee Harvey Oswald on Sunday, or yesterday's unprecedented funeral. There was little coverage of the new President. Page three had a brief article about his taking the oath of office, and his short speech when Air Force One returned to Washington. He wasn't surprised; a little disappointed, but not surprised. He'd hoped for at least page two. He'd made a conscious effort to stay in the background, standing behind Jackie and Bobby, looking sad, but still Presidential. The world needed to see that the new President of the United States was fully capable of taking over as the most powerful man in the world.

Every wrong move, incorrect gesture, would be studied by cameras broadcasting to the entire world. He couldn't make a single wrong move, not one. He wasn't the lead but he was a featured player in the first, continuous, live-broadcast in American TV history. According to the *New York Times* article he was reading, almost ninety percent of homes that had a TV watched from when Walter Cronkite broke in on *As The World Turns* through the funeral procession to Arlington Cemetery, three days later.

He'd never upstaged anyone, never exercised the power of his new office to any of the two hundred and twenty dignitaries from ninety-two countries. He made no statements to the press, and his public image at home, and international persona, was perfect.

Satisfied, he tossed the paper to an empty chair, and finished his coffee. Three limousines waited outside. Since Friday's total failure, the Secret Service were omnipresent, two inside, four between the house and the car, and six more in the cars, all travelling with him to his office at the Eisenhower Executive Office

Building. They, like many, weren't convinced the assassination wasn't a first strike. The military remained on high alert, the FBI and CIA were working twenty-four-hour days, and the Secret Service had doubled normal protection.

Everybody was worried. The new President was not.

LBJ was riding in the Presidential limousine, the American flag on one fender, the Presidential seal on the other. Traffic was halted and police were at every intersection. The destination, however, wasn't the White House and the Oval Office. Until Jackie and the kids left for Hyannis Port, Johnson decided to conduct business from his Vice-Presidential office in the Eisenhower Executive Office Building. His day would be very hectic, every minute scheduled. Meetings were set by order of importance, and the first meeting was with the Joint Chiefs. It would establish him as the Commander in Chief, clarify his position on defense, and satisfy the concerns of the entire military industrial complex.

He gazed out the window, and as the motorcade passed the Jefferson Memorial the boy inside of him, the one who woke every morning on an old torn mattress, put on pants that were too big and a shirt that was too small, smiled.

The clock, hanging on the wall opposite his desk, indicated he was twelve minutes late for his meeting. He'd been on the phone talking non-stop but was well aware he was keeping very important men waiting. Johnson stood up, scratched, and leisurely put on his suit coat. He took a step to leave, and a Secret Service agent immediately opened the door.

He was walked down the corridor to room 208, the EEOB conference room. Waiting for him were the Joint Chiefs who were not accustomed to meeting anywhere but the White

House. A makeshift seating order had been arranged by LBJ's staff and had the Chairman of the Joint Chiefs, Army General Maxwell Turner, sitting in the center of one side of the conference table. On his right was the Vice Chair, Air Force General Curtis E. LeMay. Admiral Anderson represented the Navy, and the Comandante of the Marines, Shoute, flanked their positions. Turner was Chairman, but the voice of the Chiefs was LeMay. His voice was the loudest, most demanding. He also held radically different views of world politics than the now deceased former President.

The men, to the man, were soldiers and patriots, and they were also the predominate experts in matters of war. They met regularly discussing positions and policy and often disagreed. However, the decisions reached, when made public, were always unanimous. Any dissenting votes were heard in their private meetings but decisions always sided with the Vice Chairman, a hawk and devoted anti-communist.

The door burst open and the officers stood like first lieutenants, snapping to attention.

Johnson let them stand. He didn't say, 'Don't get up, or please sit,' he let them remain fixed and facing forward. When he took his seat, across from the chief, the men in uniform sat.

Curtis LeMay remained standing a bit longer than the rest, looking offended by the new President's first power move.

LBJ saw it and catalogued LeMay's small act of defiance.

No one spoke.

Johnson looked at the men one at a time, focusing on them, studying their faces. His stare was uncomfortable for men in their positions, men who were used to exerting power, and never subjected to this kind of close order scrutiny.

LBJ finished his inspection, then broke the silence, speaking slowly and calmly like he was addressing a TV audience. "Gentlemen, we have a great challenge ahead of us. The world changed on Friday, and your President, and you, the joint chiefs, who represent the most powerful military force in the world, must do everything in our power to guide this country to peace."

LeMay immediately got red-faced. His body twitched at the word, "peace". The other joint chiefs, including the chairman, appeared more patient.

"You know that as Vice President, I did not attend the strategy sessions you held with President Kennedy. You also know I did not participate in many of the decisions made by the President. You also know that in my role as Vice President, I supported President Kennedy in all of his policies."

LBJ had to look down for a second to suppress a grin. He had noticed LeMay was ready to pop a blood vessel. "Until today, this group has not heard my views on our situation in the world, and what I believe to be the dangers that threaten... world peace." He said the word one more time, just for fun.

LeMay's hands knuckled.

"Gentlemen, I have read the briefs from recent meetings of the Chiefs and I know there are many subjects that need discussion, but one of them needs action now, and is the reason I called this special meeting." He paused for effect. "The most pressing issue on my agenda is to finalize National Security Memo 273."

He had their full attention.

"I'm going to suggest changes to what has been drafted." He paused a second. "Gentlemen, I do not share President Kennedy's view of the ability of the United States to combat the threat of a communist takeover of the Republic of Vietnam."

LeMay exhaled, the sigh audible.

"My position on 273 is this: I will not allow Vietnam to fall into the hands of a communist regime."

LBJ removed a copy of the memo from his jacket pocket. He laid it flat, then slid the memo to the Chairman. The document was face up and had LBJ's handwritten notes, reversing the withdraw of troops from Vietnam were visible to all.

"I was aware of President Kennedy's desire to remove our military advisors from Southeast Asia immediately after next year's election. I also know this body did not agree with the former President's position on using our military power to help stabilize legitimate governments being threatened by our enemies."

LeMay spoke low, but loud enough to be heard. "He was a plywood patrol boat captain."

LBJ didn't flinch. "I recognize your expertise, and your commitment to the safety and security of our country."

LeMay unclenched and started nodding agreement.

Johnson then leaned forward. "I know some of you had difficulties with the previous administration's instructions. Some of you may have let those... hesitations, influence your response in administering the orders given by the President." He stood up. "From this day on, once a decision by the President is ordered... you will execute... immediately... and without question."

He looked around the room, again slowly, face-by-face, making them uncomfortable.

CHAPTER 40

DECEMBER, 1964

EDWARD CLARK HAD BEEN MAINTAINING distance from the President for almost two years, retreating to his law practice in Austin. He couldn't remove himself completely from Johnson's life, the past made that impossible. They'd agreed to wind down the business outside of politics. There was the possibility of exposure from Estes and Baker, but in reality, the foundation of LBJ's financial independence had been built. Johnson had gone from poverty to one of the richest Presidents in history. Clark rode the money train and would also never have to worry about money. He'd stayed away but some of the subjects he needed to discuss now could never take place in the White House or even in Washington. The only safe haven was Johnson City and the ranch.

"Lady Bird, it is always my great pleasure to see you." Clark smiled his hundred dollar an hour smile and shook hands with the First Lady.

"Where have you been hiding, you rascal." She had taken his hand but pulled him close, insisting on a cheek kiss.

"How is the President?"

"Oh, Edward, you know him, he's working much too hard. Always on the go."

"Saving the free world."

"Ed." LBJ burst through the front door. He was covered with Texas dust but had a smile and seemed genuinely happy to see his attorney.

"Mr. President."

They shook hands— the memories of old exchanged in a flash.

"Bird, I'm gonna' take Clark for a ride but we'll be back in time for the barbeque."

She pointed a finger. "You'd better be."

Clark knew he'd be dragged out for a ride in the Lincoln and, as so many times before, he dreaded the prospect. Together, they exited through the front door, went down the wooden steps onto the stone driveway. The waiting car, covered with dust and dirt from a previous jaunt, was parked right in front. Clark grimaced as he wiped the dirt off the passenger seat with a handkerchief. He shook his head because he should have known better than to wear a suit. It wouldn't be the first he would ruin on an LBJ ranch tour.

The six Secret Service agents stationed in various locations were easy to identify, because they were the only men in Texas who'd wear black suits in the Texas sun. LBJ got in the driver side of the Lincoln convertible and the suits clown-loaded into a four-door sedan to follow.

Before LBJ turned the key, he looked at Clark. "I know you didn't drive out here for another tour of the ranch. Is it serious?"

Clark nodded.

Johnson set his hat firm, and hit the gas.

They bounced along about a mile or so, conversation not possible, finally stopping in a clearing near a big pond. The President and his lawyer got out and started walking toward the water's edge. Four suits deployed up and down the dirt road and two suits followed close behind. LBJ waved them back. They obeyed and, when they were out of earshot, he nodded at Clark.

Clark looked down, anticipating a bad reaction. "I found out Bobby Kennedy was feeding information to the federal investigators about Bobby Baker's connection to Clint Murchison, and General Dynamics on the defense contract for the F-111. Lyndon, it's a seven-billion-dollar contract, and Kennedy was trying to tie you, Murchison, and Baker to a kickback scheme."

"Does Clint know?"

"For months. He didn't tell you?"

"No… we haven't had any contact since…" He didn't finish.

"When Kennedy resigned in September that investigation stopped, but the IRS is looking at Baker for tax evasion and fraud. They're slow and it will take a while, but in a year, maybe eighteen months, they'll indict. My guess is Bobby will plead guilty for a lighter sentence."

"What about Estes?"

"A little tougher there. As you know, he got twenty-four years on a twenty-seven-count indictment, but his appeal looks good, and that should cut the sentence in half. Estes is quiet… still not talking."

"You wouldn't drive out here just for this… what else?"

Clark dug in. "The response about the Warren Report has been about as expected. Polls show it was a relief to most but there is a growing number of private investigations looking into Russia, Cuba, the Mob, even the CIA has been thrown into the mix. Some of them are credible."

LBJ picked up a stone and tossed it into the lake. "Like you said, it was expected."

"You're not concerned?"

"Someone once told me that 'confusion is the best illusion.'"

Clark had his head down.

LBJ leaned in. "Clark, what else? I haven't seen you for months and suddenly you have to meet face-to-face."

"I received disturbing information when I was at the races last week at Pimlico."

"Edgar?"

Clark nodded, then grinned. "By the way, making Hoover FBI Director for life was a very smart move."

"That wasn't a choice." Johnson waved him off. "What did he tell you?"

Clark looked straight ahead. "There is a fingerprint from the sixth floor that could be a problem."

LBJ turned, faced the water, and waited.

"A print of a little finger was found on a box in the sniper's nest. Every other print was identified by printing the employees or finding them available within the usual law enforcement files. However, this one print remains a mystery. Edgar said it's because the person who left it has top secret clearance, so fingerprints, like everything else, are not available to anyone, ever. Only a very few people have access to those files. Obviously, Edgar is one of them."

LBJ looked pale.

"It belongs to the man from California." Clark started to talk fast. "Somehow, he got into the sixth floor and left one print, the little finger on a left hand. One has to ask oneself how is it possible that he left no other prints... anywhere. Just that one little finger. I think it is possible he did it on purpose."

Johnson shook his head in disbelief. "Why would anyone knowingly leave something that would identify themselves, especially there, in that place. No... that's impossible. I don't believe that."

"I think he did it because he knew we would never let it be associated with him. It's still listed as unidentified, and will stay that way as long as Wallace's prints remain classified top secret.

No investigating entity, public or private, will have access. So, it's not an issue… right now."

"Can it be destroyed?"

"No. Not possible. It's already catalogued and published in the Warren Report."

Johnson stopped and looked at Clark. "Did he?"

"No… no. Wallace was there because Cliff was asked for a favor for our friends. All Wallace was supposed to do was pick Oswald up and drop him off. His contact was limited and there was absolutely no reason for him to be anywhere near the sixth floor." He paused. "Lyndon, I think it is insurance."

"I don't get that. Explain?" Johnson's voice got loud.

"I've had a week to think about this. Remember, Wallace is a really smart guy, smart enough to get a doctorate. He did a lot for us in the beginning. I know because I was there. But his problem has always been that he's a drunk." He and LBJ started to walk. "Consider this: the fingerprint puts him on the sixth floor, at the window where Oswald took the shot. Wallace was also convicted of murder, a conviction from which he walked away. There has always been rumors that we had a hand in that verdict. With the controversy about the Warren Report, if his fingerprint shows up in that location, there will be a firestorm and you will be front and center." He paused a second, thinking. "What did you say earlier… confusion is illusion… if that print is identified, your Presidency will be over."

"Was that it, just the print?"

Clark shook his head. "No. The FBI collected every photograph they could by anyone who had a camera. Bill Beal, a photographer from the *Times Herald,* naturally took hundreds of photos in Dallas. One of the random shots he took was of Malcolm Wallace standing in front of the Baker Hotel. Wallace's name is on the register which puts him in Dallas on the 21st through the 22nd."

Johnson gripped Clark's arm. "Jesus Christ, he set us up."

Clark nodded. "I think so."

"What if something happens to—."

"No…Can't happen. The press is already reporting that thirteen witnesses have died under mysterious circumstances since the assassination, not including Oswald. The *London Times* calculated the odds of that happening to be astronomical. We have to keep in mind that as long as his classification stays, he's anonymous. And—"

"And what?"

"And we would be foolish not to consider, if he was smart enough to pull this off, what do you think will happen if he is taken out?"

Johnson stayed quiet but kept walking. He picked up another stone and tossed it. "Clark, I don't… I mean we didn't…" He kicked the dirt, then exhaled a long breath. "Kennedy made a lot of enemies. Nobody could have stopped it."

"Cliff was asked for a favor. He didn't know they wanted us tied to it. It was a ride. All Wallace was supposed to do was pick someone up and drop him off."

They walked in silence for a while. When the sun proved too much, they headed back to the Lincoln.

LBJ got in the driver's seat. "He's a pretty smart guy."

"He was totally unexpected."

The car started.

"Lyndon."

Johnson turned to face his attorney.

"I came here out of loyalty to you. But this is the last time. I want out. I want far away from any inquiries, any investigations, anything that might put me in a spot where I would have to testify under oath."

LBJ grinned. "How does Ambassador to Australia sound? Far enough?"

Clark looked forward. "That'll do."

CHAPTER 41

HIS BLOOD PRESSURE was very high. The white house physician who had his stethoscope on LBJ's arm knew better than to speak, but his head shaking was ill received.

Johnson had a phone in his free hand. "I don't care what he says. You tell him that the President of the United States is telling him to get it done." He slammed the phone into the receiver, then tried to yank his arm from the doctor's grip. However, the physician was holding it with both hands.

"I need a pulse, Mr. President."

"I have one. Now get out, and leave me the fuck alone."

The doctor released his patient, waved both his hands in disgust, and packed up his equipment.

"Geraldine, who's next?"

LBJ's executive assistant yelled out from her desk in the outer office. "Chief of Staff, Army General Wheeler, and Joint Chief General McConnell are in the Cabinet Room."

His mood darkened immediately.

W. Marvin Watson had scheduled the meeting and he and

his boss knew it would be very difficult. "We've had a rough month Mr. President."

LBJ jumped to his feet. "Rough. It was hell. First, Cliff Carter resigns out of nowhere, McCarthy almost beats me in the primary, then Bobby decides to resurrect the Kennedy dynasty and announces he's gonna run against me. Now, these two generals waiting down the hall have to justify how the My Lai Massacre could have happened." The President rubbed his face. "My God, they killed over 500 men, women, and children... our boys... our troops." His voice trailed off and he plopped into his seat at the desk. A sudden sharp pain made him wince.

He opened the drawer and, with his hand inside the desk, found a prescription bottle. He popped the lid and removed a nitroglycerin tablet. He turned to the window and, unseen, slipped the pill under his tongue. He took a few long breaths, the tightness in his chest eased, and he began to feel better.

He stood up. "You go ahead, I'll be right there."

Watson nodded and left.

LBJ leaned his head back and looked up at the ceiling in the Oval Office.

"Mr. President."

He responded without moving. "What is it, Geraldine?"

"Mr. Murchison is on the phone. He's in D.C. and wants to meet you tonight. Shall I fit him into the schedule?"

"It just keeps getting worse and worse." LBJ ducked his chin to his chest. "Okay, but at his hotel. Not here."

The Willard Hotel resembled every other monument in D.C. It was old and built of stone and marble in a Neo-Classical style. Unlike the government buildings, this one didn't get the same care and had seen better days. In spite of its shortcomings, it remained the most exclusive hotel in D.C. and LBJ had gotten used to being summoned by Murchison whenever the oil giant felt it necessary to have a face-to-face with the leader of the free world.

It was after nine o'clock when the motorcade arrived. Three cars with flags flying came first, black suits frantically darting in and out of doors, alleys, and every shadow. LBJ had wanted low visibility. No press. No exposure, and nothing to explain, but that was not possible. A small crowd lined a secure entrance. Flash bulbs popped and questions were yelled out with no responses forthcoming. He was the President and was usually in complete control of every meeting but this was unexpected, and he hated the unexpected.

The suits that had cleared the front of the hotel moved to the tenth floor, examining and securing every room. They had security clearances on Murchison's body guards but the suits made them wait in the hall, outside of the meeting room.

Lyndon Johnson and Clint Murchison were now alone in a hotel room that had a slight odor of mold. They spared each other pleasantries and got down to business.

Murchison had a glass of bourbon next to his chair. He picked it up and jiggled the ice cubes. "You want one? It's a 40-year-old single malt."

LBJ, used to having what he wanted handed to him, rose to get his own. He didn't ask his host if he wanted a refill. He poured a glass then returned to a chair that was a little too small for him, and a little too delicate.

Murchison took a sip from his glass. "Smooth."

"What do you want, Clint?"

"Do you know who's on the top four floors of this hotel?"

LBJ's frustration showed on his face. "No. Who?"

"Nixon's election headquarters."

"Good for him." Johnson did show a little surprise.

"Do you know how he can afford offices in this hotel?"

LBJ's voice got louder and more annoyed. "I do not."

"Oil... Texas oil."

That stunned him.

"Lyndon, I'm gonna cut to the chase here. Our group has a lot of concerns."

LBJ reacted to the affront of his loyal allies throwing their support to an arch enemy. "I don't give a flying fuck what the 8F group thinks or does anymore. I'm the President of the United States and in fact... I have concerns about you." He was back peddling as fast as he could.

Murchison grew a small sly grin on a round fat face. "You need to hear me out. And for the record... I am speaking for the group."

Lyndon took a drink.

"From giddyup, we've backed you all the way."

"True, but I won in '64 with the largest popular vote in history, without anyone's help."

"That you did. That you did." Clint rattled the ice again. "But, there's not a chance that'll happen in '68. The war is a problem."

Lyndon objected. "You support the war. You want the war."

"True. Communism is our biggest threat." Clint held up his hand. "But... that's not the issue here. Not at all. It's your health."

"What?" Lyndon again was stunned by the unexpected.

"Everybody saw you pop that nitro tablet during the State of the Union."

Johnson's voice got calmer. "It's under control."

Clint veered. "Humphrey is VP. We hate Humphrey almost as much as we hated Kennedy. He's a liberal Democrat who will undo everything you've put in place for us."

"You just don't like my efforts in Civil Rights and Medicare."

"We don't give a shit about any of that nonsense. 8F, and others, are concerned that you will drop dead before your term ends and we'll get stuck with Hubert for the balance of your term, then eight more years."

LBJ shook his head. "Never happen."

Murchison fired right back. "Too big a risk."

There was a silence stalemate. Neither spoke.

Lyndon finished his drink and started to get up to leave.

Clint stopped LBJ in his tracks. "You're not going to run for re-election."

Lyndon's immediate reaction was to laugh, but when he realized it wasn't a joke, he stopped and turned. "You can't be serious."

"We are very serious. If you die, Humphrey will end the war. You're not going to run, and we are going to support Nixon. He's already onboard."

Lyndon stuttered. "What… about… Bobby?"

Clint shook his head dismissively. "We'll cross that bridge, if we get there. Either way, it's Nixon. He's business, he's oil, he's win with honor."

"Well just what the fuck am I? That's what I've been doing all along."

Murchison put his glass down. "You have, you've been all that. But… going the way you're going; you'll be dead in a year." He stood up. "We're supporting Nixon."

Lyndon watched as Murchison walked toward the door. He took a firm stance, then spoke loud and slow to Murchison's back. "I won't do it."

Clint turned, his cane holding him up straight. "You will, and you'll do it now. If you don't, we will ruin you." He pointed the cane. "We don't want to do it, but we will. We won't take the chance of you living out the term. Do what we tell you. Don't run."

He tapped on the door with his cane and it opened. His bodyguard grabbed his elbow and he disappeared into the hall.

March 31, 1968

LBJ held his speech in front of him, but he was reading it from the teleprompter. The red light went on in prime time, delaying the Wednesday Night Movie, and bumping The Beverly Hillbillies and Kraft Music Hall. Most of America had expected another boring speech from a boring speaker who had little to say that interested them. And they were right. Right up until the end.

He saw the last paragraphs begin to appear on the screen, and until that moment he hadn't decided to read them, or just skip to the end, and sign off.

"...*What we won when all of our people united must not now be lost in suspicion, and distrust, and selfishness, and politics among any of our people.*"

He gulped a short breath of air, then looked directly into the cameras.

"*And believing this as I do, I have concluded that I should not permit the Presidency to become involved in the partisan divisions that are developing in this political year.*

With America's sons in the fields far away, with America's future under challenge right here at home, with our hopes and the world's hopes for peace in the balance every day, I do not believe that I should devote an hour or a day of my time to any personal partisan causes or to any duties other than the awesome duties of this office— the Presidency of your country.

Accordingly, I shall not seek, and I will not accept, the nomination of my party for another term as your President.

But let men everywhere know, however, that a strong, and a confident, and a vigilant America stands ready tonight to seek an honorable peace– and stands ready tonight to defend an honored cause– whatever the price, whatever the burden, whatever the sacrifice that duty may require.

Thank you for listening.

Good night and God bless all of you.

It was all over.

CHAPTER 42

HE FELT at home for the first time in many, many years. It was the place where, once, the script for his life lay in front of him, and he had been turning the pages one at a time. It was when he walked the quad with Andre at his side, feeling taller, back straighter, chin higher. A place where football was king, but where he had ruled a different realm.

On any Saturday, back in the fall of 1944, the quarterback was the hero of the University of Texas. However, on any Monday, when the futures of the fans of the gridiron were being decided, Malcolm Wallace, Student Body President, was the man to know. He was the example that the physically normal followed, a man who'd reached the pinnacle of collegiate potential. He'd made it to the top, undergrad work complete, a master's in sight, and the girl of every boy's dream at his side. His paper chase was at its end, and the real world was beckoning.

However, his life after college hadn't followed script. No professor's advice would be sufficient to help guide his future into the waiting uncharted territory of deceit, deception, and lies. Looking back from here, now, at where it all began so many years ago, he could almost feel the force of the tide he had never envisioned. He was back where it began; his youth gone, his soul tainted, and his love deserted.

But he wasn't dead yet.

"Well, hello."

His attention was diverted from the past. "Good morning, Angela."

She had auburn hair, red lipstick, and rouged cheeks. "I got you coffee."

Someone dropped something and the crash echoed around the cafeteria. "Thanks." He sat down at her table, and picked up the cup. "I needed this."

"Long night?" She tilted her head and smiled.

"No, actually. Couldn't sleep."

"You can't still be having a time zone issue."

"Indeed." He took another sip.

"I had a bit of trouble with that too… after my divorce. I moved back to our alma mater, from Chicago."

"That's the same time zone, Angela."

She grinned. "You know there are a lot of other ways to deal with that sleep problem."

He didn't respond but he imagined his face gave away a bit of interest.

"How are you getting along with being an Adjunct Professor of Economics?"

"Fine, it's a good change for me. The students are attentive, but my office is a coat closet."

She giggled a little too hard. "Oh my, you're so funny."

He looked at his watch.

She reached out and touched his arm. "Will you walk me to the library? I go on duty in a few minutes."

The giggle was why his interest was fleeting, but it was still there. "Sure."

When they got outside, she looped her arm through his. "You know having a friend that is the librarian has its benefits."

"I'll bite. What are the benefits?"

She did a Marilyn Monroe impression. "Well, if you ever have an overdue book, you can always negotiate the fine. Anytime."

His intellectual hesitation to Angela dissipated. "I think I do have—" He stopped talking abruptly.

She looked up at him. "What's wrong?"

He gently pushed her arm away. "I'll catch up with you later." He stepped away and started walking back the way they came.

She half waved, confused. "Well… goodbye then."

A man in a long trench coat breezed past her.

Mac hit the stairs to the McCombs Building, climbing steps two at a time. Inside and walking the corridor fast he suddenly realized it was dumb to run. Trench Coat was here and there was no place to hide— best to just get it over with.

He stopped and turned around facing the front door. Students walking the hall diverted around him like fish in the ocean. He saw Trench Coat come in, stop, look, then come toward him slowly.

Mac waited until he got close. "Follow me."

Trench Coat nodded.

Mac went right, then left, then up a short set of stairs into an empty classroom. "We have thirty-eight minutes before the next class."

Trench Coat acted as if he was deciding. A few seconds went by. He unbuttoned his coat.

For a half of the next second, Mac thought he was dead.

The man took off his coat, tossed it on an empty seat and sat down. "My name is Hunt. Howard Hunt."

"Mr. Hunt, what do I owe the pleasure?"

"Where do I begin? How about, you fucked us in Dallas."

Mac blinked but didn't panic. "Really, how did I do that?"

Hunt chuckled. "I have to hand it to you, though. I've been doing this for a long time and what you did was really smart."

"And what was that?"

"Come on, we only have thirty-five minutes. I'm not gonna' waste them on bullshit. You left your fingerprint on the sixth floor. That was impressive."

Mac shrugged, but grinned just a little.

"You know your Top-Secret clearance won't protect you forever."

"I'm not too worried. It's buried within millions of documents. Besides, one has to have a suspect to have a print to match... and nobody we know is going to say anything about me."

Hunt paused. "You still sober?"

"Not a drop."

"Hmmm. Why Texas? Why not Italy, or Canada, anywhere but here?"

"When Johnson announced he wouldn't run, I knew sooner or later you'd show up." Mac shrugged. "So, why not here?"

Hunt paused, again.

Mac looked out the window. Two men in black suits were standing by a car in the parking lot. "They with you?"

Hunt nodded.

"Do I have two choices this time?"

Hunt's eyes narrowed. "Oswald and Ruby are dead."

Mac nodded.

"Cliff Carter is dead."

"I heard, died suddenly."

"Very sudden." Hunt added, "Cliff Murchison is dead."

"Not suddenly enough."

Hunt leaned a little forward. "And President Johnson is at the ranch, but not doing well."

"Am I supposed to feel bad about that?"

"You should. He's the reason you're still walking around."

"I don't think that's entirely true."

Hunt stood up, legs spread and leaning in. "We need to know what else you have."

"Who's we?"

"You don't need to know."

Mac stood up and walked to the window. "Then you don't, either."

Hunt lowered his voice. "Edward Clark is working for Nixon. He wants you to come in and talk."

Mac was surprised and showed it. "So, you being here means Clark told Nixon about me and you work for Nixon."

The man stayed silent.

Hunt broke first. "I'm former CIA, and I currently work with members of the staff of President Nixon. After Johnson announced he wouldn't run, Edward Clark changed sides and supported Nixon against Humphrey. Since then, Clark has become a valued member of the President's advisory staff and will soon be appointed to the General Advisory Committee of the Arms Control and Disarmament Agency."

Mac nodded a satirical grin. "Lofty."

"You don't understand what's happening, do you? You're almost out of time. Whatever you have... if you have anything at all... will soon be irrelevant. Almost everybody who had any knowledge is dead."

"What do you want?"

Hunt seemed relieved. "Like I said, Clark wants you to come in and be debriefed. He said he would guarantee your safety and help you return to a normal life."

Mac smiled. "Did you have to practice that?"

Hunt's face broke just a little. "Actually, I did."

Mac walked back to his chair and plopped down. "You know what? I'm pretty tired of looking over my shoulder." He took a breath and began. "I'm not going to talk to Clark because I don't trust him. He was LBJ's trusted friend and he did a lot of the heavy lifting. His hands are just as dirty as anybody's."

Hunt showed no emotion.

"You probably know a lot of this already, but this is what happened to me. Johnson came from nothing. He made deals with rich, powerful people to get every office he ever held, bar none. I know this because I helped. Every one of those arrangements left footprints that can be traced back to him and Clark and…. me. Johnson made enemies along the way, including Bobby Kennedy, and somebody started looking and looking hard. Then just when everything was going to turn to shit, all the looking stops when LBJ suddenly reaches the political pinnacle, the Presidency. Lyndon Johnson becomes the leader of the free world and as a result ceases to have a past. He is the President, an icon, and everything that happened before that event disappears. Now fast forward. Your boy Nixon made deals with the same people. And the same people that were after LBJ are after Nixon, which is why Edward Clark wants me to come in. If Lyndon Johnson and his allies turn out to be complicit in the murder of John F. Kennedy, the fallout might take down Nixon too."

Hunt started to speak but didn't.

"Clark is worried, which makes Nixon worry, which is why you're here." Mac paused. "Today, right now, if you start to worry… I get dead."

The bell tower announced the top of the hour, and students began flooding the quad, footsteps were in the corridor.

Hunt looked at Mac. "So, do I have a reason to worry?"

Mac shook his head. "No, you don't… and they don't. I've had a plan for a long time. The timetable got moved up when

Johnson decided not to run. And... moving back to Austin, instead of Italy, was actually part of my plan."

"Can I ask what it is?"

Mac grinned a little. "No, but I will tell you this: after my trial in '61, I asked my attorney what I should do. He gave me some advice that I should have listened to then."

Hunt shrugged. "What was that?"

"Disappear."

CHAPTER 43

JANUARY 7, 1971

TEXAS STATE HIGHWAY PATROLMAN RONNY LOUGH had the window of the cruiser down, and one hand on the wheel. He had borrowed his teenaged daughter's transistor radio for the night shift, and was singing along with Tom T. Hall.

One time I spent a week inside a little country jail And I don't guess I'll ever live it down I was sittin' at a red light when these two men came and got me And said that I was speeding through their town.

He couldn't sing a note, his dog barked at him when he tried, and his wife would throw things. So, he restricted himself to only letting go when on night patrol, while driving the red-eye shift on Highway 271.

Well, they said, tomorrow morning you can see the judge then go. They let me call one person on the—

"Oh my God." The headlights of the cruiser lit up a car that looked like it was growing out of a concrete pier. He slowed down and hit the blue and reds. There was no movement in or outside of the wreck.

Ronny grabbed the radio mic. "Headquarters. Car 4 2. Car 4

2. I'm 10-23 at highway 271 and the Hadenfield Branch Creek. Investigating a one-vehicle accident. Will advise."

"Roger, Car 4 2."

Ronny dropped the mic and hustled to the driver side of the car, one hand resting on his holster and one hand holding a flashlight.

The body in the driver's seat had fallen over sideways but Ronny could see that the head of the victim was crushed and horribly misshapen. He reached inside and pulled a wallet from the man's back pocket. He saw no need to check for a pulse. Instead, he flashed the light around the area in case there was a passenger in what was left of the front and back seats.

He hustled back to the cruiser. "Headquarters, Car 4 2. Car 4 2."

"Go ahead Car 4 2."

"It's a 10-53, accident with fatality. Dispatch an ambulance and tow truck."

"Roger 4 2. 10-53, accident with fatality. Dispatching requested vehicles."

He hesitated then added. "Better send the chief out here, Betty. This is a bad one."

The radio crackled a bit. "Okay Ronny. Chief Bentley will be informed of your location."

State Highway Patrolman Ronny Lough threw the mic back inside, leaned on the car and tilted up his hat.

He had no song to sing.

No cars had passed by in either direction so traffic control wasn't an issue. The ambulance arrived in about twenty minutes, a couple of minutes before the tow truck. Chief Bentley took a bit longer. Patrolman Lough held everyone on the highway, except the medic, who, upon arrival, approached the vehicle, reached inside, then returned moments later.

"He's dead but," he scratched his head, "he's been dead a long time, I think."

Headlights from Chief Bentley's car illuminated the group.

Lough asked, "How long?"

The medic still looked confused. "That would be something the Medical Examiner will know for sure, but could this have happened yesterday?"

"Yesterday?" Lough shaded his eyes against the headlights.

The chief's car rolled to a stop and he got out fast. "What do we have, Ronny?" He was a big fella, wore a big hat and had a big voice.

"Single car, single fatality. The medical crew went down there to confirm death, and no one else but me has approached the vehicle. I have the victim's wallet. Texas driver's license, an address in Dallas. Malcolm E. Wallace."

"Ease up Ronny. No need to be so formal. You're not on the radio."

Ronny blew a sigh of relief. "It's my first, Chief. Trying to do it right is all."

The chief put his hand on his shoulder. "Good so far. Did you check for tire marks?"

Ronny stood straight. "No sir."

"Then go do that and take the tow truck driver with you to help. Keep him away from the scene." Chief pointed at the two EMTs. "Who's senior?"

"I am, Chief."

"Okay, you come with me. Walk down to the passenger side door. I'll go to the driver's side. Don't touch anything till I tell you it's okay."

The front end of the car was almost split in two by the edge of the abutment. The doors were bellied and jammed shut. The windows and windshield had been shattered. Glass was everywhere.

Ronny could see the chief leaning into the car and using a flashlight to look at the area around the crash. Up on the highway, looking for skid marks didn't take that long. He walked back to the chief's car and waited for his boss to return.

Fifteen minutes went by before the chief came back.

Patrolman Lough reported curtly. "I didn't see any skid marks."

"What does that tell you?"

"Well Chief, I think the driver was either drunk or fell asleep at the wheel."

"Possible." The chief leaned back against the car. "Possible." He nodded at the EMT. "Can you estimate time of death?"

"No sir, I can't get to the body for an accurate internal temperature reading."

"Best guess."

"Yesterday… day before." His eyes shifted back and forth. "I know that doesn't make sense but I would expect a crash this bad… I mean… there's blood puddled on the seat and floor but it really should be everywhere, like splattered. It's hard to explain."

"Yep. Something ain't right." The chief pushed off his car. "Okay, take pictures, then wrap it up Patrolman. Get some help to get the body out, then tow the car to the yard."

"Yes sir."

The chief tipped his hat. "Good job."

"Yes… sir."

The chief climbed into his car. "Something ain't right." He started to back out, stopped and leaned out the window. "Patrolman, how old was he?"

Lough took the wallet from the front seat of the patrol car and looked at the license. "He was 49, chief. 49 years old."

"Something ain't right."

PITTSBURG GAZETTE
DALLAS MAN BECOMES
FIRST FATALITY OF '71
Pittsburg, Jan 14 Camp County recorded
its first fatality of 1971 on January 7th,
Tuesday, at 7:38 a.m.
Malcolm E. Wallace, 49 of Dallas, was
dead on arrival at Medical & Surgical
Hospital.
State Highway Patrolman Ronny Lough,
who investigated the accident, reported
that Wallace apparently lost control of
his car, it ran off the highway, and struck
a bridge abutment.
The accident occurred on US Highway
271 about 13.5 miles south of Pittsburg.
The highway was neither icy nor wet,
the patrolman reported. Only one car
was involved in the accident.

Ed Clark dropped the newspaper on his desk. The Ambassador, as people in his office in Austin still called him, was visibly upset. There was sweat on his forehead and his demeaner agitated which was a complete departure from the cool, calm, elder statesman. "This is unexpected. I thought you had this under control."

"I do and it is." Howard Hunt, sitting across from him in a client chair, looked a little bored.

"Sorry?"

Hunt leaned a little forward, trying to take command of the

situation. "It wasn't an accident, and actually I'm kind of impressed."

"Impressed?"

Hunt nodded and pointed to the paper. "That was no accident. I think it isn't Wallace."

Clark fell into his seat. "Explain."

"When I spoke to him, he was under complete control, confident, and certainly not suicidal. I read the police report. No alcohol, no drugs, and no skid marks."

"There was a positive ID?"

"There was a driver's license, car registration, and little else. Wallace's brother, who by the way hadn't seen him in years, identified a body with an unrecognizable face. Oh, and the brother didn't know his brother's birthday, or his mother's maiden name, and he didn't sign the death certificate."

"Fingerprints?"

Hunt started laughing. "No... No matching fingerprints."

"But he was arrested in Texas, a couple of times. How could that—"

"Records were expunged, remember? There are no official records... for murder, or drunk driving. He was well protected." Hunt paused and added satire. "He also had really good lawyers."

Clark was absorbing but still very agitated. "So, who's the body?"

Hunt held up his hand. "Wait, there's more. I spoke with our man at Ling Industries. There was supposed to be two subcontractors set up to pay the various interests that allow the contracts to move forward. In late 1968, Wallace set up another one. A quick audit determined that about a half a million dollars was filtered to a non-existent business. I am pretty sure he secured new papers, new driver's license, and a birth certificate before he left Ling eight months ago. The false company has folded, and all the accounts emptied."

"If he had the money and a new ID, why did he show up here, in Texas?"

Hunt chuckled again. "Wallace left California for a job teaching at the University of Texas." Hunt wagged a finger. "I didn't get it either at first, but I do now."

Clark was focused.

"The University of Texas has a very good school of medicine. As an adjunct professor, Wallace had access to almost everything on campus."

"And?"

"And... he took a cadaver."

"What?"

"Bodies are donated to universities for medical research. Your alma matre had one go missing over the New Year holiday and the staff figured it must be a fraternity stunt and thought it would show up in the dean's swimming pool and never reported it."

Clark sat still, frozen in thought.

"This guy is good. I wish I had him on my team."

"So, what does all this mean?"

"The only thing Wallace needed to accomplish is to create an illusion. This accident would be easy to pick apart. It would be found out as a setup in a couple of days, but... he knows we won't let that happen."

Clark's voice got lower. "Why?"

"Don't you see the irony here?" Hunt leaned across the desk. "If we expose him, we expose us. We'd be gutted like a fish. He knows we have to do everything possible to make sure this stays listed as an accident, that Malcolm Wallace is dead, and we just let him disappear into the night. He did it in Texas because its where we have the most influence. Its fucking brilliant."

Clark's voice was shaky when he repeated Hunt's word. "Brilliant."

Hunt stood up with half a smile. "Oh, by the way, guess what he named the phony company."

Clark shrugged.

"The 8F Group."

"Jesus."

CHAPTER 44

JANUARY 7, 1973

LBJ WAS WATCHING a replay of the 1969 Presidential inauguration. He couldn't get past a republican taking what was supposed to be his second term, especially Richard Nixon. Like many democrats, he hated the man. He didn't fear him like his republican colleagues did. He just plain out hated him.

"You know Mike, McNamara and I had peace talks all set up. I wanted to end the war before I left Washington. We had Ho Chi Minh ready to go to Paris and then that som-of-a-bitch fucked it up." He threw his pillow at the TV.

Mike Howard, Secret Service agent and part-time nurse, retrieved it and tucked it under Johnson's head. "You should turn that off, it's not good for you, Mr. President."

"Nixon had one of his storm troopers tell Minh that he could get a better deal after he was elected President. Ho Chi Minh stopped talking, and we couldn't get them to the table."

Mike tucked the pillow again. "Yes, Mr. President."

"Som-of-a-bitch."

"I'm needed at the security center, sir." Mike started for the door. "If you need anything use the intercom. It's right by your bed."

"I know. I know." LBJ looked at the box then at Mike. "Is Bird still shopping?"

"Yes sir. She said she'll be back later this afternoon." Mike shut the door quietly as he left.

LBJ pulled on the blanket and found it was tucked under the mattress. He yanked it harder and the TV remote-control box fell to the floor.

"Goddamn it." He reached out but it had fallen half way to the dresser.

Nixon's voice filled the room. *"After a period of confrontation, we are entering an era of negotiation. Let all nations know that during this administration our lines of communication will be open. We seek an open world--open to ideas, open to the exchange of goods and people--a world in which no people, great or small, will live in angry isolation."*

LBJ threw the pillow again and, suddenly, pain electrified his body.

He pushed the intercom button. "Send Mike immediately."

There was no one in the room when Lyndon Baines Johnson took his last breath

CHAPTER 45

DETECTIVE HENRY LARSON pulled up behind an ambulance parked at the curb. Two men in white uniforms were loading what he presumed to be someone who no longer required medical assistance. The body on the cart was covered head to toe with a white sheet.

Several people appearing to be from the suburban neighborhood had gathered to gawk, but were respectful and stayed out of the way. He walked quickly toward the house, stopping briefly at the curb.

Larson nodded to the medic. "Cause of death?"

The white uniform pulled the back door closed. "Appears to be natural causes after a prolonged illness. Best guess, cancer."

"Thanks." Larson headed up the sidewalk leading to the duplex with an open front door.

A uniformed officer stood watch. "Detective."

"Witnesses?"

"A woman stopped by this morning to check on her and found the body upstairs."

"She had a key or was the door unlocked?"

The uniform showed why he was still a uniform, and shrugged.

In the living room, Larson found a small black lady perched on a chair, her hands holding a white handkerchief. There was a cloth bag on the floor beside her.

"Ma'am, I'm Detective Larson. I'm with the Criminal Investigation Division of the Dallas Police Force and I need to ask you a few questions."

She sucked in panic air and her hands went palms up. "Lord have mercy, am I in trouble?"

Larson immediately lowered his six-foot-two frame down, taking a knee and her hand. "No...no. You're not in any trouble. Please... it's okay."

She took a breath but there was still panic in her eyes.

"What is your name?"

"My name is Mabel Harris. I worked for the Mrs. off and on for a few years."

"Is that why you had a key?"

"Yes, sir. Mrs. Akin has the consumption... I mean cancer," she pointed to her head, "of the brain. Been real sick." She picked up the handles of the bag. "I brought her some chicken soup. She always liked my chicken soup." Tears began rolling down her cheek.

"I have to ask some questions, Mrs. Harris. It is Mrs., correct?"

"Yes." She looked confused. "How did you know that?"

He held up his finger and pointed to his wedding ring then pointed to hers. "I'm a detective. Mrs. Harris, I'm here because, if someone di... passes, alone, with no witnesses an investigation report needs to be filed. Okay?"

She relaxed. "Yes, sir. I understand."

"She was really sick then?"

"Yes sir. Should have been in the hospital but she wouldn't go. She was skinny as a rail but determined, you know what I mean? She could get around, bathroom and personal things, but no stairs. That's why I'd come here. She was a stubborn woman. Yes sir, mighty stubborn."

"Mrs. Harris, what was her full name?" He took out a notebook.

"Mrs. Delmer Lee Akin. That were her husband's name. He passed back in '75."

"Do you know her first name?"

"Andre. Her full name was Mary Andre DuBois Barton Wallace Akin. She used to fool around whit it sayin' it was like a royal name. That's why I remember it so well." She paused and looked toward the stairs. "We had some good times, we did."

"Did she have any regular visitors? Any children, friends?"

"She had three childs, but they be working a lot and… don't get me wrong, they come by. Just not during the day. That's why I comes by." She nodded and smiled a little smile.

"Friends, neighbors?"

"The woman two doors down brought some soup once or twice." She leaned over and whispered. "It wernt very good."

He smiled a little. "Yes, Ma'am." He continued while writing a few notes. "So, no friends then?"

"No… not really."

She hesitated, which caught his attention. "Not really?"

"Well, last time I stopped by I saw a man leaving that I never saw before. I didn't think much of it but when I axed the Mrs., she didn't want to talk about him."

"That was the only time you saw him?"

"Well… I gots to thinking about it and I remembered another time a month ago or so when I passed him on the sidewalk. And you should remember, I couldn't come here every day, so, maybe more times, I guess."

"Can you describe him?"

"Older white man, maybe fifties. He was a good-looking man with a whole head of hair. And… he wore those black kind of glasses. You know…" She held her hand up to her face, "like that Superman on TV." Suddenly her face lit up. "Clark Kent. He looked just like Clark Kent."

Larson was busy writing.

"So, you have no idea who he was or what he wanted?"

"No sir, I sure don't. Like I said she wouldn't talk about it."

She looked hesitant again, and Larson pressed a little more. "Mabel is that all?"

"Well sir." She leaned in again to share another secret. "After he was here… she seemed very happy."

Larson nodded and wrote

Mysterious Clark Kent made Andre very happy.

THE END

EPILOGUE
THE FINGERPRINT

On March 12, 1998, A. Nathan Darby announced in a press conference, that the only unidentified fingerprint on the sixth floor of the Texas School Book Depository on November 22, 1963 belonged to Malcolm E. Wallace.

A. Nathan Darby was a certified latent print examiner with decades of experience. Darby started fingerprint examination as a Captain in the US Army. He then spent the next thirty-four years in law enforcement, rising to the rank of Lieutenant Commander for the Austin Police. He was a member of the International Association of Identifiers and a Certified Latent Fingerprint examiner and was chosen to help design the Eastman Kodak Miracode System of transmitting fingerprints between law enforcement agencies. He has testified as an expert witness in state and federal trials. His testimony was never contradicted or subject to a mistrial. He was an expert in his field.

The announcement was published in several newspapers and stated that Darby signed a sworn, notarized affidavit stating that he was able to affirm a 24-point match between the unknown fingerprint and the print card submitted to him. It was a blind study.

Darby's fingerprint report was forwarded to the FBI. Eighteen months after the submittal, the FBI verbally declared it a non-match. The FBI did not publish its findings, and had no further comment.

TIME LINE

TIME LINE FOR THE EVENTS DESCRIBED IN *WHY*

- June 26, 1944. - Lyndon Johnson visits University of Texas – introduced by Mac Wallace
- March 8, 1945 - Mac Wallace leaves University of Texas without graduating
- September, 1945 - Wallace enrolls in New School for Social Research
- October, 1945 - Wallace goes to work for National City Bank
- January, 1946 - Wallace enrolls in University of Texas master's program
- June 4, 1947 - Wallace marries Mary Andre Dubose Barton
- September, 1947 - Wallace enrolls at Columbia University
- July, 1948 Lyndon - Johnson wins Democratic Primary – Box 13 scandal
- June 29, 1948 - Andre Wallace files for divorce

- August, 1949 - Andre Wallace withdraws divorce application
- September, 1949 - Mac Wallace gets a job with the Department of Agriculture in Arlington
- 1950, - Mac Wallace begins affair with Josefa Johnson
- August 10, 1950 - Andre Wallace files for divorce
- 1950-51 - Andre Wallace has affair with John Douglas Kinser and Josefa Johnson
- October 22, 1951 - Mac Wallace murders John Kinser
- February 28, 1952 - Wallace convicted of first-degree murder, gets five-year suspended sentence
- June 6, 1952 - Mac Wallace and Andre divorce
- September, 1952 - Mac Wallace employed by TEMCO gets Top Secret Clearance
- November 15, 1952 - Mac Wallace, on parole, is drunk in judge's chambers.
- December 21, 1952 - Mac Wallace and Andre remarry
- 1955 - Lyndon Johnson becomes Majority Leader of Senate
- December 10, 1958 - Mac Wallace and Andre divorce again
- February 8, 1959 - Naval Intelligence investigation begins
- December 31, 1959 - Mac Wallace and Andre remarry
- November 17, 1960 - Mac Wallace and Andre divorce for the last time
- February 19, 1961 - Wallace moves to California hired by Ling Electronics
- June 3, 1961 - Henry Marshall murdered
- July, 1961 - Naval Intelligence investigation begins again
- December 25, 1961 - Josefa Johnson dies - buried the same day at LBJ's ranch

- September, 1961 - Naval Intelligence visits Andre Wallace
- January, 1963 - Virginia Ledgewood, a student interning at Ling Electronics, gets pregnant
- April 15, 1963 - Billy Sol Estes sentenced to 15 years in federal prison
- April 20, 1963 - Mac Wallace marries Virginia Ledgewood
- May 31, 1963 - Mac Wallace arrested for drunk driving in Rusk County, Texas
- November 1, 1963 - Virginia Ledgewood leaves Mac Wallace one week after baby born
- November 22, 1963 - John F. Kennedy murdered in Dallas Texas
- November 23, 1963 - Henry Luce orders all copies of Holland McComb's Life Magazine article exposing Lyndon Johnson destroyed
- November 24, 1963 - Jack Ruby murders Lee Harvey Oswald
- November 25, 1963 - President Lyndon Johnson signs National Security Memo 273
- November 3, 1964 - Lyndon Baines Johnson elected by 61.1 percent of the vote. Largest margin of victory of any President from John Adams through the present day.
- January 20, 1967 - Bobby Baker guilty of fraud and tax evasion
- March 31, 1968 - Lyndon Johnson announces he won't run for President
- August 1, 1969 - Mac Wallace moves back to Texas
- January 7, 1971 - Mac Wallace dies in car crash
- January 22, 1973 - Lyndon Johnson dies of natural causes at his ranch.

- January 2, 1979 - The House Select Committee on Assassinations concludes JFK assassination was most likely a conspiracy
- June 5, 1980 - Andre Wallace dies – Dallas police report a man fitting Mac Wallace's description seen leaving her house days before
- March, 1984 - Billie Sol Estes, testifying in Robertson County under immunity, accuses Lyndon Johnson, Cliff Carter, Edward Clark, and Malcolm Wallace of conspiracy in the murder of Henry Marshall, Josefa Johnson, and John Fitzgerald Kennedy
- August 14, 1985 - Federal Judge Peter Lowery rules Henry Marshall's death changed from suicide to murder.
- March 12, 1998 - Forensic expert A. Nathan Darby holds press conference and announces the only unidentified fingerprint on the sixth floor of the Texas School Book Depositary belonged to Malcom Wallace.
- 2013 - A Gallop poll indicates that 72.9 percent of American people believe that Lee Harvey Oswald did not act alone.
- December 15, 2022 - President Joe Biden authorized the release of the documents, but will continue to block some materials from public view. "I agree that continued postponement of public disclosure of such information is warranted to protect against an identifiable harm to the military defense, intelligence operations, law enforcement, or the conduct of foreign relations that is of such gravity that it outweighs the public interest in disclosure."

White House memorandum Alexandra Hutzler and Justin Gomez. – ABC News

REFERENCE MATERIAL

Books, Videos, Articles

Faustain Bargins – Joan Mellen
 The Man who killed Kennedy – Mike Colapietro
 Death of a Fixer - Texas Monthly – Robert Draper (Nov 1992)
 LBJ Mastermind of the Kennedy Assassination – Philip F. Nelson
 Blood, Money, & Power – Barr McCellan
 The Day Kennedy was Shot – Jim Bishop
 Warren Commission Report – U.S. Government
 The New Yorker – Robert A Caro, April 2 2012
 East Texas Journal – Dec 16 2020 – Hudson Old
 History Channel – *The men who killed Kennedy*
 Winter Watch – December 22, 2022 – Russ Winte
 A. Nathan Darby – *March 9, 1998* – *Affidavit to State of Texas* –
Fingerprint match

Internet Websites

Whitehouse.gov

Millercenter.org
Lbjlibrary.net
Jfklibrary.org
Wikipedia.com
Spartacus Educational.com

About The Author.

This is the fourth book published by Paul Eberz. **WHY** deals events surrounding the assassination of JFK. He also published a mystery trilogy. *Smoke – White Collar Crimes*, was the first, published in 2020, *Reckoning*, was next in 2021 and *Henry* followed 2022.

Eberz retired from the construction industry where he held executive positions in Fortune 500 companies, and also traveled the country working with Native American Tribes. Born in Philadelphia, he now resides in Virginia.

Contact the Author

Email: Paul_Eberz@yahoo.com